Levine flung
knelt over he
one hand whil
tearing her clo ... . body. She
did not struggle because it was hopeless
– just closed her eyes because she did
not want to see. In her mind she saw the
face of a tiny totem, her own creation,
something that had not existed before
she had begun work with her carving
knife. And she prayed to it; not for help
because that would come too late even
if it were possible.

Her prayer was that her god would
take a terrible revenge, not just on this
man but on all his kind, that it would
strike them down with a terrible wrath,
and that their children, and their children's children, would rue this day.

FOR DEBBIE

MANITOU DOLL

Guy N. Smith

Hamlyn Paperbacks

A Hamlyn Paperback
Published by Arrow Books Limited
17–21 Conway Street, London W1P 6JD

A division of the Hutchinson Publishing Group

London Melbourne Sydney Auckland
Johannesburg and agencies throughout
the world

First published in Great Britain by
Hamlyn Paperbacks 1981

Reprinted 1985

© Guy N. Smith 1981

Printed and bound in Great Britain by
Anchor Brendon Limited, Tiptree, Essex

ISBN 0 09 943800 3

PROLOGUE

September 16, 1868

The fifty men had been ten days out of Fort Wallace, Kansas, when they hit the flood plain of the Arikaree River. They were a straggling cavalcade, showing little of the discipline demanded by General Sheridan of those who served under him.

There had been Indian signs all along the way, whole villages on the move, a mass retreat. Before long the redman would be forced to turn and fight. Or surrender. Major George A. Forsyth hoped it would be the latter, his company was in no shape to engage in combat. Small, almost boyish in appearance beneath his dust-grimed uniform, he turned in the saddle to survey his men. Half of them were civilian scouts, the remainder hand-picked men from Fort Wallace, chosen for their fighting qualities and for no other reason. They would hunt the Indians down the way Sheridan wanted them hunted down: pursuing and harassing them until the last one lay dead in the blood-soaked dirt. For this was a revenge campaign against the Plains Indians who had conducted their guerilla warfare so effectively in the last few years.

Forsyth reined in his mount at the bottom of the incline and waited for the others to catch up; they were too strung out, and that wasn't wise even in open terrain. Lieutenant Beecher was trying to close them up. Beecher was a man who understood the Indians, thought the same way as they did, anticipated move after move and had been largely responsible for keeping the enemy on the run. He didn't hate them, though; it was just a job that he was doing the

5

best way he knew how, unlike Sheridan, who wanted to see them exterminated. Levine wanted it that way, too: the Indian an extinct species.

Levine was big but there was no surplus flesh underneath the worn buckskins, only muscles that rippled with every movement. His mass of black hair gave him a bear-like appearance at a distance: the moustache and beard hid the lower half of his face, the uneven fringe falling out of the wide-brimmed hat shielded the upper. You just saw the eyes, small and mean. Everything about Levine was mean, the way he kicked his horse's flanks, raking with his spurs and making the animal's eyes roll. For no reason except that he liked to hurt. But when you ran into trouble he was a good man to have around. There was none better.

They struck camp along the river bank, a wide open space where there was no chance of a surprise attack from the rear. If attack came it would have to be along the river-bed itself, perhaps from behind the rocky bluffs in the distance. The river-bed was now just dry sand, except for a shallow stream in the centre that trickled lazily as though tomorrow it might decide to dry up too. In full spate the river divided and made an island some fifty yards long by twenty wide, a narrow strip that was cut off from either bank, just scrub, a few alder and willow, and a lone cottonwood. It didn't even have a name because nobody wanted it, not even the Indians.

Forsyth ran his gaze over it and dismissed it because it did not figure in his plans. Tonight camp would be a hasty affair. Only essentials were unpacked; the heavily-laden pack mules were unloaded and the baggage stacked near-by, five thousand rounds of Spencer rifle ammunition and medical supplies. In addition, each man carried 140 rounds, with 30 rounds for his Colt. They were taking no chances. No fires, no cooking, just biscuits and tack and water from what remained of the Arikaree River. Four night guards to be relieved before dawn. The others divided into bunches and unrolled their blankets.

Forsyth waited for Beecher to come across and unroll close by. It was expected, though never mentioned; a segregation of officers and men.

Levine had moved away from the others, a natural loner. They didn't want him and he didn't want them, by mutual understanding. But he felt a sense of superiority: it only needed a redskin to show up and they would be looking to see where the big scout was.

He stretched out, chewed tobacco and spat, and waited for it to grow dark. He liked the night best because that was when a man like himself had an advantage over others. If you moved quietly nobody saw you until it was too late; you could hide under the cloak of darkness.

Levine sniffed the air with wide nostrils and smelled Indians. Not so much an aroma as an intuition, a sixth sense warning him that the Cheyenne and Sioux were a lot nearer than the encampment twelve miles upstream which McCall had reported when he rode in. A cluster of tipis meant nothing unless you knew the full strength of the enemy and made sure that they were all at home. Levine didn't like it one little bit, camped in here and set up like a desert buck for the slaughter. He spat more tobacco juice and reached for his Spencer repeating rifle, laying it alongside him. When he got the kind of feeling he now had, he liked to have his weapons close at hand.

The tall Indian closed the flap of his tipi so that none might see inside, his majestic hawk-like features softening into a smile as he regarded the young girl sitting cross-legged on a pile of army blankets, the ones they had brought back from the raid on the supply train less than a week ago. His heart was filled with a mixture of grief and joy every time he looked at Mistai, for she would soon be the image of her mother who had been cut down by the rifle fire of the horse soldiers at Wolf Creek. Mistai was too young to remember that cowardly ambush, in which seven squaws and a sick brave had died, but the tall Indian vowed that nothing like it must happen again. Mistai must be sent away before daylight, before the combined Cheyenne and Sioux force attacked the soldiers' camp. There was no safety even in victory.

7

The girl looked up, held out something in the palm of a brown hand.

'My father, I have carved this for you,' she smiled. 'It has taken me a day and a night but I am glad that I have finished in time. Keep it with you at all times in battle.'

He took it, scrutinized it. The wood was unseasoned alder but the carving was exquisite – a human face, features so lifelike with every detail perfect, the lines beneath the eyes, nostrils twin dark holes that seemed to breathe, lips curved into a half-smile. It was neither Indian nor white man and almost frightening because of that; one was either red or white or a god. He felt it was familiar, as though he had seen the face before but could not recall it.

'My child, it is a good thing that your carving is so beautiful. It rivals the workmanship of the totem poles that we left behind when the whites drove us from our homes.'

'It *is* a totem, father,' her expression was serious this time, 'one that will protect you in battle. The eyes shall see for you, the ears hear so that the mouth can warn you of danger, and when that danger is so cunning that neither eyes nor ears can detect it then the nose shall smell it out. Let my father, Bat, whom the whites call Roman Nose, be safe under *my* protection.'

He dropped to his knees beside her, took her arm in his, then turned his head away so that she should not see the wetness of his eyes. For a few moments he was not the feared and respected Cheyenne chief but a father succumbing to his emotions, the safety of his daughter of paramount importance. But when he turned back to her his eyes were dry again and the quiver had disappeared from his lower lip.

'Tonight you must leave this encampment, Mistai,' he spoke in a whisper. 'I have ordered Young Bear to accompany you, following the river as far as the big bend where you will camp for three moons and await my coming. When we have driven back the cruel horse soldiers I will join you there.'

Roman Nose fell silent, his thoughts too powerful for words, remembering his instructions to the tall boy who

8

looked older than his years. 'If I am not with you after the third moon, Young Bear, ride north and join the Oglala Sioux, but guard Mistai from their lusting braves. Protect her with your life, for now that she has undergone the puberty rites of our people she is open to many dangers. The chastity hide must remain around her loins for two more seasons and then you may take her for your wife.'

'You are worried, father,' Mistai's voice broke through his thoughts. 'It is for your safety that I have carved you this totem. You will come to me before the third moon.'

'I will come,' he rose slowly to his feet. 'But in the meantime you must make ready to ride with Young Bear.'

Levine awoke with the instinct of a wild animal that has sensed danger even in slumber, every muscle tensed. His strong, rough hands caressed the cold metal of the Spencer. His nostrils flared and he smelled Indian again, sharp and sour like the sweat under his own armpits. *And very close*.

His eyesight adjusted to the faint starlight that precedes the dawn, when shapes are barely distinguishable in the shadows. But Levine only needed shapes. He could make out the sleeping soldiers and scouts blissfully unaware that danger lurked so near, restless mules and horses, four guards trying to make something out of the blackness and failing.

Then Levine spotted the figures slowly advancing beyond the range of normal night-time vision; saw the four Indians belly-crawling their way towards the tethered horses. Silently and swiftly, he brought the barrel of his rifle to bear on the nearest brave, some thirty yards away.

The report shattered the stillness, a blinding flash that lit up the scene like forked lightning. The Indian was thrown over by the impact of the heavy slug and lay kicking like a wounded rabbit. The other three leaped up like angry wraiths, turned to flee. The three shots sounded as one, the flashes so close together that they seemed like a single jet of flame.

People were running, shouting, horses tugging at the ropes that tethered them. But Levine had not moved, crouching there in the darkness, the trickle of smoke from the barrel of his Spencer repeating rifle acrid in the humid atmosphere.

'What happened?' Forsyth appeared at his side followed by Beecher. 'Was that you shooting, Levine?'

'Sure,' the scout laughed, a deep rumbling sound. 'Don't worry, there were only four and I got 'em. They were after cuttin' the horses loose and stampedin' 'em, which means the Injuns ain't as far away as McCall would have us believe.'

'What d'you suggest, Levine?' Forsyth's voice was low; he didn't want the others to hear him asking the scout's advice but there were occasions when a commanding officer was forced to rely on the experience of someone like Levine. 'You reckon they're planning to attack us?'

'If they ain't, then old Roman Nose has suddenly turned yeller. I'd say right now they're massed behind them bluffs ready to ride in on us at first light. They won't attack in the dark, not because they're afraid of losin' their souls but simply because it's more difficult.'

'Which means we've got about an hour to prepare.' Forsyth looked up at the sky but the stars had not yet begun to fade. 'OK, Levine, you know the Arikaree better than most, what do you suggest?'

'Only one thing we can do,' Levine stood up, slipping a plug of tobacco into his mouth and biting on it with uneven stumps of broken yellowed teeth, 'and that's to git across to that island whilst we still can. It ain't much but it's better'n bein' caught out in the open. They'll come downstream, outnumberin' us ten to one, but maybe if we can keep up the fire with these here repeaters we can hold 'em off.'

The scout watched Forsyth and Beecher move away and start giving orders for men and supplies to be moved to the island. Levine did not hurry, moving catlike, drawing the heavy skinning knife from his belt and searching out the nearest Cheyenne. The brave was bleeding badly from a neck wound, incapable of movement, maybe half-an-hour's life left in him. Levine chuckled softly as he bunched the long dark hair, felt the brave tensing and

10

erecting a psychological barrier against pain. The big man didn't need to see, he'd done it many times before, sliding the scalp and nicking round in a circle until the shallow cut was a complete ring; one swift pull and he had the bloody scalp off, dangling it in his left hand as he went looking for the others.

In less than three minutes he had rejoined the company, the four grisly trophies stuffed into his saddlebags. He wasn't deliberately hiding the scalps but he had no cause to boast. He had collected them for his own satisfaction.

The entire party was on the small island before the first stars began to pale, Forsyth and Beecher organizing the defence. Twenty rifles covered the downstream approach; there were ten on either flank, and the remainder formed a rearguard in case the attackers circled and tried to come in from the lower end.

Levine had moved across to the single cottonwood tree. He contemplated climbing to its topmost branches in order to achieve a telling angle of downfire, but decided against it. That way he would present a better target to the enemy, and, atrocious as Cheyenne and Sioux marksmanship was, there was always the possibility of a stray bullet finding its mark. He settled down on one of the flanks, checked his rifle and laid it on the ground in front of him. He was relaxed in every way, eagerly anticipating this encounter between red and white.

Dawn came slowly and lit up the sky with its cold grey light. Another hour and the sun would be up, scorching an already parched land.

The Indians came with unbelievable suddenness, a bunch of seventy or eighty riding madly along the watercourse from behind the towering bluffs. They were shooting before they were in range, a ragged volley that split the still air, interspersed with wild whooping. They had expected to find the whites on the island. It made no difference where they were; they would be slaughtered to the last man.

Soldiers and scouts had their rifles at the ready, fingers circled lightly around triggers, awaiting Forsyth's orders to fire. He let the enemy get close, almost forty yards from them before his command sent a hail of leaden death into the approaching ranks. The Indians split and veered, a path cut through their midst by the fire-power of the Spencers.

The war-cries turned to yells of surprise and rage. Wheeling their mounts, the Indians thundered back whence they had come. A tiny pall of smoke hung over the island in the middle of the Arikaree River.

'Holy Jesus!' a soldier emptied his rifle after them. 'That sure taught 'em a lesson. Guess they never met up with repeaters afore.'

'Cool it,' Lieutenant Beecher was already reloading. 'They won't be put off just like that. No, sir! That lot were sent in to test our fire-power and now they know what to expect. Now they'll fight us a different way, more cunning. Starve us out if they can.'

The defenders were silent as they awaited the next attack. As Beecher had said, it wasn't going to be as simple as the first assault. This could turn out to be a long siege. And General Sheridan at Fort Wallace would have no idea of the trouble his men had run into.

Mid-afternoon. Cheyenne and Sioux had been massing for the past three hours, making no secret of their strength in numbers, lining the flood plain on either bank of the river. This time the attack would not be concentrated on the tip of the island; it would come from all directions, several hundred white-hating braves not caring whether they lived or died because their land, their buffalo, and many of their squaws were gone. They had only one motive: revenge.

The red men took their time, gathering under Bat's orders, as disciplined as any US army regiment, only awaiting his signal to kill. And he would be riding at their head, a tiny wooden totem face hanging from the necklace inside his shirt to give him invincibility.

Roman Nose paused for a few moments to remember Mistai and how she was safe, many miles from here with Young Bear. Then he raised his hand and gave the order to annihilate the white men on the island.

The gunfire was like thunder, rolling across the plain and echoing and re-echoing in the far mountains. Incessant. And this time the Indians were not driven back. They wheeled, regrouped, wheeled again, circling the island and returning the fire. Ponies went down, riders thrown or jumping clear, scurrying to find a patch of scrub cover and rejoining the battle on foot.

Surprisingly the casualties on both sides were light. On the island three scouts were dead and two soldiers injured, including Major Forsyth who had been struck in the leg and in the neck. Lying on his blanket shielded by a large rock, he continued to direct the battle, conveying his instructions to Lieutenant Beecher.

'It's no good, sir.' Beecher, grimed with sweat and powder smoke, his uniform torn, returned to his wounded chief towards sunset. 'We're not going to drive 'em off. They've drawn back for now but they'll be at us again at first light.'

'How long do you think we can hold out?' Forsyth's face was twisted with pain.

'A few days. Food will run out before the ammunition does but we can get all the water we need from the river.'

'Then we'll have to try and get through to Fort Wallace and let General Sheridan know what's happening. Two men, lieutenant, might make it under the cover of darkness, travelling separately. The two best men we've got.'

'Levine and McCall, sir?'

Forsyth nodded, closed his eyes momentarily. He'd never thought his life might depend upon the scum of the land but he had no choice.

Levine moved silently in the darkness, stopping to listen every few yards. He'd made it easily enough through the Indian lines and now he was following the bank of the trickling watercourse. He laughed softly to himself; there was nothing he would have liked better than to have gone on a killing spree, taking them one at a time, leaving a trail of scalped and mutilated corpses in his wake. But he'd get through to Fort Wallace, show them he did a job better

13

than anybody else. Better than McCall.

McCall was somewhere out on the flood plain taking a different route. He'd make it, too, but Levine would be first at Fort Wallace by a day at least.

Sunup. He'd left the Indians way behind but he still moved cautiously because there was always the chance of running into the odd party of renegades. Then, as he topped a rise, he smelled Indian, very strong. Instinctively he was ducking for cover, crawling, easing his knife out of its sheath.

Then he saw the Indians, two of them, a youth and a strikingly handsome young girl who could barely yet have achieved puberty. He pursed his lips in a silent whistle even as he recognized them as Cheyennes. A smile, a movement of the thin lips beneath the matted beard, wolfish and lusting. He moved closer, using the brush to shield his progress until only two or three yards separated him from the couple sitting in the shade of a stunted cottonwood tree. He listened to their conversation, understanding their language as well as his own.

'My father promises that one day you shall have me, Young Bear,' Mistai pushed away the hand which crept on to her thigh, 'but until that day you must be patient. I will wear the hide until then.'

The listening Levine grinned again. The girl wore 'the hide', the rope chastity-belt used by Cheyenne maidens which meant two things; she had attained puberty and she was a virgin.

Levine rose to his feet and stepped forward quickly, towering over them before either noticed his presence. His dark eyes flicked from one to the other, settled on Young Bear.

'Injun scum!' he spat tobacco juice. 'As cowardly as the rest of 'em.'

Young Bear did not hesitate. In one perfectly co-ordinated movement he leaped at the buckskin-clad white man, drawing his hunting knife, his arm going back for the death blow.

But Young Bear's move was slower than his enemy's.

14

Levine's left forearm came up, diverting the descending knife whilst he plunged his own blade deep into the brown, flat stomach of his attacker. The steel went deep, twisted, grated on bone. And then the scout was straightening up, still holding his knife, the blade crimson, Young Bear inert at his feet.

'*No!*' Mistai backed away in horror, felt grief and terror rising up to her throat like vomit. She saw the motionless youth, his gaping wound pumping blood, his eyes wide with horror because he knew he had failed her, broken his promise to Bat. And he realized only too well what was going to happen to her.

Levine laughed loudly this time, bent to clean the blade of his knife on the parched grass, and sheathed his weapon because he knew he would not need it. From now onwards it was going to be very easy and *very* pleasurable. He reached out, grabbed the girl and pulled her close, jerking her head back by her long, dark hair. She did not scream because she knew it was futile and with Young Bear dead she wanted to join him. But there was no way she could hide the hate and contempt in her eyes. She closed her lips, determined not to respond to his vile stinking kisses, wanting to retch at the foul odour from his mouth.

'Squaw!' his free hand tore her clothing, baring shapely young breasts, began to fondle them roughly, squeezing them so that the nipples bulged as though they would burst out of the flesh. 'You goddamned Cheyenne hussy!'

She kicked at him but her moccasined feet rebounded off his powerful legs, hurting her toes. As he held her up against his own body she felt a hardness pushing at her loins and she knew only too well what was going to happen to her, not that she had ever been in any doubt.

Levine flung Mistai to the ground and knelt over her, pinning her down with one hand whilst with the other he began tearing her clothing from her body. She did not struggle because it was hopeless, just closed her eyes because she did not want to see. In her mind she saw the face of a tiny totem, her own creation, something that had not existed before she had begun work with her carving knife. And she prayed to it; not for help because that would come too late even if it were possible. *Her prayer was that her god would take a terrible revenge, not just on this man but on all his kind, that it would strike them down with a terrible wrath and that their children, and their children's children, would rue this day.*

She felt him snap the cord around her loins as easily as if it were a slender thread, pull her apart with a roughness that brought a cry almost to her lips. But she checked it just in time: he would never see her humiliate herself by screaming or pleading.

A slap across the face jerked her eyes open so that she was forced to gaze upon him. His filthy trousers had been pulled down below his knees, exposing grimy flesh pimpled with blackheads. But her eyes were riveted on the size of that which she would be compelled to take inside her, its length and thickness almost rivalling the handle of her father's tomahawk. He was grinning, rubbing it and delighting in her revulsion. Then he knelt close and lowered his body on to hers.

The pain was like a war arrow searing her tender, previously-untouched flesh, destroying her soul with every inch it penetrated. The thrusts came harder and harder; her body vibrating, head jerking from side to side, her lower lip bitten until the blood flowed freely. Then he was convulsing on top of her, grunting like a wild animal, clawing her breasts with his ragged fingernails, his fetid breath upon her face.

It was some moments before she realized that he had withdrawn from her, that their bodies were no longer in contact. She opened her eyes; they were swollen and she had difficulty in seeing. He must have punched her but so terrible had been the degradation and the agony elsewhere that she had not been aware of it.

Levine was fastening his trousers, breathing heavily, his features shiny with sweat. He glanced down, met her gaze and his lips curled cruelly.

'I ought to kill you, Injun,' he pulled out his knife, wiped some blood smears from the blade with thumb and forefinger, 'but I ain't going to. No, I want you to live and remember the time you was fucked by a real *man*, not some scrawny boy brave. And every time one of 'em has you, it'll be *me* fucking you. That's somethin' you'll never shake off!'

Mistai knew that he spoke the truth. Her hide belt was broken and none would want her except the bands of roaming renegade half-breeds who looted and raped whenever they could; no better than this white man.

She closed her eyes and when she opened them again he was gone without leaving so much as a footprint in the hard ground. His only marks were on her own body, scars that would never heal.

And as she lay there in the hot sun she saw her totem again, its expression changing according to the angle from which it was viewed, lips that moved and spoke, words you only heard if you listened hard enough.

I will repay!

The occupants of the island could not hold out much longer. The chief who was known to his own people as Bat and to the white men as Roman Nose was certain of that. The casualties amongst his own warriors were slight, less than a dozen killed, twice that number wounded. The soldiers, however, had suffered far greater losses. This last charge, or maybe the following one, would over-run them.

He raised his arm, held his rifle aloft, and kicked the flanks of his mustang, hearing the chorus of savage cries as the mounted throng behind him responded.

Even as he splashed into the shallow muddy water-course, Roman Nose realized that he was going to die. It did not come as a shock; he was too philosophical to feel any terror of death or what lay beyond. Just a sadness that he would no longer be able to remember his wife nor to gaze upon her living image as Mistrai became more beautiful day by day. Those were his only regrets. A warrior anticipates that every battle will be his last.

The whites held their fire until the last moment. Ponies reared, riders fell and were thrown. Something jogged against Roman Nose's neck. He glanced down, saw the totem face carved by Mistai swinging free of his shirt on its leather thong, spinning, seeming to leer at him in its gyrations. Blurred lips that spoke. *And cursed*. And he was frightened because Mistai had carved it.

Roman Nose had barely got his mount under control when the Spencer bullet tore into his throat, severing the jugular vein so that he was spouting blood even before he hit the ground. A broken, dying man, lying beneath a forest of plunging hooves, awaiting death and praying, not for himself but for his daughter whose innocent hands had trespassed into the world of the spirits and by chance stirred a demon in its ancient slumberings.

September 1874

The woman had walked the desert lands for several years now, the frayed blanket draped over her head to protect her from the fierce rays of the sun. . . or to hide her face in its dark shadow. By the hand she led an infant girl, neither wholly white nor red, who stared up at her with sullen dark eyes.

The squaw was known from Bent's Trading House to the Rio de los Animos, and for a dollar she would lie with any man, young or old, red or white. The Kiowas referred to her as *wihia* (the whore), and in the saloons and gambling dens she was blamed for spreading 'the disease'.

Her face was lined, ingrained with dirt so that it was difficult to guess her age, but her breasts were still young and tender. Yet her body was emotionless, a thing with which to copulate; none had known her to reach orgasm.

Men suffered and died from the disease but there were always others willing to mate with her, regardless of the rumours. They paid for their pleasures and sometimes in addition they purchased some of the quaint wooden carved figures which she carried in her medicine bag. There were always those who awaited her return, some even going into the desert to search for her.

Fall drifted into winter and when spring came there was no sign of the Indian harlot. Those who awaited her coming were impatient and frustrated so that in the end they sought out the prostitutes in the towns and paid five dollars for what they needed.

None knew her fate. Few cared. And the Indian child who was found wandering the streets of Sand Creek down the Kansas Pacific Railroad from Fort Wallace was in no way connected with her. The carvings found in the pouch strapped around the girl's waist were taken from her by an unscrupulous sheriff who was killed the following night in a saloon gunfight. The wooden figures were never seen again.

The child grew into a woman, learned the ways of saloon towns and how a living could be made without leaving one's bed. And then one day she, too, disappeared and was never seen again.

1
BANK HOLIDAY MONDAY

The fairground was an eyesore, a shabby cardboard world, its gaudy paint fading and peeling, its constant blaring music harsh and hurtful to the ear. But it was impossible to ignore the mind-blowing din that called the young like a Pied Piper. If your children did not drag you inside then somehow you found yourself there.

It had the lot, an untidy assortment of cheap amusements and rigged slot machines, hungry contraptions that gobbled holiday savings and only spat out twisted coins. Bingo halls and pool tables, stalls that offered prizes which could have been purchased for a third of the stake money. A menagerie that had somehow escaped the attention of those dedicated to preventing cruelty to animals: a lion who had long given up roaring, its cage so small it could not even pace the floor in frustration; an elephant who had once squirted water at its leering audience but had since had its liquid rations reduced to allow only sufficient for drinking; an ageing gorilla who sat with its back to the crowds in open contempt of Man; smaller, less dangerous creatures who lay on the floor of their smelly prisons, resigned to their life sentence. Once there had been a large notice, bold red lettering on a white board: DO NOT FEED THE ANIMALS. Jacob Schaefer, the proprietor, had ordered it to be removed because he saw by its absence a way to cut his feed bills.

Schaefer had lived in this artificial world of his own creation for almost a decade. He hated it, every square yard of it wherever it was erected, but he loved the money it brought in. Several times he had promised himself retirement, but there was always just one more season to see through and the takings were always up on the last one. A tall, raw-boned man, it was difficult even to guess at his nationality, and as if in a deliberate attempt at disguise he had allowed his beard to grow long and straggling. The upper part of his face was lined and wizened and he was probably at least sixty, many thought older. He kept to himself, avoiding conversation. When it was necessary he spoke in thick guttural tones with an indefinable accent – perhaps East European – a stump of dead cigar clinging to his bottom lip, bobbing up and down. His hands were like the talons of a bird of prey, half-clenched most of the time, the fingernails black and broken. He appeared to shuffle rather than walk, scraping worn carpet slippers along the ground and somehow managing to keep them on his feet.

Most of the time Jacob Schaefer remained in his caravan at the rear of the Kiddies' Kastle, a large inflated rubber edifice that wobbled like a jelly on a plate, an outsize trampoline for children to jump and roll on. Usually on the first night at a new site he went on a tour of inspection, seeing, nodding, mumbling incoherent words of approval or disapproval (nobody knew which) that somehow got absorbed in the soggy end of his cigar. But he never interfered because the money rolled in anyway and that was all that mattered.

There was only one place he would stop off before

returning to the solitude of his shabby caravan; a tent that had a hint of pride about it, small and colourful, neat inside because there was little to get untidy, just a trestle table, a couple of straight-backed chairs and a neatly-laid-out assortment of small wooden figures, hand-carved and painted so that you found yourself admiring the workmanship, wanting to reach out and pick one up, examine it closely. Your hand was half-way there when the occupant of the tent stopped you with a '*do not touch, please*'. And you stopped because when you saw her you were half afraid.

Logically, there was no reason to be, although children cowered behind their parents, peeping round at the strange dark-skinned woman dressed in hand-woven blankets that cascaded down to her feet. Fortune-tellers were supposed to be benign elderly women of Romany origin who relied on ambiguity to preserve their reputations. They told you what you hoped to hear and you left feeling that it was money well spent.

Not so with 'Jane'. None knew whether it was her real name (except possibly Schaefer) and her gypsy-like appearance was unconvincing, the skin too dark, the features denoting a wilder origin than the rural lanes of Britain. If her eyes flashed in anger you saw a savage, almost heard the thundering hooves of unshod war ponies and the blood-chilling cries of painted warriors. The sign over her tent-flap told you all you wanted to know: JANE, THE RED INDIAN FORTUNE-TELLER. It promised tribal mystique, an art handed down by the old witch-doctors, the real goods! So you ventured inside.

And underneath those blankets Jane was young. And beautiful. On occasions it had been hinted that that was why Schaefer went to her tent or caravan but the suggestion was ludicrous, too repulsive to be taken seriously. Both of them were loners, hermits once the fairground had closed down. Perhaps sometimes they experienced the need to talk. Nobody knew and nobody really cared. Somebody had nicknamed Jane 'Calamity', a jest that had turned sour when it had reached Jacob Schaefer's ears. Now it was only whispered.

Jane was in her tent long before the fairground was officially open to the public, sitting at her table working nimbly with a small bone-handled knife. Carving. She cut good-luck charms out of chunks of wood, working fast as though her livelihood depended upon it. Yet a tiny figure or emblem could be purchased from her for a pound – a day's work, possibly longer because none knew when she started or finished. And she never seemed to have more than one finished item on her table at a time, parting with it as unemotionally as though it was some object of mass production, stuffing the note somewhere in the voluminous folds of her gaudy attire, smiling, and saying softly, 'Keep it with you at all times. It will protect you from evil spirits.'

Life was a cycle that went in weeks and fortnights. Moving, erecting, taking down and loading the entire show on to a fleet of dilapidated lorries. New sites, but the scenery was always the same, towering sectional wooden and hardboard buildings that shut out everything around them.

And the Indian girl just carved impassively and told those who queued into her hot and stuffy little tent what was likely to befall them. If the tidings were bad then she withheld them because that was the way Schaefer wanted it. She smiled but somehow it was only a movement of the lips, her dark eyes yielding nothing. But the listener felt uneasy.

Today was exceptionally hot and extremely busy. She worked steadily. Possibly she was not even aware that it was a Bank Holiday.

The bikers had started to arrive early on Sunday afternoon, singly and in small groups, queue-jumping the mile-long line of cars and coaches trying to squeeze into an already-overcrowded resort. Nobody paid much attention to them in the beginning. Motor cyclists were commonplace enough, perhaps there was a rally on somewhere. But if you watched them closely they didn't appear to have any definite objective. A sort of drifting arrogance, clustering

22

on the promenade, obstructing traffic and pedestrians, parking their machines and pushing their way through the crowds, shouldering holiday-makers rudely to one side. No real trouble, though, not enough for the under-staffed police force to intervene. They merely watched apprehensively and hoped.

Towards evening the noise of motorbikes was threatening to drown even that of the fairground, a rivalry that was becoming more noticeable by the hour. The sun began to sink behind the western hills as though it wanted no part of this holiday scene. The weathermen had forecast more changeable conditions by Tuesday. But at the moment there was no hint of that change taking place.

It was dark before the first fight broke out, one of many that had been threatening for the past couple of hours. To the average seasider the bikers were much of a muchness, their uniforms of soiled denims bearing a variety of emblems and four-letter words. Had they scrutinized the invading army more closely they would have noted distinct differences between the separate factions. The East London Chapter wore their skull and crossbones on both sleeves and they were mostly clustered on the landward side of the promenade, small groups beginning to amalgamate. The Gladiators, with just a single death's head on their backs, had been the first to arrive but they had been outnumbered within the hour, and reluctantly they had begun to group together, bunches of nondescripts, imitators who were wishing that they had not come after all. The hardcore Hell's Angels were determined to rout the 'amateurs', remove them from the scene, before they concentrated on the town, its inhabitants and its visitors. And the fair.

Fat Fry was the undisputed leader. He'd come a long way, the throttle on his BSA was starting to slip and he had to take it out on somebody. He spat and heeled a blob of phlegm into the sand-covered concrete. Maybe they ought to begin their preparations in the pubs, put them in the mood. A trial run.

The grossly overweight twenty-year-old never got that

far. Something struck him in the face, something soft and sticky that smelled sickly sweet, adhering to his nose and eyes, clinging to his fingers as he tried to claw it away. All he could see was a mass of pink that blotted everything else out. Even his roar of blasphemous rage was muffled in the thick splodge of candy-floss.

'Oh, I'm *so* sorry.' He saw a woman, late twenties, the conventional respectable suburban housewife, an expression of horror on her prim face. Revulsion. *Fear!* 'I'm most terribly sorry. I didn't mean. . . .'

Of course she didn't, she wouldn't have the guts to hit him with the stick of candy-floss she was buying for her pimply darling little bastard of a child. The kid was starting to cry, pointing up at Fry's plastered face as though he wanted his mother to scrape it off and let him lick it off her fingers.

'Mummy!'

'It's all right, darling. Mummy will buy you another.'

Fat Fry saw red. Literally. Through it he saw two faces that represented the class of people he hated most in life; a species that couldn't stand up for itself and hid behind the law, went to church and tried to make out it was better than the kind that stayed away, physically weak, with soft hands that never got soiled. All this mingled in a cauldron of hate and came bubbling to the boil. He didn't even reach for the coil of oily chain in his pocket. He couldn't wait; he had to do something about that prig-awful female face quick.

A bunched fist powered by every ounce of fat and muscle in his body shot forward. The woman knew it was coming but was too terrified either to scream or get out of the way. A sickening thud; Fry felt it but didn't hear the crunch of breaking bone because others were yelling. He left his fist there, watched her face bounce off it, a flattened nose that was pouring blood down into the mouth beneath it, a tooth hanging out over her lower lip by a single thread. He sleeved some more candy-floss out of his eyes with his other arm, and he knew that his fury was only just beginning, that it was uncontrollable, and he would not have had it any other way. The arm went back, braced for a second blow,

24

and then his intended target keeled over and hit the ground. Fat Fry looked round for somebody else to hit. The nearest person to him was the kid (he couldn't have been more than eight), and the biker never hesitated. He swung his foot, caught the child in the solar plexus, sent him flying back against the refreshment stall.

The boy was bent double, then straightened up suddenly, arching his back, arms waving wildly as though he was unsure which part of his anatomy to clutch. He twisted round and at that moment his attacker saw the full extent of the wound he had inflicted. Something sharp, possibly a protruding nail beneath the counter-flap of the stall, had driven right into his back, ripping away the T-shirt then boring up into the spinal cord, gouging skin and exposing a knot of bone.

The child ran two steps then collapsed and writhed on the ground, his chances of walking again exceedingly remote. Fry stepped forward, couldn't stop himself as he put the boot in, his steel-capped toe unerringly, instinctively, finding the spinal wound and bludgeoning the exposed disc of bone. Only then was he satisfied.

Fat Fry turned, wiped some more of the clinging fluff from his eyes and tried to take in what was going on around him. Mother and son were on the ground behind him; he looked for the father. A mêlée. People fighting, somebody swinging a cheap cricket bat and trying to keep a couple of Hell's Angels at bay, failing, and going down beneath a windmill of heavy chains. Two more had got hold of a teenage girl wearing a bikini. One had her arms pinioned behind her back whilst his companion was removing her two-piece; she kicked out in desperation but he got in between her flaying legs and chopped viciously upwards with the flat of his hand. She sagged, her eyes closed, and the one holding her let go so that she fell in a heap on the concrete.

Everybody running for cover, nearby vendors hastily dropping the screens on their stalls. But the fairground's music dominated, a scratched Gene Pitney record of the early sixties ' . . . *yeah, I wanna love my life away.* . . . '

25

On the ground a sobbing, bleeding woman was trying to pick up the unconscious body of her son, screaming for somebody to help her. Nobody heard. Except Fat Fry.

He looked down, grinned through a pink beard, and his boot went back. The woman threw up a frail arm but it was smashed as though it was made of balsa-wood. The steel toe went in, buried itself in her abdomen, squashing an embryo that had not yet made its presence known to onlookers (not that that would have troubled Fry), and ended its life before it was begun.

Then everything stopped. Except the music, ' . . . *love my life away. . .* '.

A harsh penetrating sound somehow managed to cut into the end of the record. *Bee-bor, bee-bor*. . . . Flashing blue lights, cars and motor-cycles easing their way through the watching crowds, uniformed, helmeted men on foot. Police.

Angels and Gladiators alike were retreating, a mass stampede seawards, spilling over the sea-wall on to the soft powdery sand ten feet below, their feud forgotten temporarily in the face of a common foe. There were plenty of places to hide and the majority of them had intended spending the night on the beach, anyway.

The police let them go. A task force that wasn't big enough and didn't dare to poke the sleeping lion. Everywhere they looked there were denim-clad youths who might or might not have been involved in the fighting. It would just be a waste of ratepayers' money to attempt to round them up; ninety-five per-cent of them would get off because there was no evidence and the other five per-cent would get nominal fines. The brawl was broken up: that was good enough for now. Tomorrow would bring its own problems.

The Chief Inspector glanced round, saw the three injured people and radioed for an ambulance. His men would comfort them until it arrived. And in the meantime he would have to try and arrange for reinforcements to be sent over for Bank Holiday Monday. He knew there was going to be trouble in a big way. It had already begun.

Jacob Schaefer stared out of his caravan window and pursed his lips. He did not like the way things were shaping. He'd seen it all before. Margate, Southend and other places. It followed a pattern, a steady build-up of Angel forces on the Sunday preceding the Bank Holiday, then all hell let loose on Monday. And there was no way it could be stopped. You couldn't throw everybody in biking gear off the fairground, and if you closed up for the day they would still wreck the place. He blamed the police; he blamed the police for most things. They didn't do their job. Used any excuse. Because they were scared out of their uniforms. But they were only too eager to do you for minor infringements of the law; no road-tax or selling cigarettes to a twelve-year-old kid who looked every bit sixteen.

Angels and Gladiators were riding the roundabouts. Hell, there was a notice so big you couldn't miss it that said nobody over sixteen was allowed on the horses, but you couldn't blame old Everitt for not trying to stop 'em. They were sparring up on the dodgems, too, attempting to knock hell out of one another and the cars as well. A group was clustered around the shooting range, getting their eye in. When it all exploded, which could be in five minutes or five hours, they would be using the .177s and they wouldn't be shooting at the silhouette ducks.

And there wasn't a damned copper in sight. Schaefer locked the door of his caravan although he knew the old lock would not stand firm under pressure. All he could do was to wait . . . and hope.

Angels and Gladiators had segregated, formed into groups and taken up strategic positions. They had cased their battleground and now they were ready. The public had sensed what was happening and had moved out. But still the police did not come.

Fat Fry knew that his Chapter were looking to him to give the signal. He belched, knocked another duck off the belt and thought he could still taste candy-floss. Right now he could have done with some chips, a whole bagful, preferably fried in dripping. His real addiction, the reason he'd got his nickname. But he didn't mind that.

'How much longer are yuh goin' to wait?' Stap, his pock-marked lieutenant, spat and almost hit one of the ducks. 'The boys're gettin' edgy. Them fuckin' Gladiators are ready for the takin' but we don't want the fuckin' fuzz showin' up before we get started.'

'I'm ready,' Fry grinned. 'And we'll take this fuckin' place wiv 'em. Don't leave nothin' standin' that'll come down. Get me?'

Stap liked it when his leader was in the mood. Today was going to be real *fun*!

Fry cocked his air-rifle again, took his time adjusting the sights; the weapon had been deliberately set to shoot an inch to the left, but unless you knew something about guns you'd never guess. And Fry knew a lot about guns; like how to line up on a moving wooden duck, follow it across the whole line of fire and then suddenly swing up on to a human eye three yards away, snapshooting instantly, deadly accurate.

The balding attendant gave a loud piercing scream as the leaden wasp slug ploughed its way into his eye, splattering blood in its wake. Clutching at his wound, staggering back, knowing that he was a living target and there was no escape. A fusillade of shots, the whole line of target shooters suddenly taking their cue from Fat Fry, neck and cheeks punctured, the slugs from the air-rifles with powerful springs penetrating the flesh, the weaker ones striking and falling to the ground like bees that had exhausted their stings. The wounded man fell to the ground screaming.

The battle had begun! Only those actually engaged in the fighting knew friend from foe; to the distant crowd of spectators, many ghoulishly expecting to witness a blood-bath, one denim figure was the same as another. But up on the big-dipper Angels were engaged in deadly combat with Gladiators and it was only a matter of time before the first body came hurtling down like a cast-off rag-doll, cart-wheeling crazily until it struck the hard ground at full force, breaking up into a bloody mass of pulp.

Two bodies were draped lifelessly over the waltzer cars;

one slipped, got caught on the lower roundabout until the skull cracked against a steel pillar. On the ground, knives and chains were inflicting gory wounds. One combatant had an eye hanging out but retaliated with his knife, slitting an artery in his attacker's arm and spraying those in close proximity with blood.

A police panda car passed by on the adjoining road, drew into the kerb a hundred yards or so further on. The driver began talking into his radio. It was going to require a mass invasion by the law to break up a gang-war on this scale. No way was he going in alone.

Fat Fry watched the fighting for a few minutes but made no move to join in. The injured air-rifle attendant had crawled beneath the target stand, a trail of blood leading to his hiding place. Had there not been so much noise it would have been possible to hear him groaning with pain and terror. Given time, they could have some real fun with him!

Fry saw the tent with the Fortune-Teller sign hanging across the closed entrance flaps. His eyes narrowed as he remembered the Indian girl he had seen on his trip around the fairground yesterday. A sudden idea . . . he broke into a fast walk with Stap at his heels.

One swift tug was sufficient to break the cord which closed the entrance. The flaps fell back, and Fat Fry pushed his way through, stood just inside the door.

'Well, well,' his lips curled in a sneer, 'didn't really think there'd by anybody home. A real live Injun at that!'

The girl regarded him stoically. She was squatting against the far wall, dressed as she always was in her multi-coloured blankets, her head bared to reveal jet-black hair woven into two plaits. Her dark eyes flashed. 'You have no business in here!'

'Ain't we now?' Fry laughed loudly. 'The lady says we ain't oughta be 'ere, Stap. Come on in and close the door so we can all be nice and cosy.'

Stap did as he was ordered, the tent becoming darker as the sunlight was excluded. The smaller man felt uneasy, little shivers running up and down his spine. If it had been up to him he wouldn't have stayed. But it wasn't. Fat Fry was the boss and it could be very dangerous to disobey him.

Fry moved to the table, picked up a small wooden figurine, the head of which was almost the size of the rest of the body, features grotesque in their crudeness, eyes that seemed to watch and understand.

'Jeez!' Stap muttered. 'Them kinda things give yuh the creeps!'

'Lovely little dolly,' Fry mimicked a child's voice. 'Mam, it fair scares the shit outa me!'

They both laughed, then suddenly Fat Fry's smile faded. 'What a fuckin' awful piece o' carvin',' he sneered. 'I could do better'n that with me penknife. What's it supposed to be, squaw?'

Jane did not answer, looking at the intruders in silence, tight-lipped and angry but with no visible trace of fear.

'Well, we ain't got time to discuss the art o' carvin',' he dropped the chunky wooden figure into the side pocket of his denim jacket, 'but if this hussy ain't goin' to play along wiv us then maybe'll we'll get back to the subject o' knives and things!'

Stap swallowed. He would not have followed Fry in here if he'd guessed that the Indian girl was inside. He'd presumed she had fled like most of the fairground people. Now it was too late. He'd seen it all before, seen what their leader did to girls on a big raid like this one.

'Hold 'er, Stap!'

'Fry, maybe we could. . . .'

'*I said hold 'er!*'

Stap moved to obey on legs that had suddenly gone very weak, stepping round behind Jane, grabbing her wrists and pulling her to her feet. She didn't resist, it was almost as if she didn't care. Or else she had resigned herself to her fate.

Fry grasped the outer blanket, tried to rip it but it would not tear. He cursed, started to become angry, searched for a fold and found it. Underneath the Indian was wearing a sari-style garment fashioned out of some kind of hide. He couldn't tear that either and had to fumble with three separate rawhide thongs. As he loosened the last one the whole dress fell away and underneath it Jane was stark

30

naked.

Fat Fry pulled her close, pushed himself at her, let her know what he wanted; looked for a reaction. But there was none, not a single flicker of fear in those eyes. Fry saw and understood. Then he spat in her face, a blob of greeny/brown tobacco juice and spittle, a river of contempt trickling down her chin and dripping on to her breasts.

'Damn you, squaw,' he hissed, his rage coming up to boiling point, 'now you'll fuck until you can't fuck any more!'

Stap closed his eyes, half-turned his head away; he wished he didn't have to watch this or be any part of it. He almost let go of the girl and turned to run, changing his mind even as his grip slackened on her wrists. It wouldn't be any good; not when you were in the East London Chapter. There were too many of them, not just in London but all over the country. One word from Fat Fry and they would hunt you down like a pack of ravenous wolves, picking up your scent wherever you hid. And when they finally caught up with you . . .

Jane was pushed down to the ground, making no attempt to struggle even when Stap stood back. The smaller youth thought that he was going to throw up, the sight of Fry naked from the waist downwards was a revolting spectacle, a creature dominated by lust, violence and greed.

Fry went down on to the Indian girl, smothering her with his revolting hot kisses as he found what he was looking for and forced his way in. He started to jerk, his rolls of fat shivering and shaking, the interior of the small tent heavy with the smell of sweat. Stap didn't want to watch but it was a kind of compulsion because it was so horrible. Beauty and the Beast mating. Just *evil*.

Fat Fry was finished in a couple of minutes. It was always the same. He'd never been known to make it twice in spite of his constant boasts. He eased himself off his victim, spitting again in contempt of her closed eyes, kicking her bare thigh roughly as he struggled to fasten his jeans. But she did not open her eyes, her lids did not even flicker.

'All yours, Stap,' Fry jerked a thumb down at the

motionless girl.

'No,' Stap's mouth was dry and his stomach muscles were bunched into a tight ball. 'I . . . I ain't in the mood, Fry.'

'Please yerself,' the big youth turned away. Now that he had satisfied his sexual desires it was as though he had forgotten all about the girl's existence. 'Let's see what's goin' on out there.'

They stepped back outside. The fair was like a battle-ground. Sideshows were smashed or overturned. The big-dipper and the waltzer had ground to a standstill, some-body had turned off the motors. Maybe it would have been preferable to have left the big wheels turning because now the wreckers were able to go about their acts of vandalism more steadily, hacking at the wooden ornamentations without having to hang on with one hand to keep their balance. Only the music continued unperturbed, one record following another as though business was continu-ing as usual.

There were few Gladiators to be seen. Most of them, outnumbered by the combined forces of Angels, had fled back to the promenade, some even as far as the beach. Only the injured were left, bodies that crawled or lay on the ground and were kicked and beaten every time they moved.

But now a new enemy had entered the field of conflict: *police*.

Over a hundred uniformed officers were moving in, the advance party armed with batons and riot-shields. No longer was the battle one of unorganized violence; there was an unnerving efficiency about the way the law fanned out, converged, and came to grips with their foe.

'Christ!' Fat Fry experienced a rare stab of fear at the spectacle. 'We'd better get clear, Stap.'

Stap didn't argue, following in his leader's footsteps down an avenue of wrecked sideshows. It was clearly going to be a case of every man for himself and Fry wasn't worrying about the fate of those who had ridden in here with him. There were a good many who wouldn't be riding out again. Stap wondered what Fat Fry felt about them—

maybe he didn't care how many Angels got hurt so long as he escaped unscathed. Maybe he even saw it as a means of thinning out the ranks and getting rid of unwanted followers; the unworthy were always the first to fall in battle.

The Punch and Judy theatre lay on its side, the wooden figures sprawled grotesquely as though they too had fought and lost. Judy's head was cracked; Punch lay nearby clutching his truncheon. The policeman was sprawled between them as though he had tried to intervene and had been struck down also. But that was just plain bloody stupid, Stap told himself. All the same it was bloody weird that they had fallen that way. Jesus, the sooner he was away from this place, the better!

Suddenly his terror hit a peak, a mind-blowing deafening escalation that had him cowering, almost fleeing blindly and to hell with Fat Fry. A roar that threatened to shred the ear-drums, a sound of bestial fury and hate. Even Fat Fry had pulled up and was starting to cower.

'It's only the fuckin' zoo,' weak relief but the fear still lingering. 'They . . . can't get out!'

Stap stared, saw the mangy old lion, head back in preparation for a second roar, an ageing MGM that had suddenly discovered its basic instincts again. Something long and grey snaked up over a ten-foot steel barricade: Attila, the elephant, responding to the call of his king. A thumping, hollow like some huge drum: George the gorilla no longer sat with his back to the bars of his cage; he stood erect for the first time in years, proudly beating his matted hairy chest, eyes glinting with a malevolence that had slumbered for too long. The animals all remembered their mutual enemy, their cruel gaoler – Man.

'Come on,' Fry managed to make his limbs respond to his brain's command to move, 'let's get outa here.'

They slunk back towards the promenade, the sounds of music and the fighting growing fainter all the time. Neither of them could account for their sense of growing depression. Police intervention had been inevitable, they hadn't expected it to end any other way. And they had smashed the place up good and proper, shown what they were capable of. Yet deep down they were both afraid – not of being picked up by the law, that was all part and parcel of a day like today. It was something they couldn't explain. Like an inner wound that would grow and spread, a malignant cancer the seed of which had just been sown. As they found their bikes and climbed into the saddles the first heavy spots of rain splattered down. The darkening skies and freshening wind coming in from the sea caused them to shiver. The atmosphere had an air of foreboding, almost a warning that had come too late.

Jane, the Indian girl, lay on the ground for some time after the two men had left. Eventually she gathered up her clothing, and slowly dressed. Her wounds, both physical and mental, were just beginning to hurt but with a supreme effort she ignored them, shut them out in the same way that she had divorced herself from the dirty, stinking youth who had lain on top of her. Those few minutes had been a total blank, as though she had died and then been resurrected when he had withdrawn from her. She did not know how she did it, only that she did, as though at some stage in her infancy her mother had taught her how in preparation for such a day. There was only one thing she could not control. *Her hate*. Not just for those two; they were bad but only representative of the white race, a race that was bent on dominating older civilizations – using physical violence to subdue culture.

She glanced at the small table, saw that the carving, the one she had completed less than an hour ago, was gone. The big fellow had stolen it, she remembered the contempt he had poured on it.

Jane's eyes narrowed, her nostrils widened with the breath she expelled. Her lips barely moved, the words that came forth in the old Cheyenne tongue scarcely audible, a torrent that ended as quickly as it had begun.

And then she was seated composedly behind her table, the pain driven from her mind and body as effectively as the police outside were routing the last of the invading Hell's Angels. She continued to sit there. Waiting.

34

The traffic was at a standstill a mile outside the small seaside town, long queues of cars stretching out of sight in either direction, engines switched off, the force of the rain restricting the vision of drivers and passengers alike. Frustration was building up, the incessant downpour prevented people from getting out to stretch their legs, or from walking up the road to satisfy their curiosity about the cause of the hold-up.

Then the ambulance came, forcing its way through the double row of vehicles, scraping a Fiat which was too near to the middle of the narrow road, but not stopping. Everybody knew then that there had been an accident and some regretted that they would be unable to view it before the carnage was cleared away.

It had taken the ambulance three-quarters of an hour to reach the scene of the accident. Every vehicle in the local fleet had been called in to the fairground battle and this one had been summoned from twenty miles away. The torrential rain had forced the driver to cut his speed to a crawl.

'Hey, Joe,' the uniformed man in the passenger seat turned to the driver, an expression of concern on his suntanned features, 'I think you scraped that Fiat.'

'Sod 'im.' The driver had to slow to negotiate a parked caravan that was protruding at an angle. 'Sod 'em all! Stupid buggers, if they'd stop at home Bank Holidays there'd be a few less killed and injured and we could be doin' sommat useful. Here we are now . . . *Lord Jesus*!'

Even the two hardened ambulancemen paled as they drew on to the grass verge beside a mangled heap of wreckage. A harassed policeman was attempting to keep back the occupants of nearby cars. There were just two bodies – at least they *looked* as though they might have been bodies once – laid out by the roadside covered with a blood-saturated blanket. Motorcyclists. The ambulancemen saw the remains of a couple of machines, tangled and twisted where they had hit a Land Rover head-on, catapulted into the air, caught up together and then struck the road with unbelievable force.

Somebody had to sort out the bloody smashed corpses

and if you happened to have received the call then that was *your* bad luck. Joe told himself that it was just routine work and steeled himself to go in closer for a look. A big fellow and a smaller one, his experienced eye was already weighing up the extent of the injuries and how they had been caused. The riders had been thrown, then the spinning machines had kicked back up gutting them in mid-air, an almost unbelievable double coincidence but it had happened. Paunched like a couple of snared rabbits the bikers had got hooked up on their airborne machines, spraying blood and entrails everywhere, but even then they weren't finished. Coming down at all angles, bikes finishing up on top, grinding the human remains into the black tarmacadam, sharp and torn metal like slashing knives and axes. Even so, a *double beheading* . . . not impossible but highly improbable. *But it had happened*.

Not speaking, even to each other, the two men returned to the ambulance, got some polythene sheeting and sacks, a stretcher. There was no hurry, nothing that wouldn't keep.

'Hey, what's this?' the man called Joe picked something out of the grass beside the heap of torn flesh and blood-soaked clothing. He held it in his hand, turned it over.

'Some kind of kid's toy.' His companion welcomed a diversion, anything that was not connected with flesh and blood. 'A mascot of some kind, maybe.'

The driver gave the object another quick look, then dropped it in his pocket. A hand-carved figure, crudely done if you placed importance on proportion; the head was far too big, the body squat and ugly. Maybe his young grandson would enjoy playing with it. Nobody was going to miss it. It could have been lying there by the roadside for weeks.

Their grisly task completed, they set about turning the ambulance round, a matter of some difficulty even with the assistance of the policeman. The rain didn't help either. It was one of those Bank Holidays when everybody wished that they had stayed at home and been miserable in some degree of comfort. Already the long trek home for the fortunate had begun.

The ambulance moved off slowly, passed the dented Fiat which was now nearer to the verge, its driver leaning out of the window and shouting something as they drove by.

By the time they got clear of the traffic jam the rain was easing off to a fast drizzle. Joe glanced towards the horizon but even with the passing of the thunderstorm there was no clear sky to be seen.

'Don't look like. . . .'

Joe never finished what he had been about to say. Instinctively his foot was stamping hard on the brake pedal as an elderly man in a rain-drenched Panama hat suddenly stepped out into the road, hurrying with the blind urgency of senility.

Tyres squealed and failed to secure a grip on the slippery surface. Slewing, skidding, cannoning off a parked cara-vanette, ploughing into the side of an Avenger estate on the opposite side, a frail figure bowling over in the middle of the road like a shot rabbit.

A few seconds of silence followed the crunching and tearing of tortured metal and the showering of broken glass. And then the crowds were gathering, the screaming beginning again.

Death. And death again.

2
MONDAY EVENING

'Fai . . . fai . . . fai. . . .'

The small red-haired girl was shouting and pointing excitedly, apparently oblivious of the driving drizzle which was already beginning to dampen her flowery cotton dress. She stood there at the gate of the insignificant boarding-house hopping from one foot to the other in her excitement, a tiny double hearing-aid emitting a shrill high-pitched whistle as her movements disturbed its frequency. 'Fai . . . fai. . . .'

'*Rowena*!' a tall woman in her mid-thirties appeared in the doorway. Her hair was the same bright chestnut colour as her eight-year-old daughter's and there was an underlying sadness permanently stamped beneath the mass of freckles on her face. 'Rowena, will you come in out of the rain at once!'

'Fai . . . fai. . . .' The girl heard her, turned, but such was her excitement that obedience was the last thing on her mind.

'Yes, I know it's a fair.' The woman came out, grasped her daughter lightly but firmly by the wrist. 'But you must come in for now. Perhaps tomorrow Daddy will take us all to the fair. Come on, now.'

Rowena was staring into her mother's face, barely hearing the words but lip-reading with an expertise which even the teachers at her Partially Hearing Unit marvelled at. She nodded, somewhat reluctantly allowed herself to be led into the narrow hall and up two flights of badly-carpeted and poorly-lit stairs. Liz Catlin was weary, Rowena's perpetual exuberance now bringing on a feeling of near-exhaustion. It hadn't been an easy journey down; blazing stifling heat for two thirds of the long crawl, then hours of suffocating delay in pouring rain. The last five miles had been the worst, first that motorbike accident (she was glad they hadn't been close enough to see any details), then the ambulance colliding with an old man. She couldn't help wondering if the old man was still alive.

'That's better.' Roy Catlin, stripped to the waist, was towelling himself by the wash-basin in their double-bedroom. 'Nothing like a drop of clean water to wash a journey out of your skin.'

Liz closed the door, leaned against it. She had washed earlier but it had not had the same effect. Seldom did she get depressions these days but this one was really eating into her. And holidays were one helluva time to start feeling like this.

'What's up with Rowena?' Roy Catlin glanced at the child who was still in a euphoric state. 'We're not going on the beach this evening, not in this weather.'

'It's not the beach,' Liz replied. 'It's the fair. You know what she's like where fairs are concerned. It looks a pretty tatty one to me. I thought perhaps a tornado or a tidal wave had come in from the sea and wrecked it but Mrs Hughes down below was telling me that there's been a massive battle earlier today, hundreds of these Hell's Angels yobs rioting. It took the police nearly two hours to get them under control. Two of the rioters . . . ' she checked to make sure that Rowena could not see her lips and lowered her voice, 'were *killed*. Several more were taken to hospital, including three policemen.'

'Serve 'em bloody well right.' Roy Catlin pulled his shirt over his head. 'The yobs, I mean, not the coppers. Just what the hell is this country coming to? I say bring back hanging, the birch, conscription and. . . .'

'Oh, don't go into all that again, *please*!' Liz moved across to the dressing-table and began brushing her shoulder-length hair.

'And what's got into *you*, first day of the holiday?'

She rounded on him, saw Rowena standing watching them, and checked herself with an effort. 'Nothing. Just tired after the journey, I suppose.'

Roy Catlin lowered himself into the tatty armchair and lit a cigarette. This holiday wasn't getting off to the start he had planned, quite obviously. Not that he *enjoyed* holidays, but as the head of the family one had to give the impression of being reasonably enthusiastic. It wasn't easy. Life was all a process of acting, from the time you were born until you died. Some had to do it more than most.

He hated being 'just average', had fought against it all his life. Sometimes he thought it would have been preferable to be 'below average'. At school he'd never ever been top of his class in any subject; or bottom. Somewhere around a middle placing; and he never managed to shine in the athletic events or the annual cross-country run. It was the same after he left school. Four 'O' Levels, high enough to qualify him for middling jobs but not enough for a top post. He'd done his damnedest to avoid the mediocrity of conventional clerical work. The police force had appealed to him, a chance to work his way up the ranks by sheer hard graft. He never even got the chance because he'd failed his medical, and that also ruled him out of any of the armed forces. The field was a bit limited after that, and in the end he'd had to take a 'temporary' job. Solicitor's Cashier. It had a ring of prestige about it but right from his first day at the offices of Balfour and Wren he'd placed both feet firmly in the rut. They already had a cashier, a guy in his mid-thirties who had every intention of remaining there until retirement age and longer if he was allowed to. Roy Catlin's duties were basic and were unlikely to be upgraded. He was just a glorified messenger with a carrot dangled frequently, sometimes threateningly, by Mr Balfour on his sporadic appearances at the office. 'Of course, Catlin (never *Mister*), you will have to learn *Mr* Stafford's job because I must have someone who can take over during his absences.' Not that Stafford was ever absent; he'd never been known to be away sick, and even during his holidays he came in for a few hours most days 'just to make sure that there aren't any problems'.

So Roy Catlin had his own problems. He stared at his reflection in the mirror as Liz prepared herself for the evening meal. He had to be honest, he wasn't really *bad-looking*; neither was he handsome. A sort of in-between. Average. Had his eyes been half-an-inch further apart, his jaw set a little more squarely, then, with a tan (which he hoped he would acquire before the end of the week), he reckoned he might have borne a fair resemblance to Alan Ladd, his boyhood screen hero. Twenty years of idol-worship just because he wanted to be somebody else, fifteen years of deterioration in the musty Dickensian offices of Balfour and Wren. His temporary job had stretched into permanency. And Liz wouldn't even come clean, tell him he was a failure. She just told all her friends that he was 'with Balfour and Wren', and avoided any direct questions about what he actually did there. Was *she* happy? He didn't even know that much; she said she was but never enthused about life. Maybe secretly she blamed him for Rowena's deafness from birth (sorry, partial hearing, you had to get it right although it was virtually the same thing). And now it was too late to change. The years were ticking away too fast. He was firmly entrenched in the 'average' bracket.

'Are you ready?' she turned to him.

'The gong hasn't. . . .'

A muffled metallic clanging from somewhere below. Three resonant sounds that died slowly away. Roy eased himself out of the chair, smoothed back his corn-coloured straight hair. Holidays were just another routine. Breakfast at nine, a packed lunch to eat on the beach, an evening meal at six. It didn't give you much of a chance to do your own thing.

The food at the Beaumont Private Hotel was as Roy had expected. Average. They advertised it as 'Good' but they couldn't be blamed for that; so long as it wasn't bad they were safe.

'Is it still raining?' Liz twisted in her chair as she drank her coffee and tried to see out of the small bow-window.

'Doesn't look too promising,' her husband saw the grey opaqueness that had come in from the bay and settled on the coastline. 'Drizzling. Maybe it'll clear up tomorrow.'

'Maybe,' she turned back, glanced at Rowena who had opted for orange juice. 'But we'd better go out somewhere this evening. It's only a quarter to seven. We can't stop in our room until bedtime.'

Roy thought that they could have done that and also thought of a lot of things that they might possibly have done if they hadn't been Mr and Mrs Average from Conventional Town. But Liz wouldn't do those sort of things so it was a waste of time thinking about them.

'Well, we don't want to go out anywhere in the car, that's a sure fact,' he grimaced at the prospect of roads solidly jammed with disconsolate day-trippers who were lucky enough to have the option of going home. 'Maybe we could take a walk in the town and keep under cover of the shop

41

fronts.'

'Fai . . . fai.' Rowena, who had been watching his lips closely, suddenly shrieked loudly so that heads in the small dining-room turned, disapproving stares from those who had no conception of the problems involved with a deaf child.

'Shh, darling,' Liz dropped a restraining hand on to the child's arm and glanced back at Roy. 'Well I suppose it's an idea. There are worse places to go on a wet evening and certainly there won't be any rowdies left there.'

Roy groaned inwardly and knew that they would be going to the fair. Liz had decided and that was that.

Rowena gave one final jubilant shout. '*Fai*!'

Jane had carved steadily since mid-afternoon. To the observer she appeared perfectly relaxed, if uncommunicative, and none would have guessed that only hours before she had been violently raped. She had told nobody, neither the police nor Jacob Schaefer when they had called to check on her. It would have served no purpose. And, anyway, they too were white. She didn't blame individuals, just a race. A race that had slaughtered her own forefathers, pillaged and raped and stolen their lands. She had heard the stories from her mother who had heard them from her mother in turn, and she from her mother before her. That was sufficient. So she continued with her carving because there was nothing else to do.

'It is a terrible mess,' Schaefer had said, 'but we have experienced it before. Perhaps you could help to repair some of the carvings, some of those which were originally done by yourself. The Punch and Judy Show is the most important if we are to put on a performance tonight. Just disfigurations mainly. No problem for you, Jane, I am sure.'

Jane worked slightly faster than she usually did. Judy and the policeman were already repaired. Another half-hour would see Punch ready for the next show. And then she stopped, looked up, suddenly aware that somebody was in the entrance to the tent watching her. It was strange that she had not been aware of it before. Frightening, in fact, a hint that her senses were being dulled by an artificial existence.

She saw the child standing there, and again experienced a peculiar sensation which she could not describe. Certainly not fear . . . something else. A kind of understanding that did not require words, and for some seconds she stared at her visitor in silence. Children rarely came in here on their own. Jane saw the small hearing-aids, recognized a shyness in the other, seemed to forget her animosity towards the white race.

In those few moments, both felt a bond of sympathy between them. Rowena dropped her gaze, raised it again, then let her eyes travel around the interior of the tent. Seconds later she was backing away, a look of horror on her face; the Punch and Judy characters propped up against the canvas, they seemed to *see* her. *They seemed alive!*

'Do not be afraid, little one,' Jane followed Rowena's gaze, saw the reason for her fear. 'They are only wooden figures. Dolls. I made them. They were broken so now I must mend them.'

Rowena smiled but could not stop the faint trembling. She knew that Punch, Judy, the policeman were only wooden effigies. She'd seen a show once, last year on the sands at Torquay. But the characters there had been so different from these; these seemed to take on a personality of their own, she felt it emanating from them like invisible waves reaching out to embrace her, as clammy coldness. Eyes that saw and were *hostile*. She almost turned and ran. She didn't know why she stayed except that perhaps the dark-skinned lady was so kind, offering her protection so that no harm would befall her.

'*Rowena*!' there was a note of panic in the shout that came from outside, bordering on hysteria.

Rowena heard it in the depths of her limited hearing, recognized her mother's voice, but she made no move to answer.

'Is your name Rowena?' Jane smiled.

The child nodded but still did not speak.

'Somebody is calling you. Perhaps you had better go.'

Rowena shook her head. She did not want to leave. She liked it here, apart from the three carved figures, but the lady wouldn't let them do anything to harm her, because she was kind and understanding.

'*Rowena*!' the tent flap was pulled back and Liz Catlin looked in, her expression of anguish changing to one of relief. 'Thank goodness! Whatever are you doing in here? Daddy and I have been searching all over for you. You shouldn't have gone off on your own like that. *Roy*!'

Roy Catlin appeared, pushing his way into the confined space. 'Thank God!' he muttered. He was sweating as though he had been running. 'Come on, Rowena. It's time we were going, time you were in bed.'

'*No*!' Rowena stood her ground.

'*Rowena*!' Liz's tone was sharp. She stretched out a hand, grasped her daughter's wrist firmly.

'She is quite safe here,' Jane's voice was low yet firm.

'She's too young to know anything about fortune-telling,' Liz snapped, 'and anyway I wouldn't allow her to dabble in that sort of thing.'

'She is interested in the carvings,' the Indian's features were impassive, only her eyes revealing an inner annoyance at the sudden parental intrusion. 'It is good that a child with any kind of disability shows a keen interest in things around her.'

Liz's expression said '*How dare you*', yet somehow she did not voice her feelings. She experienced a strong sense of awe bordering on fear, akin to her feeling about the headmistress of the High School when she was a pupil there. You wanted to say an awful lot of things but when the opportunity arose you merely fumed in silence.

'Look, Mummy,' Rowena tugged at the hand which restrained her, pointing excitedly at the wooden puppets, her fear of them now gone. 'Nice dolls.'

Ugh, Liz thought, they're horrible. Gruesome. Not for children.

'They're rather cute,' Roy smiled and moved further inside the tent. 'Real craftsmanship there. Did you . . .

carve them?' He sensed an atmosphere of embarrassment, felt he ought to say something to this attractive girl whom Liz had apparently taken a dislike to, blaming her for Rowena's disappearance. His wife always jumped to conclusions, usually wrong ones.

'Yes,' Jane smiled for the first time. 'Unfortunately there was a big fight here today and they got broken. Not seriously, but it is necessary for some work to be done on them so that they can perform this evening. See, Punch has had an ear broken so I have recarved it. It leaves him with a disfigurement but what does that matter? Why do you not take Rowena along to see the show?'

'It's her bedtime!' Liz snapped. 'Past it, in fact.'

'Oh, I don't see that we have to maintain strict bedtimes on holiday.' Roy spoke casually, but there was an underlying stubbornness in his voice as he instinctively seized the opportunity to undermine Liz's family domination. Maybe he'd left it too late, but he was determined to test her. 'Come on, we'll all go to the Punch and Judy show.'

A momentary conflict. Husband versus wife, Rowena siding with her father, leaping up and down excitedly. Jane's mute encouragement that they should go along to the puppet show, a kind of casting vote.

'All right,' Liz found herself conceding and hated herself for it. She wanted to argue, knew she could come up with a score of reasons why they should keep away. Those figures, they were positively *horrible*, could give a child nightmares. And Rowena had always been prone to nightmares. It was the Indian's fault. You felt her domination of your own will, but you were powerless to fight against it. 'I hope it won't go on too late, though.'

Roy Catlin wasn't listening. He was looking at Jane, aware of the power in her eyes, a kind of seduction. You couldn't imagine yourself going against her will. Not like Liz's domination; in a strange masochistic way he enjoyed the Indian's.

'Thank you for looking after our daughter for us,' he spoke softly, having to concentrate to put the words together. His brain was confused, muzzy. That was because

45

he was tired.

'You are lucky to have such a lovely daughter,' Jane favoured him with another smile. 'We have got on so well together. Please bring her to see me again, we should both enjoy that very much.'

Liz tensed, fists clenching, a sudden helplessness which she wanted to fight against but could not. Everything seemed to be slipping away from her, husband and daughter alienated from her by this slut of a squaw. But the seething cauldron of rage inside her would not come to the boil.

A thought crossed Roy's mind; he wondered what the Indian would be like in bed. He felt the early tremors of an erection but it was gone almost as soon as it began, leaving him with a sense of shame instead. He was still looking into her eyes. That was where the brief thought had come from, almost as though she had deliberately planted it and then withdrawn it.

'Thank you,' he said again.

'It is a pleasure,' she didn't smile this time. 'Perhaps another time you would allow me to tell your fortune.'

He nodded. 'Yes, I'll do that.' Then he was turning away, following the tall striding figure of Liz who pulled Rowena along with her.

Outside, clear of the tent, Liz Catlin turned and never previously had Roy seen her in such a rage. Her flaming features matched the colour of her hair, her lips a thin bloodless line, opening to pour out a torrent of contempt and fury.

'Are you mad?' she shouted but the blaring crackling music rendered her words barely audible. 'Rowena should be in bed but instead you allow that . . . that squaw to cajole you into letting her watch those vile puppets demonstrating violence and everything else a child shouldn't see. Maybe even *sex* as well! I won't stand for it. D'you hear, *I won't allow it!*'

Suddenly Rowena had flung herself at her father, arms around his waist, her head pressed against his shirt. He could feel the sobs which shook her. Liz had overlooked the fact that Rowena could lip-read. The child had seen and understood.

'We can't go back on our promise.' He tried to make himself heard above the din, could see that she was still spitting out her protests but was determined to defeat her on this issue. 'We've got to go along to the Punch and Judy whether you like it or not.'

Liz Catlin's rage subsided slowly and she nodded. There were no tears in her eyes, only a dry burning hate. Oh God, she hated that Indian, the way she'd brought all this about. All for one purpose. *Because she was determined to lure Roy back to her*. She wanted to get him back to her tent, to work on him with her guile, the dirty little hussy! And Roy had already fallen for her charm, that much was evident. She wasn't attractive, she was weird. And she wasn't going to succeed, Liz Catlin was determined on that. No way. It appeared they had no alternative but to go along to the Punch and Judy. Well, at least she wouldn't be there. And after that they weren't coming anywhere near this fair-ground again for the rest of the week. It was a cheap, nasty, low-class form of entertainment for mindless holiday-makers, cheating them out of their hard-earned savings. If people had any sense they would boycott fairgrounds, force them to close. And the yobs who chose them for their battle-grounds would be forced to look elsewhere.

Nevertheless, tonight she, Roy and Rowena were going to the Punch and Judy Show. After that they would forget that this noisy fairground even existed!

The show was late starting, an audience of some forty or fifty people becoming restless, a few beginning to drift away to the sideshows. Possibly they would come back later. More likely they would not.

The Catlins had seats in the front row of the open-air theatre, the menagerie behind them, a line of parked vans and lorries shutting off the rest of the fairground. In its own way it generated a claustrophobic atmosphere, the din hemming everybody in so that they got the feeling that they couldn't escape even if they wanted to.

47

Children sat on the laps of their parents, some already asleep because of the unaccustomed lateness, everybody staring fixedly at the square wooden structure with gaily painted curtains, urging the show to begin. Movements. Once those curtains billowed outwards as though the foot-high puppets were on stage and as restless as those who awaited their performance. Of course, there was a man down there beneath the stage, possibly two, another stationed in an elevated position, probably screened by that big square of chipboard, to work the wires. The humans were the real actors, the puppets taking the credit and the applause, the abuse when Punch's violence became intolerable. Today everybody had seen enough violence but it was a drug, an addiction, and they flocked here hungry for more.

A gasp of mingled relief and expectation; the curtains were opening, parting slowly, jerking as though they snagged on ragged wires. The scene was set. A room, windows navy blue in an attempt to depict nightfall, a luminous smiling moon peeping in. Sparse furniture, two chairs and a table, and a cradle in the foreground; the top of a tiny head was just visible above the side. Some of the audience had already climbed on to their chairs to view the wooden baby inside it. Already sympathy for the infant was growing. Everybody was aware of the baby-battering which would follow.

Enter Judy, clad in a flowing apron that scraped the floor as she tottered across to her offspring, concern in her posture as she leaned over it, head nodding jerkily. Her lips seemed to move; perhaps they were spring-loaded or it could have been an illusion. Any second now the villain would appear, intent on destroying the bastard of his creation, removing an unwanted burden from his life of crime.

Judy stooped as though to lift the child to her bosom. *Too late*! A screech of fear drowned by a roar of rage as the clown-like Punch materialized on stage. Catcalls and abuse from the crowd, a child somewhere at the back was starting to scream.

48

Roy Catlin found himself tensing, slipping a protective arm around his daughter. *That face, the way it turned towards the audience, leering, threatening. You felt yourself cowering away from it, pressing yourself back in your seat.* Liz's hand had uncharacteristically found Roy's, squeezing it; he felt her body leaning against his. *Oh God, I'm scared!*

Punch's attention was now focused on the baby in the crib, sheer hate blazing from his black eyes, baton upraised. Judy forced herself in front of him, tried to fight him off with puny windmilling fists that rattled like castanets. Shrill screams. *Those lips were definitely moving!*

Baton upraised, crashing fiercely down, spilling the cradle and its contents, the infant rolling across stage, bouncing back off the far wall. Punch was after it, weathering Judy's attack as his staff found its mark. Once, twice. Thrice. Incessant blows that it was impossible to count. The deed was done!

Now he turned his attention to the berserk Judy. Two pairs of eyes dominated, had Roy Catlin clutching both Liz and Rowena close to him. It was stupid, he told himself, inanimate objects having this effect on him. *It was the eyes which were doing it; living orbs!*

Judy was down and coming up again, desperately fighting a battle which could have only one possible outcome.

Screams of fear, yells of terror from the audience. It couldn't be, but it was there for all to see. Blood! Bright and crimson, oozing out of the baby's head, now pouring from Judy as she slumped and fell lifeless to the ground, spreading and forming into a pool in the centre of the stage.

A trick of some kind, Catlin tried to convince himself and hoped that he would be more successful with his explanation to his wife and daughter. A bloody clever ruse, probably a well of tomato ketchup inside the figures' heads which opened on impact and released its contents. It had to be that, it couldn't be anything else. *Jesus Christ, it was awful!*

Rowena was squirming herself into a ball, hiding her face against her father. Liz was gripping him fiercely, murmuring her disgust, her fear. More children were screaming, a small boy had vomited over the man sitting in front of him, but nobody moved. Nobody left.

Cheers. For once the police topped the popularity poll in the figure of a burly wooden officer, his uniform a shade too blue but that didn't really matter. Optimism from the audience; he would not succeed in arresting or even thwarting the horrendous villain but for a few moments anyway he would exert his authority. Already the law was brandishing its truncheon, the two squaring up like fencers seeking just one opening. *But there was no getting away from the blood that oozed around their feet . . . they were even finding it difficult to keep a foothold.*

Blow for blow. A sudden roar of encouragement from the crowd, the figure in blue had the upper hand, driving his adversary into a corner with a spate of vicious thrusts. Agony on Punch's face; his lower lip seeming to split, a dark spreading stain.

'It's awful!' Liz Catlin muttered. 'Can't we leave?'

Roy did not reply. He couldn't take his eyes off the duel. Rowena pressed against him but her head, too, was turned towards the stage, transfixed almost to a state of hypnotism. Everybody wanted to leave but nobody was doing so. They were kept here by some unseen power.

Punch was not on the defensive for long. He weathered the attack and then struck back with even greater venom, an over-arm swing that landed on his opponent's helmet. The officer was down, unable to get back on to his feet, blows raining on him.

And now only Punch remained standing, battered and victorious, turning to face the audience. People cowered, gasped aloud, threw their hands up as though he might suddenly launch an attack on them. He tottered to the edge of the stage, stood there looking at them. His mouth was definitely moving, muted mutterings of hate that were directed at *them*. His eyes narrowed, blazed their venom like twin miniature searchlights.

The curtains were trying to close, snagging again, as though that same invisible force was determined that this scene of unbelievable, inexplicable carnage should not be hidden from human eyes. The murderer himself stepping between the curtains, laughing insanely.

Blood was oozing from beneath the helmet of the inert policeman, a steady flow that was starting to congeal already.

'Bloody disgusting!' a man's voice from somewhere on the back row. 'Children shouldn't be allowed to watch this sort of thing!'

'Hear, hear,' Liz Catlin muttered.

Then the curtain was closed and all that was visible was Punch's shadow behind it, a grotesque moving shape, club raised. *But the show wasn't over yet*; the stage lights were producing an eerie shadow show on the frayed fabric, all the more weird because the audience knew what lay behind, three corpses and a psychopath who was not yet finished with his foul deeds. Death . . . *then mutilation*!

Thud . . . thud . . . thud.

Even the fairground noise seemed unable to mask the final vicious blows as Punch pummelled his victims, working himself up into a frenzy. A woman was screaming, children were crying.

And then suddenly the whole scene was plunged into darkness as though those who manipulated the strings had realized that they had pushed the audience to the very brink.

Angry spectators conversed in low tones, children were carried, clinging to their parents fearfully. Roy had Rowena in his arms, aware how her body was shaking, Liz was holding his arm with fingers that trembled. Yet nobody went forward to lodge their complaints to those responsible, the men behind the screens who had worked the strings of the puppets.

Roy Catlin breathed a loud sigh of relief once they were clear of the theatre, felt the welcoming freshness of a sea breeze fanning his cheeks. Then for the first time he was aware that it was raining, a steady heavy drizzle. With amazement he noticed that his clothes were wet. So were Liz's. And Rowena's. And everybody else's.

It had been raining throughout that strange and terrifying

3

TUESDAY

Roy and Liz Catlin had undressed in silence, spread their damp clothing over a radiator that was cold and likely to stay that way. Maybe if it was fine tomorrow the garments could be hung from the window sills to dry in the sun. *If* it was fine.

'I wish we'd never gone anywhere near that fairground,' Liz spoke for the first time as they climbed into bed. 'It's Rowena I'm worried about. She's really scared. Perhaps we ought to let her sleep in our room tonight.'

'She's probably already fast asleep,' Roy shivered with a damp coldness that seemed to have penetrated his skin. 'She'll be all right.'

'I just hope so,' Liz paused to listen but heard no sound from the adjoining bedroom. 'Whoever put on that show was a sadist. There was no need for all that . . . that *make-believe* blood.'

'No,' Roy agreed. 'But I guess it's a sign of the times. Violence and more violence. Anyway it wasn't appreciated by the audience, so maybe the fairground people will drop it for future performances.'

'I think we ought to complain.'

'It wouldn't do any good.'

'Which is what everybody is saying today. Nobody has the guts to stand up and say what they think. It's the same all over. You're as bad as anyone else. Old Balfour snaps his fingers and you come running. "Yes, Mr Balfour, I don't mind working late. Of course I don't expect any overtime. I'm only too pleased to change my holiday dates

52

to suit you. And if you want me to come in at the weekend I'll do that for you. Don't you worry about me, Mr Balfour. I'm only the junior clerk so you can do what you like and I won't complain. Because I *love* my job!" '

Roy tensed, the bitterness biting deep. Here we go again, he thought. I can't even get away from it on holiday. It was her bloody suggestion that we went to the fair and now she's blaming me for the Punch and Judy. He didn't argue, he'd given that up long ago. Let her have her say and maybe in the morning she would have forgotten about it.

'Well, *we'll* complain!' Liz moved close against him but he knew it was only because she was feeling cold. 'In the morning you can go back there and you can find the man who worked the puppets and tell him just how revolting everybody found it, that all the kids were scared, *and* the parents.'

'All right,' he sighed. 'But I thought you said we weren't going anywhere near the fair again.'

'*We* aren't. Not Rowena and myself. *You* can go across after breakfast, tell them exactly what we think and that the whole thing was in exceptionally bad taste and then that'll be that.'

Roy turned over, faced the wall. As usual he was to be the spokesman. Well, he'd sort something out tomorrow but in the meantime he needed some sleep. His brain was racing like a car engine with the choke out and sleep wasn't going to be easy.

Tuesday morning. It was raining hard. A sea mist had drifted in, almost impossible even to see the end of the pier less than a quarter of a mile away. A grey incoming tide with an even greyer sky above it reflected the mood of the day that had struggled to dawn.

The atmosphere in the dining-room of the small hotel was depressing. Nine tables with the occupants of each lingering over toast and marmalade, squeezing extra cups of tea and coffee out of depleted pots because it all used up time. And time was likely to hang heavy throughout the day. Even the children sensed it, aware that there would be no beach games, no paddling or sand-castles.

'Mummy, can we go to the fair?' a boy's voice broke the silence.

'We'll see,' the answer was non-committal, reluctant. 'We'd better explore the town first. It might brighten up later.'

Rain lashed the windows as though the elements were determined to destroy that faint hope, and the sullen silence settled again. Secretly you wished you were back home but you would never admit it. Only to yourself.

'Maybe we ought to take a drive inland,' Roy Catlin drained the last dregs of coffee from his third cup and felt in his pockets for his cigarettes. 'This is probably only a belt of coastal rain. We might find somewhere drier.'

'Possibly,' Liz was watching Rowena intently. Their daughter had been unusually silent throughout breakfast. She looked tired. That was because they had kept her up late last night. 'But first . . . well, you know what you have to do first!'

'If you insist.'

'I do.'

'All right. But there's no hurry, it's going to be a long day.'

Rowena looked up, glanced from her mother to her father. 'Fai . . . fai. . . .'

'No, darling,' Liz didn't manage entirely to keep the sharpness out of her voice. 'Not today.' Or ever again.

'Punch and Judy. I want the Punch and Judy.'

A shocked silence, Roy and Liz looking to each other.

'No, love,' Roy smiled, ruffled Rowena's chestnut hair. 'It's finished. They won't be showing it again.' A downright lie, one that made him squirm inside.

'They won't,' Liz was tight-lipped. '*You've* got to see to that.'

Roy drew hard on his cigarette. It was bloody ridiculous the way she got these fixed ideas, as though it was all his fault. He stood up, almost knocking his chair over. 'I'd best go and get it over with then.'

Wearing his anorak with the hood pulled up, Roy Catlin

stepped on to the rain-whipped promenade. God, it couldn't be worse! Sickening. It didn't appear to be making much difference to the fair, though; if anything, it was reaping the benefit of the adverse weather. Crowds of kagoule-clad figures jostled for places on bumper-cars and merry-go-rounds, feet squelched in mud and splashed in puddles. Artificial gaiety, forced happiness because it cost too much money to be miserable on holiday. And deep down everybody was wishing they weren't here, except the kids who saw in the rain a golden opportunity to indulge in pastimes which otherwise their parents would have dissuaded them from.

Catlin pushed his way through the crowds, took a short cut through the menagerie. The lion and the gorilla were indoors, the elephant standing dejectedly in its enclosure. He was surprised that there was no admittance charge but it was obvious really. The large beasts in themselves were crowd-pullers, the atmosphere and the children doing the rest. If every holidaymaker was tempted to spend even 20p the proprietors were on to a winner.

He slowed in his tracks, felt a quickening of his pulses. The tent, the gaudy one with closed flaps. In his mind he saw the Indian girl again, her wild beauty and savage eyes, the way she searched you out, knew more about you than you did yourself. Which wasn't surprising if she was a genuine clairvoyant and Roy Catlin had no doubts regarding that.

He had to make a conscious effort to drag himself away, and again he experienced that faint hint of an erection. It was exciting to know that he even thought that way; eroticism was something that just happened now and again. Marital sex had become more of a duty than anything else and Roy often wondered if Liz would care if it never happened again. She hadn't always been like that. In fact he couldn't really remember when their relationship had died. It had been more of a gradual process that had crept upon them, destroying, leaving only glowing embers of the fire that had once burned within them. Possibly one day it would come back again but it wouldn't be easy. They would have to work at it and that was something his wife apparently was not prepared to do. Her respect for him, like her love, had withered. It was all due to Balfour and there was precious little he could do there. One had to have a job to keep a family, and Balfour and Wren only employed the kind who . . . he winced . . . the kind who served in the old tradition of the profession. Devotion.

His despondency killed his erection stone dead. A few yards further on he saw the Punch and Judy site. In the dampness of a sobering rainy day it looked drab and uninviting, a space behind parked vehicles and a row of sideshows, uninspiring in every respect. A wooden box on stilts, the gaily-coloured curtains hanging like wet washing, just a man in a mud-splashed torn raincoat picking up litter and straightening rows of chairs. Last night was like a bad dream that had evaporated with the coming of daylight.

The man looked up, saw him. A typical shabby fairground hanger-on. A sniff, wiping his nose with the back of his hand. A blank stare.

'Excuse me,' Roy Catlin hesitated, half-wishing he hadn't come, that he didn't have to associate with fairgound scum. 'I'm looking for. . . .' Oh, Jesus, what the hell did you call the people who operate Punch and Judy puppets? 'I want a word with the . . . the Punch and Judy men.'

'What the 'ell for?'

'I. . . .', taken aback by the blunt rudeness, revolted at the way the other squeezed one nostril shut and blew the other loudly. 'I want to talk to them.'

'Why?'

Oh God, this was ridiculous! But it was quite obvious that this scarecrow of a fellow wasn't going to concede information willingly. All right then, bloody well tell him, stop cringing like it was old Balfour standing there and tell him.

'Because we've got some complaints about last night's performance.'

'Oh yer 'ave, 'ave yer? And 'oo the bloody 'ell are you to start complainin'?'

'I am making a complaint,' Roy Catlin drew himself up haughtily, a flood of sudden anger firing his courage, 'not just on behalf of myself but on behalf of everybody who watched that disgusting show last night!'

'Then it's me yer gotta talk to.' The man's eyes narrowed and his broom fell to the ground in a threatening gesture. 'I works the bleedin' things and if people ain't satisfied then they can bugger off. What's wrong?'

'The violence,' Roy felt his breathing quickening. 'It went too far, it upset the women and children watching and. . . .'

'There's always violence. That's wot Punch and Judy are all about. . . .'

'Not to that extent. The blood was revolting, sickening.'

'*Blood*?'

'Yes, blood. That revolting mess of ketchup or whatever it was.'

'Then yer bloody barmy. There weren't no blood, never 'as bin. Yer want yer bleedin' eyes tested.'

'There *was*!' almost a shout. 'I saw it. We all saw it.'

'Look, chief,' he trumpeted with the other nostril, 'there weren't no blood, I'm tellin' yer.'

Catlin sighed, looked towards the crude wooden theatre with its rain-drenched curtains hanging limply down. It didn't look nearly so appalling in the starkness of daylight, the heavy drizzle lashing it. Harmless.

'We'll soon see.' He turned, strode angrily and purposefully towards it.

'Oi!' The man turned and shambled after Roy, dragging his left leg behind him. 'Oi, you mind yer own fuckin' business. I'll 'ave the police on yer. I ain't standin' for. . . .'

Whatever the puppet man wasn't standing for it was too late. Roy reached the stilted structure, pulled the curtains wide, almost afraid of what he might see. The next second he was standing there foolishly, looking at the bare wooden boards of the stage, weathered, chipped timber. *But not a single crimson stain.*

'There, what did I fuckin' well tell you!' The attendant pushed up against him, giving off a stale odour of sweat and clothes that were worn night and day, old man's B.O.

'You've washed it all off!' Roy Catlin turned on him accusingly. 'You've cleaned up in preparation for tonight's show!'

'Look, guv,' The other was breathing heavily as though he wasn't used to sudden movement . . . or else he was *afraid*. 'There weren't no blood and there ain't goin' to be none cause it don't figure in the show and even if it did I wouldn't waste me time messin' with it. Get me? Now piss off!'

Catlin was turning away, feeling foolish, when something caught his eye, made him jerk his gaze back beyond the stage. Sitting there, propped up in a row on a sheet of corrugated iron across some oil drums were three wooden puppets. Judy, the policeman, and Punch. Nothing extra-ordinary about that, it was the place one would expect to see them, except. . . .

Their *expressions*! They should have been wooden, static features carved by the Indian fortune-teller. But there was . . . *something* about them, the eyes which seemed to look straight at him. Living, *understanding*!

Judy's expression registered *fear*. The policeman's frustration that bordered on terror – like a Christian who had just been hurled into an arena full of man-eating lions, determined to fight but knowing there was no way he was going to win.

Punch seemed to return Catlin's stare, two tiny black eyes that blazed evil, flickering and hating!

And in that instant Roy Catlin knew that there had been blood spilled on the previous night and that it had not been simulated. Yet there were no stains remaining on the stage boards.

He shuddered, had to drag his eyes away.

'D'you 'ear wot I'm saying, mister. Piss off!' A dirty, smelly hand shoved him but he welcomed its touch because . . . *because he had experienced something akin to hypnotism and now the spell was broken.*

'All right.' He scarcely recognized his own voice. 'I'll believe you. I'm sorry I troubled you.'

'I should fuckin' well think so. Now bugger off and don't let me catch you 'angin' around 'ere again otherwise I'll 'ave the law on yer. We 'ad enough trouble yesterday.'

Roy Catlin found himself back in the main fairground, wandering aimlessly, his brain floundering as it tried to cope. Past the fortune-telling tent, this time not even thinking about the girl who was surely inside those canvas walls, not noticing the rain which drove into his face. He saw those eyes again, the way they had fixed and held him, conveyed their message of malevolence. *You saw the blood; next time it could be yours.*

He tried telling himself that it was ridiculous, all in his own mind. He was overworked, unable to relax now that they were actually on holiday, everything crowding in on him. The weather didn't help.

Somehow he found his way back to the promenade, had to force himself to think logically, try to get a sense of direction. The hotel. The Beaumont Hotel. It lay at the harbour end, in the opposite direction. He turned around, shook his head in an attempt to clear it.

'*Roy!*'

The sudden shout brought him back to reality, cutting into him like a whiplash. He looked up, saw Liz running across the road, a car braking suddenly, blowing its horn angrily, the driver yelling abuse.

'Roy! Oh, thank God!'

He stared at her, her usually immaculate hair windswept and rain-drenched, summer dress damp and creased, an expression of agonized frustration on her face.

'What the hell's up?' he gaped at her, a sinking feeling in his stomach, knew that something was dreadfully wrong. She hadn't even noticed the car which had almost run her down.

'Rowena!' she got the name out in a strangled breathless gasp. 'Have you seen her? *Oh God, have you seen her?*'

He shook his head, incapable of speech.

'She's missing!' The tears were welling up, starting to roll, constricting her speech. 'After breakfast . . . I couldn't . . . find her . . . she must've followed you. . . .'

He stood there, a sensation of sheer helplessness creeping over him, people scurrying past looking for somewhere to pass the time out of the rain, wishing it was the end of the week so that they could go back home. Himself included. Except that first he had to find Rowena.

'She'll be in the fair,' he was surprised at his own calmness. 'I know she will. She wouldn't be any other place.'

'*Then find her. D'you hear me, find her*!'

'She's probably perfectly safe,' he had to prevent Liz becoming hysterical at all costs. 'Probably wandering around the sideshows quite happily. Come on, let's go and look for her.'

He turned back, knowing that his wife would follow, not caring if she didn't. Rowena was all that mattered to him these days, he had to come to terms with that, although he had known it for a long while. He walked fast, not looking behind him, suddenly knowing just where their missing daughter was going to be found.

The flaps of the fortune-teller's tent were closed as Roy Catlin hurried towards it. He slowed his pace, stopped. It was as though they were a deliberate barrier to keep him out. But that was silly. Anybody could go in there.

'Go on,' Liz hissed. 'See if she's in there . . . only I hope to God she isn't!' No, I don't, I don't care where she is so long as we find her.

He moved forward, parted the canvas and saw what he had expected to see. The Indian was sitting there behind her table as if she had never moved from it. Rowena was standing in front of her, oblivious of the intrusion, clutching something to her; it looked like a tiny doll.

'Good morning,' Jane's eyes lifted and a half-smile parted her lips. 'The weather is not good this morning.'

Roy had meant to be angry but it died away, leaving him with a feeling of uncertainty. He was mentally apologizing for the interruption, stepping back a pace. I'm sorry to intrude, I shouldn't have barged in like this.

'*Rowena!*' All Liz's fears, frustration, and relief were summed up in that one shriek. Roy felt her trying to squeeze past him, her shaking body rubbing against his own. 'Rowena, how dare you go off like that.'

'It's all right,' Roy came to the defence of his daughter before he realized it. She was with Jane and that was OK, even though he had never set eyes on the fortune-teller before yesterday.

'No, it isn't all right. I won't have her coming . . . *here*!'

A mute confrontation between two women, the centuries-old conflict between red and white. Suspicion. Fear.

'She is quite safe with me.' Jane smiled with her mouth again but her eyes narrowed. 'She is lonely. She needs a friend.'

Liz was about to say 'she's got plenty of friends back home at the Unit' but she remained silent because she knew it was a lie. Rowena didn't have *friends* because outside school the pupils rarely saw each other, shut away in their own world of silence. She *needed* friends . . . other young children. This present relationship was dangerous, unhealthy. No good could come of it. It had to end now.

'Well, *I* don't like her coming here!' Liz was defiant, standing in front of Roy, hands on hips. 'Furthermore, I won't have her coming here again. Ever!'

An awkward silence. Rowena turned to face her parents and there was an expression on her features which neither of them had ever seen there before. More than just defiance, almost contempt, her lips curling into a sneer, head erect. 'Jane my friend. Give me doll.'

Liz Catlin saw the thing which her daughter clutched in her small hands and felt the skin on the back of her neck starting to prickle. She could just see the face through Rowena's fingers, roughly hewn out of a lump of wood, but with all the expression that a professional sculptor might have given it in spite of the obvious disregard for proportion. The nose was large and hooked so that it almost overshadowed the slit of a mouth, falling down to a square chin. Ears flat against the side of the head which was grooved to convey hair hanging down in a fringe. But when you had noted all these your gaze came back to the eyes and remained there. They reminded Liz of something she had seen lately but she couldn't remember what; they seemed to fog the memory. Two sockets carved round protruding tiny knobs, pupils so shaped that they appeared to follow you wherever you moved. Liz started; they couldn't move, it was a trick of the light, they were just lumps of wood.

The body was squat, a caricature that might have seemed humorous under different circumstances. Few details, just an effect, Indian clothing that hid everything except the protruding hands and feet. Harmless. It should have been – but it conjured up an eeriness, flickering campfire shadows in which inexplicable things lurked and manifested themselves in this strange . . . *totem*.

Suddenly Liz was once again unable to say all that she wanted to, powerless to give vent to her anger. Before it had been this strange young woman who had been responsible for it but now she knew it was the doll which Rowena was cradling to her. *Those eyes . . . you couldn't get away from them*!

'Lovely dolly, Mummy.'

'Yes, yes . . . it's lovely. . . .' Revulsion, but being compelled to lie. It's awful, hideous. I don't want you to keep it.

'I carved it especially for her,' Jane spoke softly, determinedly, as though she read the other's thoughts, 'and she watched me the whole time. It is her work as much as mine. She will treasure it long after she has grown too old for childish toys. It is a gift to her from me.'

And as Liz found herself staring back into those beady wooden eyes she knew that Jane spoke the truth. There was no way they were going to be able to get rid of that vile effigy.

'We were worried because Rowena was missing,' Liz found herself speaking calmly, matter-of-fact although she seethed inside. 'However, we had planned to go out for the day in the car. . . .'

'Of course,' Jane smiled at the child. Now run along and enjoy yourself for the day but come back and talk to me again. 'It is such a pity when people come away on holiday and it pours with rain. I shall look forward to seeing Rowena again. Perhaps tomorrow. Or the day after.'

Rowena did not resist her mother's hand, barely glancing back into the tent as the three of them filed outside. 'Lovely dolly. Lovely, *lovely* dolly.'

The wind had freshened considerably, driving the heavy drizzle into their faces, and the fairground seemed even more crowded. Fruit-machines jangled voraciously on a diet of small coinage, a bingo-caller was trying to make himself heard above the noise, everything boosted by the music without which the drabness would have succeeded in casting its mantle of depression over the whole area.

' . . . *in a world of our own* . . . 'Jacob Schaefer's world was just starting to come into its own.

'How dare she!' Liz finally spat out the words that had been roasting to a turn inside her.

'Who?' Roy had that feeling of vagueness again, a mental numbness that was somehow helping to make all this bearable.

'That Indian. Who else?'

'She wasn't doing any harm. In fact she seems to be doing Rowena a lot of good.'

'Rubbish! Rowena's lonely and that's *our* fault. Perhaps we can get her friendly with some of the other children in the hotel. But I'm not going to let her go back to that woman again.' Or you! Liz had noticed the way Jane had glanced frequently at Roy, almost furtively, something that only a woman recognized in another woman. And Liz Catlin wasn't prepared to take any chances. 'As for that doll. . . .'

'I think it's rather cute.'

'Well, *I* don't. It's enough to give her nightmares. Me as well. That face, it's like the totem-poles you see in cowboy films. You can just imagine a helpless victim roped to it, awaiting death.'

'Now you're being really bloody stupid.'

'No, I'm not. And don't swear, please, Roy. Perhaps you haven't noticed its . . . its *eyes*.'

'Can't say I have really.'

'Well, *I* have.' You were too busy ogling the Indian. 'They're like . . . like. . . .' Suddenly Liz knew what the small doll's eyes reminded her of and her brain reeled, something stabbed at her heart. *'They're identical with those on that devilish Punch puppet!'*

Roy looked away quickly because he didn't want his wife to see his own expression, the shock which he couldn't control, the trembling lower lip. It was some moments before he could trust himself to speak again.

'Well, that's not really strange considering she carved the Punch and Judy characters. A formula she works to, I suppose.'

'Nevertheless it's horrible.' Liz noted the way Rowena walked on ahead of them, not once glancing back, almost as though she was attempting to divorce herself from a parental relationship. It hurt. And it was all that damned squaw's fault. The bitch! 'I think we ought to get rid of it at the first opportunity.'

Rowena turned slowly, the carved figure pressed tightly against her breast, deep blue eyes focusing on them, narrowing.

'Lovely dolly,' she almost spat the words out.

And it was all that Liz Catlin could do to hold back her tears. She could not explain the sense of loss, almost of bereavement, which engulfed her. It was as though she had just lost something which was very dear to her, had it snatched from her grasp.

P.C. Brian Andrews had been in the Force less than a year. A rookie, and if he wasn't aware of his status then the red-faced station sergeant made certain that he was. It was a kind of traditional bullying that went back to the days of foot patrols around the town throughout the nocturnal hours, as good a way as any to train a recruit. If he was scared of being on his own in the dark then that was the most effective way to break him in. Teach them the hard way.

And Brian Andrews wasn't at all happy. The weather didn't help, that heavy drizzle had turned into a good old-fashioned downpour that hammered on the tin roof of the panda car. He checked his watch. 2.40 A.M. The radio crackled; a couple of calls but neither concerned him. It had been a long night and it was going to be even longer before he saw the welcoming dawn streaks in the eastern sky.

The fairground on his left was a giant slumbering monster, not a single light showing in the blackness of the night, silent except for the raindrops splattering in the deepening muddy puddles.

The sergeant had said to check it out *thoroughly*. It was bloody silly, pointless. A subtle form of bullying, soak a rookie and lie in your own snug bed sniggering about it. But Andrews would have to patrol on foot just to be on the safe side; *suppose* there was something wrong that wasn't discovered until morning. It didn't bear thinking about. Sanderson would really have a ball over that.

He reached into the back of the car for his raincoat. He hated wearing that almost as much as he hated the rain. Cumbersome if you got into a fight (Monday was still fresh in his memory), and you sweated so much that you ended up saturated anyway.

Brian checked his torch, got out of the car and locked the door. He ran across the pavement and ducked under the awning of the first tent. He might have sheltered there for a few minutes except that the water was pouring so fast off the roof that it was like standing under a waterfall.

A quick circuit of the perimeter, maybe a random check further into the interior. He set off, the beam from his torch glinting on the falling droplets. The stalls and sideshows were all closed up and battened down, the menagerie cages empty because the animals were all asleep in their covered quarters. He envied them.

It was creepy, far more so than any side street in the dead of night. That was because the whole setting represented a noisy carefree way of life, and without the crowds and the music it had a graveyard atmosphere. It was dead, the ghosts of the day hours lurking in the darkness, resentful of any intrusion.

He was three-quarters of the way round the outside, on the seaward end, when he heard a noise. A hollow sound like a cricket bat being beaten against an empty oil-drum, resonant, vibrating. Just once, taking its time dying away.

Andrews stopped, felt his heartbeat speeding up beneath the layers of uniform. He was sweating, too, but that was probably due to the weight of the clothing he wore and the fact that the night was sultry in spite of the rain. He stood listening but the sound did not come again. A number of explanations flooded his brain. There were endless empty drums around the fair being used for a variety of reasons or just lying around. An equal number of loose objects that could fall at any time, particularly in this downpour. It *could* happen; it was quite likely. But training college had taught P.C. Brian Andrews never to accept the obvious.

Reluctantly he turned and headed back into the interior of a dead world, an artificial towering forest with gaudy foliage, painted faces that leered in the torchlight. Silent. Waiting.

Bong. . . .

Andrews whirled, crouching, dragged his truncheon clear of his pocket. The noise was close, came from a building immediately on his right, a square structure with steps leading up to the curtained doorway. HALL OF MIRRORS.

The sound had definitely come from within. He stood there undecided, thought he heard a movement from inside, a sort of heavy shuffling sound as though something was being dragged across the floor. No lights showed behind the curtain. *You'll have to go in there, copper. It's your duty!*

Sweating heavily now, knowing the full extent of his fear. *Alone.* His walkie-talkie was still in the car and he had no way of calling for help whatever happened. The Hell's Angels battle was still vivid in his mind. The violence, the blood, and worst of all the sheer malevolent brutality that had rendered life a cheap commodity in a supposedly civilized age. All in broad daylight. This was pitch darkness, a cloak for unspeakable evil.

He climbed the steps, pulled the curtains apart. He was surprised that there was no door or barrier to prevent casual access but, there again, there was nothing but mirrors inside, nothing to steal. Brian's hand groped the wall, found what it was seeking; a light switch.

Stark dazzling light, temporarily blinding him, more frightening than the darkness had been. Looking about him as his eyesight painfully adjusted to the brightness. Seeing himself, half-a-dozen different distortions staring at him in amazement, mocking him. Angry at his intrusion. Enlarged and shrunken heads, arms that held up minute and oversize hands. *Look at us! We're not YOU, we're us!*

Vague facial resemblances, elasticated features pulled apart, shooting back to almost normal proportions then shrinking to tiny pimples on broad shoulders. Growing again, laughing as they did so.

Brian Andrews dropped his torch, heard it bouncing and rolling away, wielded his truncheon. The odds were too great but he would put up one last desperate fight. They're only reflections. Your own. Ignore them. No they're not, they're alive, *malevolent*.

Laughter. *We're real, coming to get you, copper. We're not coppers, just dressed up like this to fool you.*

He struck wildly at the nearest one but even as the blow descended the figure diminished in size so that the truncheon whistled harmlessly over its head. Enlarging again, the head coming up long and narrow with a tiny flat cap somehow balancing on the top of it. Brian stepped back, whirled round because there were more of them coming at him from behind; big ones, little ones, fat ones, thin ones, all wavy, like reflections in a mill pond that had suddenly been disturbed. Wait awhile and they'll return to normal. But there wasn't time . . . too many of them! Swivelling, striking one way then the other but they were too quick for him, navy blue wisps that eluded him, no longer resembling himself, demons closing in on him, wearing him down. Already the arm swinging the baton was tiring so he switched his weapon to the other one. No strength in that one either.

Then he saw the body. . . .

Everything slowed down, came to a standstill, even his attackers retreating until they were well beyond his reach, watching in silence. Everybody stared at the crumpled figure on the floor, a bundle of flowing robes that were stained with crimson. Andrews couldn't understand why he hadn't noticed it before, or even fallen over it.

She was dead, of course. Nobody could withstand a brutal battering like that, lose all that blood and still live. The head was pulped like a crushed boiled beetroot but if you looked closely you could see the remnants of a blood-soaked bonnet. It was impossible to guess her age because there wasn't enough left of her. Beneath her, pressed against her bosom in a death-locked hold was a tiny form, still shielded even after life had left her, a last desperate instinctive act of protection by a mother for her baby.

And even as he noticed the infant, Brian Andrews heard it cry, a high-pitched unearthly wail that was more terrifying than all the mocking laughter from these things which formed a circle to hem him in. The cry came again, louder this time, grating on his tortured brain and running all the way down his spine, paralysing him.

You're a copper. It's your duty to rescue that child.

He glanced about him. *He was alone*, they'd gone. Disappeared. A trick of some kind, gathering together somewhere to rush him, suddenly coming at him from the rear as he bent to drag that baby from beneath the weight of its dead mother. They'd killed once, they'd kill again. Hesitating.

Your duty, copper. You can't leave that baby. Go get it!

The paralysis which had frozen his limbs had suddenly thawed and Andrews found that he could move. Jerky steps like a string puppet, swaying, tottering, fighting to keep his balance. *Oh, God, what have they done to me?*

Go get that baby, copper!

Time and distance seemed to have evaporated. It was as though he was in some kind of a void, a pocket in the universe which was impervious to everything that happened elsewhere. He might have been there a couple of minutes; it could have been a couple of hours, days, weeks. Months. Years.

Reaching down, the bile rising into his throat, knowing he was going to have to touch *that* on the floor, plunge his hands into it to get the baby out. Any moment he would throw up.

But he didn't touch it. Still reaching out, groping, fingers closing over nothing. Grabbing desperately, but it was always inches beyond him.

Go get that baby, copper!

It was crying persistently now, a harsh almost inhuman sound that tortured his eardrums, like fingernails scraping on metal. Screaming, reverberating in his brain. Closing his eyes and praying that when he opened them he would not be here but back in the panda car, the crackling of his badly-tuned radio having awakened him from an exhausted slumber. *Sleeping on duty, copper?*

But it didn't happen that way. Searing fluorescent light that showed up every awful detail; the corpse, the baby kicking a leg which it had somehow freed. Glancing round. *Alone again, they'd all left, disappeared, not a single distortion remaining to taunt him.*

This time he'd get the baby, drag it free from that death-hold, run with it clutched in his arms back to the car. Radio for help.

He managed to touch that tiny flailing leg. At least he thought he did, his fingertips brushing against something that moved, a limb that was hard and solid and kicked jerkily. He heard it scream again and snatched his hand away. Run *now* get help.

Too late! A waft of icy air as though the entrance curtains had billowed up and let in a draught of freezing sea breeze, so damp and cold that it penetrated the flesh right down to the bones. One fleeting second of darkness, then the light returned – a dull glow reminiscent of the gloom in the reptile house of a zoo. He could see, but there was no detail, surrounded by deep shadow.

And Brian Andrews knew that he was no longer alone.

He straightened up, saw a figure which stood between himself and the doorway. Huge. Gaudy. A clown in billowing oversize garments with a multicoloured pointed hat that looked as though it might fall off at any second. The face . . . he cringed as his eyes focused on it. Mask-like, the colourings deep and unnatural, the wide mouth parted in a perpetual leer, the blood-red lips unmoving.

But it was the eyes which had him backing away so that he stumbled against something and almost fell. Tiny orbs set in cavernous sockets, glowing and flashing like dying twin torch bulbs, forcing him to look into them. And keep looking.

That baby was crying somewhere far away. One last despairing grasp at reason before it vanished altogether. You're a fairground clown. A murderer returned to the scene of his crime. Yelling, '*I'm a police officer. You're under arrest. D'you hear me, you're under arrest!*'

Laughter filling the room, insane babbling. The figure was advancing, a club of some sort raised menacingly in its right hand. *I killed the woman. And the baby. And now I'm going to kill you!* Words that clattered mechanically like an animated recording. The needle stuck, repeating the words over and over again. *I'm going to kill you . . . kill you . . . kill you . . . kill you. . . .*

The policeman's actions were instinctive; his brain had ceased to function but his subconscious remembered its training. Truncheon poised, watching the other's every move. A duel to the death against a terrible adversary.

I'm going to kill you . . . kill you. . . .

Andrews struck wildly at a target that made no move to dodge his swing. A resounding blow on that enlarged mis-shapen head, his baton bouncing off it with a force that numbed his arm right up to his shoulder.

Bong . . . a familiar sound, one he'd heard recently but couldn't place where or when because his reason was no longer functioning. Insane laughter, wild maniacal chattering, heavy feet scraping on wooden floorboards, the figure looming up over him, dwarfing him.

Screaming in his helplessness, Brian Andrews raised his

arm, a defensive rather than an offensive move, not knowing whether he still held his truncheon. That face was so
close now that no detail was hidden from him. He smelled
its breath, like fresh paint and turpentine. The lips moved
but that gloating smile remained fixed; even white teeth too
small for the huge mouth, nostrils that had no openings.
Finally the eyes again. *Dead eyes that lived and saw. And
hated. Merciless.*

P.C. Brian Andrews had accepted the inevitability of
death from the moment his puny blow had rebounded off
the solid skull of his attacker. Now he stood there meekly,
the terror gone from him, his strength sapped so that it was
as much as his legs could do to support his body. Waiting
for the end, a condemned man balancing on the gallows
under heavy sedation, unable to come to grips with reality
and not really wanting to.

Laughter all around. Chattering voices reminiscent of his
executioner's. He didn't know whether he actually saw the
watchers or was simply aware of their presence. He just
knew they were there. Mis-shapen figures, all sizes, all
dressed in navy-blue. Their babblings died slowly away to
silence but they were still there. Gloating. *Go get that baby,
copper!*

The policeman raised his eyes, saw the huge club.
Cumbersome. Unwieldy. But somehow grasped in that
powerful hand and poised aloft. Starting to descend.

I'm going to kill you . . . kill you . . . kill you. . . .

4

WEDNESDAY MORNING

Rowena recognized it as the place Miss Doubleday, the
PHU teacher, had described to her on many occasions.

71

That woodland glade with the ring of red-spotted toad-stools amidst the carpet of bright, sweet-smelling, almost overpowering, bluebells. She'd read the story to the class on more than one occasion, out of the big book with faded blue covers, using the Phonic Ear so that they would be able to hear the words. A delightful story but frightening in some places if you didn't know the ending when everything turned out for the best.

A young child, no more than seven judging by the water-colour frontispiece, had wandered away from her picnicking parents into the big wood. It was cool and shady beneath the entwining branches with their thick foliage, in some places almost as dark as night. She'd walked on and on until finally she realized that she was lost. She'd panicked, run one way then another, and finally ended up in this clearing. Then suddenly a number of tiny figures had emerged from where they had been hiding behind the oversize fungi, wicked little man-like creatures with pointed ears and fingers like sharp claws. Goblins! The girl had tried to run but they had surrounded her and cut off her escape, jabbering excitedly. There were a dozen or more of them and they had dragged her to the ferny floor and produced knotted creepers with which to bind her and keep her prisoner forever. However, just as they were tying her up, a squat dwarf-like man had waddled into the clearing and with screams of rage and fear the goblins had fled.

The girl was frightened of the newcomer but he calmed her and told her that he meant her no harm. He explained that he lived all alone in a cottage in the deep dark woods and if she would like to come home and have tea with him then he would be delighted. She shook her head and explained that she had not long ago eaten her picnic and would he please take her back to her parents. Somewhat reluctantly he had agreed to do so and in due course she found herself back at the parked car where her mother and father were lying fast asleep in the long grass. They hadn't even missed her!

But, as Miss Doubleday repeatedly pointed out, what

would have happened to the little girl if she had gone back home with the dwarf? There was a strong moral in the story which Rowena thought about a lot. It always puzzled her because, ugly as the little man was, he was so *kind* – so what would have been so wrong in going back to his house for tea?

And now Rowena was in the same glade and at any second the goblins were going to emerge from their hiding places. She cowered back, wanted to run, but her legs would not move. Eyes wide with terror she saw the figures emerging from the shadows, chattering excitedly. But they weren't goblins. They were . . . she didn't really know what they were; strange puppet-like beings with large heads that nodded and bobbled, rattling their string joints, poking at her with fingers that were hard and hurt her. She tried to scream but no sound came. Or if it did she didn't hear it.

Suddenly they were backing away, their jabbering turning to shrill cries of terror, turning and fleeing as fast as their stiff little legs would move until there wasn't one of them in sight.

Somebody was coming up the grassy path out of the shadows. Rowena waited, knew what was going to happen. But she wouldn't do like the girl in the story and ask to be taken back to her parents. No way. She would accept the invitation and go home to tea with the dwarf. Because she was finding her father and mother extremely boring lately.

But it wasn't the dwarf who came juddering out of the gloom. It was her own tiny carved doll, except that he wasn't so tiny now. He was at least three times larger; a living walking effigy, eyes blazing with a fury that had sent her chattering tormentors fleeing with shrill cries of terror.

Just the two of them were left in the clearing, the silence rolling back. But Rowena wasn't afraid. Not of . . . she didn't have a name for him. He was just 'Doll' in the same way that her goldfish at home was 'Fish'. Perhaps she ought to think up a proper name for him. But not now. 'Doll' would do fine.

She had a choice as she had expected. He would either take her back to her parents or else she could go home with him. Her mind was made up. Her mother was getting tiresome these days, raising all kinds of objections to everything she wanted to do and it would be a change to be away from her for a while. Daddy felt the same way, she could tell, but he just smiled and put up with it. The happiness she had known in her earlier childhood had faded. It was all too much for her understanding, so she just trailed along behind Doll.

It was a strange wood, none of the familiar beech and elm and silver-birch trees that grew in woods. The trees were much bigger, everywhere gloomier, making her feel uneasy. But she wasn't frightened because Doll was here and he would protect her. Jane had assured her of that. And Jane wouldn't have said it if it wasn't true.

Rowena had no idea how far or how long they had walked, but when they emerged from the wood it was dark. It was much warmer, too, a sultry atmosphere that was almost thundery.

They walked on and on, over rough stony ground that sloped gently. Doll paused, held out a hand which Rowena grasped to steady her balance. His fingers were hard but somehow they managed to secure a grip, pulling her along as though suddenly he was in a hurry to get to wherever they were going. It was all very exciting.

Rowena saw the glow, an orange light that came up from a hollow somewhere ahead, flickering and dancing in the night sky, welcoming yet eerie. Somebody had lit a fire, a big one, like the one the big school held on Guy Fawkes' night and invited the PHU to join. Only bigger. Perhaps that was why the air was so hot.

They topped a rise and Rowena would have held back except that Doll was holding her so firmly that she was dragged along with him. Below them were a number of conical tents, people moving about, flitting shadows in the light cast by the huge central fire. Sparks showered high into the sky, the heat seeming to hang in the air because there was no wind to disperse it.

Closer now, Rowena saw the occupants of this straggling camp and recognized them as Red Indians, not quite as majestic-looking as the ones on TV but definitely Indians. Fierce faces daubed with coloured paints, their clothing like cast-off jumble-sale garments, an atmosphere of poverty all around.

They didn't appear to notice either herself or Doll, or if they did they gave no sign. There were women, too, blankets draped around them, squatting in the shadows as though it was not their place to take part in whatever was going on.

Doll was gripping Rowena's hand firmly, as though he feared that she might try to escape his protection. Without him she would have been very frightened, but his presence alone dispelled any apprehension she had had earlier. She accepted everything she saw, not able to hear the harsh cries of the half-naked warriors. But their expressions revealed their feelings. They were very, very angry about something.

A pair of eyes drew her attention and held it. High on top of the twenty-foot totem pole, two brightly coloured orbs reflected the firelight and flashed with an anger that was greater even than that of the Indians clustered below. A bird with outspread wings and a human face, nose hooked like a beak, its arms a pair of ragged wings, its feet talons that clawed a hold on the thick tree trunk which supported it. Its feathers fluttered – but that was probably caused by the dancing shadows. Looking down, not at the two intruders but at . . . The carving reminded her of those in Jane's tent, the same fierce living expression. *And she knew it was evil.*

Rowena screamed, tugging wildly in an attempt to free herself from the one who held her, but Doll's grip never slackened. He didn't appear even to notice. He, too, was staring fixedly ahead – *seeing the man with bowed head who was roped securely to an upright stake, brushwood piled up to the thighs of his torn and filthy buckskin clothing.*

The prisoner never looked up. He could have been unconscious, even dead. Long black matted hair hid his features completely and had it not been for the ropes he would have fallen to the ground.

Doll had stopped, hanging back from the crowd which circled the captive as though even he feared to intrude. Rowena had stopped screaming, pressing herself up against him, wishing that he was bigger so that she could hide behind him. With her free hand she pointed, made noises, asking questions but not expecting to be understood.

'They are very angry,' Doll spoke and she was amazed that she could hear his guttural tones. 'That man is their most hated enemy. He has killed many of them, helping the white invaders to steal their land and drive them back into the great waters. But worse, he has wronged one of their women, a terrible wrong that cannot be erased, and for that he must pay the penalty. The one who gave me life, it was she to whom he did this terrible thing.'

Rowena felt the terror building up inside her, not afraid for herself but for . . . *Jane*. It was surely Jane of whom her strange friend spoke. Some terrible harm had befallen her. And Rowena began to hate that man as she had never hated before, wanting to hurt him in some way but not knowing how, screaming inarticulate insults, again trying to free herself so that she could dash forward and pummel him with her fists, claw at him with her fingernails, kick him. But Doll held her back, began pulling her away until at last they were back in the dark night where not even the firelight was able to reach them.

Still stumbling on. Back the way they had come, or in another direction, she did not know. Neither did she care. Only one thing was uppermost in her mind, the fact that Jane had been hurt. She wanted to go to her, to console her, but she had no way of finding her. *Unless Doll was taking her to Jane.*

She was convinced that that was where they were going. To the fairground, wherever it was, to be with the Indian girl and to try to comfort her. Everywhere was so dark that it was impossible to tell whether they walked on open ground or in the forest, following a winding footpath that only Doll could see with his strange dark eyes.

Suddenly she stopped, realizing that something was

wrong but not knowing what it was. And then she knew. She still clung to Doll but no longer was he big and commanding. *He had shrunk back to his normal size, no larger than her own hands which held him.*

She gave a little cry, held him up, tried to see him but it was too dark, an unyielding pitch blackness which closed in on her, damp and cold. Her doll was lifeless, the movement gone from his limbs, an inanimate object once again. She screamed and screamed again.

'*Rowena!*'

The sound cut into her brain, slicing through the panic, familiar, yet it didn't fit in with this strange wild place. She cowered, clutching Doll tightly against her. Hands reached out of the darkness, grabbed her, shook her. But she wasn't going to let them take her doll away.

'*Rowena! Rowena!*'

It was suddenly light again, a dazzling brightness that had her squinting and blinking, seeing surroundings that did not blend with all that had gone before. Stark white walls, hemming her in, coming at her as though to crush her. Screaming again. Being held and shaken. Crying. A blur of faces that finally became still and merged into two, a man and a woman; *her father and mother.*

'Rowena,' Liz Catlin's features were twisted with anguish. 'Wake up. You've been sleep-walking again!'

The child was sobbing, shaking so much that she almost dropped the small wooden doll. She was in a corridor, standing only a foot or so away from the top of a flight of steep narrow stairs.

'Thank God!' Liz turned to Roy, her face white so that her freckles stood out like a spreading rash. 'Another few seconds and she would have fallen. I told you we shouldn't have left her alone tonight. And she's got that damned doll with her!'

'Doll mine.' Rowena pressed it to her defiantly. 'I love it. And I love Jane!'

Liz's expression hardened, her lips compressed. It was all the Indian's fault; that carved figure was enough to give anybody a nightmare. 'You'd better come and sleep in our bed.'

Reluctantly Rowena allowed herself to be led back along the passage, her movements automatic, trance-like. The forest had been more than just a dream, everything had been so *real*. Including Doll. She glanced down at him, his eyes seeming to glint knowingly. And then her fears came surging back. Jane was in some kind of trouble and she had to go to her tomorrow, no matter how much her parents objected. Jane needed her.

The sea-mist had cleared to make way for a solid down-pour. The weather forecast, according to Roy Catlin's morning newspaper, was summed up in one word: RAIN. Further outlook: RAIN.

'We'll just have to go somewhere in the car,' Liz glanced across the table, noted the faraway look in Rowena's eyes and her brow furrowed. 'Even if we only sit on the headland all day.' The prospect wasn't inspiring but it was better than staying around here. She was beginning to experience a sort of trapped feeling, as though they were imprisoned in this small seaside town. A day away from it would do them all good, somewhere where they couldn't hear the strains of the fairground music. It got on your nerves, wore you down. That was one place they weren't going again!

'OK, I'll go and bring the car round to the front door.' Roy stood up, aware that he welcomed the opportunity to be away from his wife if only for a few moments. The prospect of being enclosed in the car with her for the whole day was not an appealing one but there was always an outside chance that the weather might ease up enough for them to take a walk.

'We'll go on upstairs and get our things.' Liz glanced at Rowena again, saw that same glazed expression. 'Don't be long.'

Roy donned his anorak and went outside, running from building to building in an attempt to dodge the rain, glancing in the direction of the fair. Two police cars were drawn up on the pavement close to the amusement arcade, both with their lights flashing. He winced. More trouble, and the day had hardly begun. But it wasn't any of his business. He couldn't care less. He didn't give a damn. Then in his mind he saw the Indian girl again, draped in blankets which failed to hide her sensuousness. His pace slowed, he almost forgot it was raining. But he'd have to try and forget her because he wouldn't be seeing her again.

He reached the car which was parked in the street immediately behind the Beaumont Hotel, had to force his key in the lock to get the door open. It had been sticking for weeks now, he'd really have to get the garage to have a look at it. Wet and uncomfortable, he slid in behind the wheel, catching his foot in the loosely-draped seatbelt as he did so. It was going to be that kind of a day, cramped and soaking wet and hating every minute of it. Right now he would have welcomed an urgent phone call from Mr Balfour to return to work; because he would have gone, no matter what Liz said, and it would have been the lifeline he needed. But it wouldn't come.

The engine started at the first attempt which was surprising. It hadn't done that for months. He let it tick over, anything to use up a few more seconds of the day. It was with reluctance that he flicked the windscreen wipers on and grasped the gear-lever. The gearbox shrieked its protest, Catlin's fingers transmitted the agony of vibration right up to his shoulder. The engine kicked and stalled. Passers-by turned their heads, grinned at one another. It was a job to find anything to laugh about today . . . outside the fairground.

'Fuck it!' Roy delighted in the use of the four-letter word, shouting it out aloud so that it echoed inside the car; he didn't care a sod if those stupid buggers in the street heard him. He hoped they did. Fuck them, too! And fuck Liz!

He had to brace himself to try the gears again, hardly daring to press his foot down on the clutch pedal, gently easing the gear stick forward, loosing it the moment it started to grind and object. This time he didn't even swear. He almost laughed; because today they wouldn't be going anywhere at all.

He lit a cigarette and sat there staring at the rain-dashed windscreen, listening to the elements beating on the tinny roof. He wasn't in any hurry, mentally writing the script for the next half-hour. I'm sorry, *darling*, but I think the gear-box has seized up. I've told you for ages, Roy, that you drive too much on the gears and, anyway, you should've had the car checked over before we came away. Even if I had they wouldn't have taken the gearbox to pieces. What are we going to do now? I'll call the AA but I expect they're inundated with calls on holiday week. So what are we going to do for the rest of the day? I'll have to stop with the car until they turn up (escape!) so you and Rowena had better look after yourselves for the next hour or two. All right, but we're not going anywhere near that fairground.

Liz was getting so bloody boring these days. He finished his cigarette, tossed the butt out into the rain and hauled himself out after it. He didn't even walk fast; he was wet already and he didn't relish the news he had to convey to his wife. The thought crossed his mind that if it hadn't been for Rowena he might just have walked away. Somewhere, anywhere. A lot of men had done just that for a lot less reasons than he had.

'What!' Liz's features suffused with blood. 'I told you the engine was jerky on the way down.'

'It was probably all the queue-crawling, stopping and starting every few minutes that did it.' Roy Catlin needed another cigarette but resisted the temptation. He was likely to get through a lot before this day was over. 'Anyway, I'll have to phone the AA.'

'If they come before tonight it'll be a miracle,' she spat out viciously. 'And what do *we* do in the meantime?'

'You'll have to find some way of amusing yourselves.' He sensed a glibness in his tone but she didn't appear to notice it. 'Why don't you go down to the harbour, sit in one of those covered shelters and watch the boats coming in?'

'How thrilling! Apart from the fact that everybody else will be doing exactly the same thing, you don't think Rowena's going to pass most of the day like that, do you?'

'I'm sorry but there's nothing else I can suggest right now. . . .'

'Fai . . . fai. . . .' Rowena was clutching the carved doll in one hand, pointing excitedly, frantically, towards the fairground with the other. Somehow she had to get in touch with Jane.

'*No*!' it was almost a shriek from Liz Catlin. 'That's one place we're not going. If we have to stand here in this porch for the rest of the day because everywhere is full up then we'll do just that. *But we are not going to the fair*!'

Rowena was silent, looking at Roy. Her eyes were wide and starting to mist up. Pleading. Daddy I want to go to the fair. You'd take me, wouldn't you, if it was up to you?

Yes, love, I probably would. But you know what your mother's like when she gets a bee in her bonnet about something. She hates the fair so that's that. There's nothing I can do about it. I'm sorry, really I am.

'There's an ambulance backing into the fair,' Liz's attention was momentarily distracted. 'I don't know what's going on in there. Police have been in and out all the time you've been gone.'

'Probably somebody's got hurt on the big-dipper or something,' Roy murmured, surprised at a sudden sense of anxiety which gushed over him. Afraid because it might be . . . no, it wouldn't be Jane because she didn't do anything except carve and tell fortunes all day. At least he didn't think she did anything else. All the same, he felt uneasy.

Rowena watched white-faced until the ambulance was hidden from view behind the amusement arcade. She began to tremble, held Doll against her wet cheek.

Something was terribly wrong. Doll had told her so last night when he had led her to that strange place on the other side of the dark forest. Somehow she had to go to Jane, no matter how much her parents tried to stop her. It was as though Jane was calling her.

'I'm sure that none of my people are responsible for the death of your constable, inspector.' Jacob Schaefer tried again to light the chewed remains of his cigar, drawing hard on it so that it hissed like damp kindling wood.

'That's a very wide statement, Mr Schaefer.' The thickset inspector with thinning hair made no attempt to hide his contempt for these fairground people. They were dirty, vagrants and social security fiddlers, they conned the public and they wasted police time with petty infringements of the law. And Schaefer was the spider who sat in the midst of the web and spun it. 'You've just admitted that there are dozens of people doing casual labour for you whom you've never set eyes on before. You don't even know their names.'

'Fairground people are honest,' Schaefer was unperturbed, almost insolent. 'I've lived amongst them all my life so I should know. Anyway, what was your officer doing in the Hall of Mirrors last night? You realize he was trespassing, don't you?'

'Checking, on *my* orders. After Monday's trouble, we'll be checking you all along the line, Schaefer. Sneeze out of turn and you'll catch one helluva cold. Now, let's go over the facts again. P.C. Andrews was bludgeoned to death in the Hall of Mirrors. The place was like an abattoir, the most brutal murder I've ever had to handle in thirty years in the Force. But not so much as a footprint nor any sign of anybody else having been in there except the dead man. It's as crazy as your mirrors.'

Schaefer gave up trying to light his cigar and let it bob up and down on his bottom lip, a flicker of unease in his eyes that was gone almost as soon as it appeared. 'I am sorry, inspector, but I am afraid I cannot help you. I have no idea what happened.'

'We'll find out,' the detective spoke angrily, with more confidence than he felt. 'Be sure of that, we'll get the killer. It may take time and if necessary I'll pull this place to pieces and question and re-question everybody working here.'

'Please do,' insolence, anger meeting anger. 'Help yourself, inspector. But in the meantime the show must go on.'

'I didn't expect anything else', Chief Inspector Landenning's lip curled contemptuously, 'from you!'

Landenning went back outside, turned up the collar of

his already-damp raincoat, stood looking about him. The weather hadn't affected the enthusiasm of some holiday-makers, not in here anyway. A crowd had gathered beyond the rope barrier which the police had erected around the Hall of Mirrors. Again he sneered silently. They were a sector of the public he despised, the kind who flocked eagerly to gloat over others' misfortunes, an added bonus if they caught sight of a mangled body or some blood.

The policeman turned, walked away in the opposite direction, steely-grey eyes missing nothing. The continual music grated on his nerves and he wondered if there was any way he could have it stopped, some local by-law which demanded that noise was kept to a certain level. He could always check, but he wouldn't because it was all too petty. Right now he had to track down a murderer. His men would work night and day on this one if they were asked to. Because the victim was a police officer. It made it kind of personal.

He sauntered on, watching everything, not knowing exactly what he was looking for. There were queues at every form of amusement. The bumper-cars were charging 75p a car, no time limit stated, left to the attendant's discretion. Thousands would be cheated and probably not even care. Easy come, easy go. Just watching the waltzers made Landenning feel sick. It was a lot of money to pay for the privilege of having your guts churned up. And if you suffered from vertigo you could get your kicks on the big-dipper. He watched it slowing down, stopping, moving on a few yards and stopping again so that white-faced people could stagger back on to *terra firma*. It took all sorts. . . .

Suddenly he stiffened. He didn't know exactly why but it was a feeling he'd had several times in his career. Some described it as a sixth sense. It went deeper than that, an *awareness*, the certainty that somebody was watching you. Not merely a casual observer (I can tell that guy's a copper even though he's in civvies), but a malevolent stare that penetrated you like radiation, had your skin goose-pimpling. On one occasion back in his early days on the beat it had saved Landenning's life. His own in-built early-warning system.

He gave no sign, walked on a few more yards then came round in a circle, so casual that whoever it was would never suspect. The feeling was even stronger. God, it was eerie! He took his time looking about him, watching a quoits stall, the way the rubber rings bounced back off the board. The hooks were too large, the rings too springy. On purpose, of course. He let his eyes travel on. A couple of youths were watching him, possibly survivors of Monday's battle, but they dropped their gaze. It wasn't them, he knew, because that tiny shiver was still going up and down his spine.

Following on round, steadily, flicking over bystanders, dismissing them. Coming to rest. Jesus, now this really is crazy! His gaze met the watching eyes and his pulses missed a beat. Two large yellow eyes, fixed, unblinking in a horse's head. A wooden horse, a ridiculous animal caricature, wildness depicted in every aspect; the flowing mane, lips drawn back in a vicious snarl, rearing with flaying hooves as though bent on trampling a hapless rider which it had just thrown. A mixture of colourings. Not a horse, *a mustang*, the favourite mount of the savage warriors of North America. *But Landenning couldn't get away from those eyes. They seemed to follow him, bore into him with a primitive hatred.*

Now you really are getting bloody stupid, he told himself. You've got the jitters, scared by a merry-go-round horse. Suddenly he was aware that he was trembling, his pulses racing, his breathing so shallow that he was consciously having to draw deeper breaths. A fleeting sense of shame, but he couldn't shake off the fear. That horse seemed *alive*, no longer wooden, its nostrils wide, teeth bared as though to savage him. *It moved!* It was the rotating stand jerking because the motor was still switched on, an optical effect brought about by the lifelike carving. Landenning gave a nervous laugh but it didn't help. He couldn't take his eyes off the creature, flinching beneath its penetrating stare. It was a horrible-looking thing if you really studied it. Probably nobody ever did, it was just a moving seat that you paid 25p to sit on, clambered off when the attendant brought it to a standstill and that was it.

Forcibly the policeman jerked his attention away. He had a lot more important things to do than waste his valuable time on fairground fixtures and fittings. He turned away, felt those eyes boring into his back, hating him for some reason. But it was all in the mind and he had to get rid of it. Fast.

The damned music, it was getting on his nerves even worse than before. If he could have stopped it he would have, closed the whole place down and done the public a big favour. But he couldn't so he had to put up with it. And keep looking until he found what he was searching for. But in the meantime he'd try and keep under cover. This rain wasn't going to let up today.

Landenning felt depressed, as though everything was a waste of time, including his own presence here. They wouldn't find the killer because they didn't have anything to work on. Not a single clue. No weapon, no motive, not so much as a footprint or a fingerprint. It was hopeless. The enquiry would cost a fortune; cancelled police leave and overtime for weeks on end, reams of paperwork that could be summed up in one word – *useless*.

He got that feeling again but it wasn't the horse because he'd moved on (out of its sight!). People all around, but nobody was paying any attention to him. Everybody was more concerned with getting rid of their holiday savings as fast as they could, swelling Jacob Schaefer's coffers.

But he was being watched all the same. A Viking figure-head on the topmost big-dipper car seemed to stare down with a hostile expression (all Vikings had fierce coun-tenances so there was nothing strange in that), as though it had singled him out from the teeming crowds; eyes that *followed* him. Jerking his head round, seeing a grinning clown's head carved on the facia of an amusement arcade. The wide mouth was a leer if you looked close enough, the eyes narrowed as though they were trying to frown, rain droplets giving the impression of moving pupils that saw. And *hated*!

85

A clatter of swinging, banging doors made him jump, whirling round. Scared! A three-carriage miniature train was just emerging from a dark narrow tunnel, parents trying to comfort white-faced crying children. The Ghost Train, a common feature in most fairgrounds, artificial terror, nylon cobwebs that brushed your head in the dark and spooks that would have been comical if you hadn't conditioned yourself to being frightened because you thought you weren't getting your 50p worth if you weren't.

One look at the faces of those scrambling from the train was enough for Landenning. There was more than just a cheap fright on their features. *Sheer terror.* Mothers clutched young children to them, fathers stared angrily back at the closed twin doors.

'Bloody disgusting!' a man shouted at the train-driver who was in the act of collecting tickets from the next lot of passengers. 'There's no call for that sort o' thing, not even in there.'

'You gets what yer pays for.' The driver pointed up at a sign above the tunnel entrance – ALL THE TERRORS OF THE SUPERNATURAL.

Angry murmurings greeted his words. 'You oughta be 'ad up for some o' the bloody tricks goin' on in there. Bloody sick, that's what it is!'

'Shaddup', the man in greasy overalls replied in an undertone and carried on collecting tickets, head hung low. Sullen.

A voice somewhere inside Landenning said 'You ought to go take a look.' That was his police training teaming up with his conscience. He replied, 'It would only be a waste of time. They're all fakes. This whole place is one big fake.' But he knew that he lied because he was afraid.

And he was still being watched. From all directions. His skin crawled as though hordes of tiny insects moved beneath his clothing. Eyes everywhere, painted wooden ones that seemed to follow his every movement. The job, maybe this particular case, was starting to get him down. Maybe he should go back to H.Q., check on a few reports. There were always reports coming in, nutcases confessing to crimes they hadn't committed. At least half-a-dozen would swear to having bludgeoned P.C. Andrews to death, becoming abusive when they were told to stop wasting police time. They even believed themselves guilty. Some threatened suicide.

God, he needed to get away from this place. One final glance back at the Ghost Train. Maybe he should take a ride and check it out. No, it wasn't necessary. Guilt again, trying to shrug it off.

A small redhaired girl caught his attention. Just one of hundreds of children, nothing really extraordinary about her. Except . . . she was clambering on to the Ghost Train alone, no sign of an adult with her. She couldn't be more than eight or nine at the most but nowadays parents generally were apathetic about their offspring, believing that nothing could happen to *their* child. Until it did. Which was why there was such a high rate of child murders. His policeman's scrutiny of her picked out her twin hearing aids. Passing sympathy. All the more reason why she ought not to be going on that train alone. She was carrying a small doll, but he dismissed it with a cursory glance.

Inspector, you really ought to take a look inside there. No, I must get back to H.Q., somebody might have come up with something urgent. Coward! He winced.

Landenning walked quickly towards the exit where his car was parked, got that creepy sensation again. His instinct was to turn around, *for Christ's sake stop watching me!* But he resisted the temptation because they were only carved wooden figures playing on his nerves. They couldn't even bloody well see so how the hell could they watch him?

As he eased himself in behind the driving wheel that child crossed his mind again, the deaf one climbing on to the Ghost Train. It was her expression more than anything which worried him. So intense, not sullen like a lot of the kids today. As though she had some specific purpose in mind.

He gunned the engine, sat there with it ticking over, again battling with his own conscience. It had troubled him today for a lot of reasons, so many things he should have done but he hadn't. *Because he had been afraid*. He had shirked his duty, side-stepped many of his own convictions. He'd reached his present position mainly by backing hunches in the days when he had been a constable in uniform. Improbabilities, half-chances that he had taken the trouble to pursue. No more than a feeling about something not being quite right . . . like today, those ridiculous effigies. A faint tingling up the back of his neck creeping into his scalp. *Warning him*.

Those weren't hunches, they were *nerves*, ridiculous things playing on his mind, a sure springboard to a nervous breakdown if he once pandered to them.

He gave a laugh, a forced one, waited for the wipers to clear the windscreen and eased out into the traffic. That girl had probably been treated to the Ghost Train whilst her parents concentrated their efforts in the bingo hall. She'd get a scare but it wouldn't do her any harm. Those carvings were nothing but lumps of wood so that was all bunkum. And with a team of the best C.I.D. men in the area on this case, Andrews's murderer might be behind bars before the end of the week. Looking at it that way, everything was under control, the way it should be.

The weather was largely responsible for getting him down. And, of course, that bloody deafening fairground music. Maybe he would see if something could be done about it after all.

5

WEDNESDAY
AFTERNOON

Rowena had given her mother the slip quite easily. Sly cunning, and it had come so naturally. Furthermore she had no regrets, nor did she fear the consequences. Because

Doll would protect her. She knew it would all work out all right.

Daddy had gone back to the car after he had made a telephone call from the kiosk across the road. That had taken some time because this morning it seemed as though everybody wanted to use the phone and there had been a queue of a dozen or more people standing out in the pouring rain. Then he had gone off leaving her and Mummy standing in the hotel entrance. Rowena tried to think of some way by which she might get away from her mother but at that moment there was no opportunity on offer. Liz Catlin was watching her daughter carefully, almost as if she guessed what was in the child's mind.

'Well, I can see we're going to be on our own for most of the day,' Liz muttered and thought that perhaps on the whole that was not such a bad thing. Roy wasn't exactly the best of company lately and he appeared to be becoming more withdrawn with every day, almost as though he was deliberately erecting a barrier between them. Possibly they were just going through a bad patch; most couples struck one from time to time.

She tapped Rowena on the shoulder, attracting the child's attention, a signal that she wanted her to lip-read. 'Would you like to go down to the harbour and watch the fishing boats unloading?'

Rowena hesitated. She didn't want to go anywhere except to the fairground but the harbour might be as good a starting place as any. She nodded, gave a half smile. 'Yes.'

'Well let's get down there then,' Liz took her by the hand.

The rain did not show any signs of relenting. Nobody expected it to. Everybody had resigned themselves to a wet week. Some of the campers on the big site towards the headland were already packed up and leaving, homeward-bound traffic jamming the promenade road. Only those with booked accommodation stayed, trapped here and determined to get some kind of value for their money. The fairground was packed by nine-thirty, the only real winner.

Liz glanced down at Rowena as they pushed their way

89

through the crowds on the quayside, saw she still clutched that awful doll. It would be a good thing if she lost it somewhere. A few tears at first but it would be for the best. Somehow it would go, Liz was determined on that.

People huddled in the harbour shelters, an odour of damp clothing and sweat permeating the salt-tinged air. Seagulls perched on the railings, even they looked bedraggled, not even bothering to flutter down and forage for food scraps. Liz shuddered; they had a vulture-like look about them. As though they were waiting for something to happen.

The shelters were crowded, not even standing room available in most of them. Children had made an early morning start on ice-cream and candy-floss. A little boy had been sick but nobody had attempted to clean the mess up, other children treading in it and not even noticing.

Rowena's eyes narrowed. There was a stonebuilt café on the opposite side of the harbour road, the queue stretching right down the single flight of steps and on to the pavement. TEA, COFFEE, ICES.

'Ice cream!' she pointed, pulled at her mother's hand.

'Well, it's a bit early yet,' Liz made a half-hearted protest. 'Perhaps later.'

'*Please*, Mummy.'

'Oh, I suppose so then. But we might have to wait some time in the queue.'

Which was exactly what Rowena knew would happen. They crossed the road, mingled with the throng, a straggling line three or four deep, everybody huddling together, using each other as psychological rain shelters but getting wet all the same. Liz groaned, thought about the perm she'd had last Friday and how it was steadily disintegrating into a bedraggled auburn mess. This holiday was going to prove costly; garages capitalized on car breakdowns and if they had to do without a vehicle for the rest of the week that meant they were going to be moping around here spending unnecessary money, like early morning ice-cream and coffees which they didn't really want. Her thoughts switched to Roy, the way he seemed to have discarded his

90

earlier ambitions (dreams) and resigned himself to being the whipping boy for Balfour and Wren. That was the whole root of their discontentment. She forgot all about Rowena for a few moments, staring vacantly up into the grey sky, never even noticed her daughter sidling away.

Rowena broke into a run once she was clear of the queue, sprinting the way she did when she competed in the infant fifty metres on Sports Day, weaving her way in and out of dejected holidaymakers, holding Doll beneath her blue anorak so that he wouldn't get wet. She relied on him, almost as much as on Jane. But she had to find Jane quickly.

She reached the fair in less than ten minutes, slowing to a walk now, breathless. Her parents would come looking for her, they would know where to find her, but it would take time. There were a number of policemen standing about but she ignored them, taking a direct line for the fortune-telling tent, gasping her relief aloud when she saw it and breaking into a run again.

Seconds later she slowed, pulled up abruptly as though she had run into some immovable object. *The canvas flaps were closed, the cords tied. Jane was not in there.*

Frustration escalating into panic, looking wildly about her, a feeling of utter helplessness. Then an idea filtered through to her dazed frightened mind. She knew the caravan where her Indian friend lived, only fifty yards or so to the right of the sideshows. That was where she would be for sure.

Sobbing her relief, running again. Seeing the caravan, shabby, the paint peeling off in places, rust corroding, grimed windows. She climbed the small flight of aluminium steps, beat on the door with a tiny fist. *Jane, I'm here. I want to help you!*

But there was no answer. Her hearing-aids did not pick up any vibration of movements within. Again the despair came flooding back, tugging at the handle but it did not yield. Pulling frantically, crying.

'*Oi*!' The coarse nasal tones rasped on her limited hearing. She turned, saw the tall angular man staring angrily at her, a stub of cigar stuck firmly in the centre of his thin lips. 'Oi, what's going on?'

'Jane!' she shrieked back at him. 'I want Jane!'

'Clear off!' he waved a fist angrily at her. 'Jane ain't around. Now you get away from these caravans.'

Rowena backed slowly away. She didn't like this man, not just because he had shouted at her, it was his eyes, his obvious dislike of children. And something more, she read in his tone, his attitude, a jealousy that was vindictive. *He resented her looking for Jane, as though the Indian girl was his own possession.*

Rowena Catlin retreated from the caravans and stood there looking back, seeing Jacob Schaefer walk away and knowing that for the time being she was not going to find Jane. But where was the Indian fortune-teller? She wasn't in either her tent or her caravan. Possibly she would return to one or the other later. But in the meantime Rowena's mother would come searching for her. If she found her, she would be dragged away and there would be no chance of contacting Jane. Which left her with only one alternative – *she must find somewhere to hide.*

Rowena experienced the feelings of a hunted beast of the chase, a wariness that had her glancing in every direction, a determination to run at the first sign of any pursuit. But nobody so much as glanced in her direction. Nobody was interested in one small child. Nobody cared. It gave her a forlorn, lonely feeling.

The size of her latest problem was evident within minutes. Amidst all the activity there was nowhere she would be screened from the view of the crowd. Roundabouts were the obvious places where parents would search for missing children and anyway they were too expensive, the rides too short.

Rowena walked along, looking about her. She was more perceptive, visually more aware than the average child. It was a useful compensation for being trapped in her own world of silence. Mentally, too, she was more alert, her powers of reasoning way ahead of her age group. Even if her reading was behind that of others outside the PHU she understood much more, gifted with an insatiable enquiring mind.

She saw the sign GHOST TRAIN and knew what the second word meant. The first wasn't important and she didn't think that ALL THE TERRORS OF THE SUPER-NATURAL were of any significance. Just a train. It went through those doors, was away for some minutes and then came back again. 50p seemed a lot of money for a ride, half her holiday pocket money, but after all this was an emergency. Perhaps, wherever the train went, she could alight and remain in hiding for some length of time. She could not decide on anything until she saw what lay beyond those twin doors which the engine buffeted on its way in and out.

She climbed on to the wooden platform. There wasn't anybody else waiting which was strange considering that people were clamouring for virtually every other kind of amusement. But that didn't matter, the fewer passengers there were the better.

She sensed the approach of the train, a shuddering vibration that made her feet tingle, saw the doors fly open, banging and clattering against the following open-topped carriages. The driver was hunched over his controls, expressionless; dirty long hair falling out of an undersized peaked cap. There were five passengers; two teenage girls clinging white-faced to each other and an older couple with a boy about Rowena's age sitting between them. His eyes were shut tightly, holding on to his parents. *Terrified*.

The train eased to a halt, the driver sitting where he was as though he was deliberately avoiding contact with the others. The girls were first out, holding hands, running. Rowena thought that perhaps they were desperate to reach the toilets. The man was half-carrying the boy, turning angrily to shout something at the driver still sitting in the engine, but his wife was pulling him away. 'Don't start no trouble, George. It ain't worth it. Ian'll be all right.'

Rowena's stomach knotted with fear, so that she felt slightly sick. But she was determined to go on that train; it was important, both for herself and Jane. She pulled the 50p piece out of her pocket, held it ready in her hand. The other hand cradled Doll beneath the unzipped front of her anorak. For some reason she didn't want anybody else to see him. They might try to steal him. He was her very own special talisman.

Something attracted her attention, held it transfixed; everything else – the frightened, angry people and the sullen driver – forgotten. The imitation funnel was moulded into an oval shape, features carved on its exterior. A face. Grooves to convey straight hair that dropped over the forehead in a fringe, hooked outsize nose like a hawk's beak, slotted mouth. But the *eyes*, they were the key to everything, protruding orbs painted jet black, dark and mysterious, glistening as the rain trickled down on them.

Rowena started, knew the face as well as she knew her own reflection in the mirror. The features were identical to *Doll's*!

She jumped, felt something touch her shoulder.

'Wake up, kid,' it was the driver, a roll of tickets in his grubby hand. 'We ain't got all day.' He didn't notice her hearing-aids, not that he would have been in the least concerned had he done so; just as Rowena did not see the small lettering beneath the larger signwriting 'Children Half Price'. He snatched the coin from her fingers, dropped it into his pocket. This was one time when he wasn't giving out a ticket. 'Go and sit in the end truck and don't get larkin' about!'

No more takers. The man checked his watch, walked up and down. It was hardly worth a trip with just one passenger, a stupid bloody half-soaked kid at that! Hang about, Frank. You got all day.

A wait in which every minute seemed an hour to Rowena. The driving rain soaked through her anorak but she scarcely noticed it. Staring straight ahead of her, unable to take her eyes off that head-shaped tunnel, her spine tingling. Jane had carved it and she needed to see Jane. Just looking at it gave her queer sensations, a foreboding which she couldn't explain.

'Ghost Train,' the driver bawled. 'Come and see all the spooks of the fair. Fifty pence a time.' He didn't mention anything about half-prices. Angry now, seeing the crowds elsewhere, the desolation around his platform. It had never been like this before, always a full train, wet or fine. He couldn't understand it. The spooks and ghouls were just the same as they'd always been. Maybe folks were getting bored with the same old stereotyped horrors. They craved something new, something *really* terrifying. He'd mention it to Schaefer the next time the boss looked in. Not that it would do much good because the mean old bugger didn't like spending money.

'Any more for the Ghost Train. Just leavin'.'

Footsteps pattered on rain-soaked wooden planks, splashing up the trousers of the approaching man. The newcomer glanced about him furtively, pinched sallow features, thinning hair that hung damply, long thin fingers pushing it up out of his eyes. His shabby clothes hung limply on a frame that had an emaciated look about it, a sodden raincoat seeming almost too heavy for the thin arm over which it was draped. No more than thirty at most, a travel-worn despondent look about him. Shifty.

'Fifty pence, the best value for money in the fairground,' the Ghost Train driver turned towards him, sensing custom, eager and pushing.

'Er . . . all right,' a vague expression on the pallid features, small bright eyes picking out the solitary child in the end truck, fumbling in a pocket which jangled coins, a sudden sense of urgency.

'Thank you, guv,' the coin was accepted, this time a ticket given in return. 'Sit anywhere yer like.'

The stranger hurried, almost ran, to the waiting train, not hesitating in his choice of the end car, sitting alongside the red-haired girl, glancing at her out of the corners of his eyes.

Rowena felt uncomfortable, knew the other was watching her, felt his eyes boring into her. She was acutely embarrassed. She didn't like people staring at her; they usually did so in cafés or on buses once they noticed her hearing-aids. Oh, just look at that poor child! The last thing she wanted was sympathy.

Embarrassment blended back into unease, the way her companion edged closer along the seat towards her, didn't speak, but she knew she was still under scrutiny. She wished somebody else would come and join the train. But it was evident that there were going to be no more passengers, for the dejected driver was already slouching up towards the engine. And if it hadn't been for Jane and the trouble she was in Rowena would have jumped off and run back into the fairground.

The train started up, grinding and jerking. The man alongside her almost fell, regained his balance and she noticed that he was another few inches closer to her. She looked away, pretended she hadn't noticed him. She often did that with people she didn't like.

The engine hit the doors at gathering speed, crashing them open, a flickering of light and darkness like some old shutter camera. Something soft and spongy brushed against Rowena's arm. She let out a scream, instinctively turning to her companion and only stopping herself from grabbing him at the last second, drawing back. Revulsion.

'Don't be frightened,' she managed to lip-read his slit of a mouth before the doors clanged shut and buried everywhere in darkness. She didn't hear him say, 'Sit close to me and I'll look after you.'

His arm came around her, a hand tipping back the hood of her anorak, damp cold fingers beginning to caress her neck. Rigid fear, unable to scream, paralysed so that she could not draw away from him. Pulling her close, imprisoning her as surely as if she was in the grip of a rogue octopus. Words hammering in her brain, a scratched recording that had been retained, *warnings*. Her mother's voice, a constant nagging, 'don't talk to strange men . . . we're not going to the fair again *ever*'. Too late!

The train was slowing, hardly moving on a circular course. Skeletons, laughable if you were in a cynical mood, luminous gawky figures that rattled their plastic bones and tried to touch you. Old hags in filthy clothing cackling and leaning over a cauldron. Corpses raising the lids of their coffins, angry at this intrusion by the living.

'Don't be frightened,' the stranger was struggling to remove Rowena's anorak but it was caught up somewhere. 'They're not real.'

One thought in her mind. *Jane!* But Jane was in trouble also. Doll had said so. Remembering her doll seemed to restore her waning courage. That was why this man couldn't get her coat off, because Doll was caught up in it, obstructing his efforts. She wished that he would come alive again, grow big like he had the other night (it wasn't a dream), and take her to safety.

The train seemed to have stopped. Blackness everywhere, stygian gloom that cloaked skeletal and witch figures alike. Darkness that was alive and vibrant with terrors beyond the commercial cardboard horrors. Even their screeching noises had died away.

And then came the demon god! Rowena felt her captor's grip slacken, felt his stale breath on her face as he gasped his terror. A figure that towered above them, its horned head suffused with a fiery glow, its contorted features the ultimate in evil. Eyes flickering redly like embers fanned by a sudden breeze, nostrils that widened and smoked, the open mouth belching hate and rage. It saw them, gloated over them.

A movement in Rowena's hand like the stirring of a cradled hamster, hard against her tender skin, breaking the trance, bringing back the fear. *Doll had come to life, was trying to warn her. Run! Anywhere!*

A roaring like an infuriated dragon that crackled her hearing-aids so that they hurt. The god was stretching out its arms, reaching for her, so close she could smell its foul stench.

She was out of the truck, running. Falling. Sobbing. A dull orange light that showed up silhouettes as though it came from some nocturnal campfire, flitting shadows as though the artificial demons fled, impostors routed by the horned lord of the dark hours.

Trees, flat ones that weren't real. Rowena crouched behind one, remembered the forest and the Indian camp. The tall totem, its bird-like shape that was a cloak for *the demon god.* The captive, roped to the stake awaiting torture and death. . . .

He was here, too! Thinner, as though his flesh had wasted right down to his bones, the bushy facial hair had withered and died, a broken lusting figure that in no way resembled the buckskin beast in the Indian encampment. Only *one* resemblance; Rowena had seen it, recognition slow to dawn. *The eyes. He couldn't hide his eyes!*

She trembled, wanted to run again. This man had done Jane a terrible wrong; he might do the same to her, something so awful that death was the penalty he faced. And yet he would do it again. And again.

The god roared its wrath, the silhouette trees shaking with the vibration, the whole place filled with an eerie glow. A stark cardboard jungle. Two beasts, one mortal, one immortal. *Herself the prey.*

She looked to Doll, squeezed his hard outline, but he remained immobile. Inanimate. Powerless against greater forces. Rowena felt her terror escalating to a peak.

Another shadow, crouching, running. *Hiding! The man, not hunting her but being hunted!* The god figure was turned away, its back to her, only a pasteboard shape like everything else in here. But it moved, breathed its fiery demoniac wrath, a living creation. Everything else cowered away from it, Transylvanian vampires frozen in the act of emerging from their coffins, their blood-lusting expressions wilting before the ultimate terror. A foul ghoul-like creature backed off its human repast, blood dripping from its slavering jaws. Skeletons trembled rather than rattled their bones.

Everything had been brought to life so that they could die. They had dared to presume immortality and now they had to answer for their crimes against the powers of darkness.

Rowena closed her eyes tightly the way she used to do when she became frightened in the loneliness of her bedroom, not wanting to see the shadows and the shapes. It was cold, her teeth chattered and the dampness of her clinging clothing was penetrating her body. She wanted to cry; the tears were all stored up behind her eyes but they wouldn't come. And then she was squinting through half-closed lids, hoping that by now everything might have gone away. But it hadn't, it was still there, the grotesque fiery manifestation dominating. The ghoul had slurped its last and fallen to the ground, vampires slipped back into their coffins, skeletons wilted and drooped like daffodils whose season had come to an end.

Only the man remained. Skulking, trying to hide from those terrible all-seeing eyes. Instead he was caught and held transfixed in a flickering light that might have come up from the bowels of hell, driving him one way then another. Fleeing, screaming, now on his knees pleading, gibbering as his sanity tottered on the brink of a chasm of no return.

Rowena huddled watching, suddenly no longer afraid. The demon god did not want her. She merely happened to be around. It sought to take revenge on he who had done this great wrong and now that moment was very near. It moved, jerky unnatural steps, massive legs that made the flimsy building shake, towering over its victim, revelling in this moment, mouth wide in maniacal laughter.

Doll seemed to come alive again, a slight movement in her hands that attracted her attention. A message that transmitted itself to her brain. *You are quite safe. Do not watch. Look away!*

She found that she could turn her head away, the terrible scene no longer hypnotizing her. She found herself staring into Doll's impassive face, sensing his protection. It would be all right, there was nothing to fear for herself. If only she could shut out the sounds which tore into her brain, the struggle between man and god, the terrible revenge of the god. But even turning off her hearing-aids did not achieve this.

Harsh animal-like grunts, laborious breathing. Thuds that reverberated, soft and squelchy like wet cardboard being pounded with a sledge-hammer. Human screams that became fainter and fainter until finally they died away altogether.

And when she looked again it was dark and the avenging god was no longer to be seen. In his place stood a cardboard silhouette, a painted gorilla with protruding fangs and waving arms. Inanimate, carelessly daubed by some hack painter, coming to life and then dying again. The ghoul had returned to its grisly feast, the vampires once again struggling to leave their coffins, all going about their scary business, the slaves of the electric generator as before; they might never have been interrupted.

The train was starting up again, the trucks clanking and rattling, the driver not even looking round; not even aware. Again a movement in Rowena's hands, Doll urging her into action, getting his message across and ensuring that it was obeyed. She made it to the end truck, pulled herself up, glanced around fearfully. But there was nobody else on board.

Nylon cobwebs brushing her face, making her crouch low. The spooks laughing and making half-hearted attempts to get at her, but she wasn't afraid of them any more. Picking up speed, swaying on the bends. Round and round, faster and faster, a crazy hell-bent ride. Recorded screams and howls of anguish, everything speeding up, witches frantically stirring an empty cauldron, vampires bobbing up and down in their pasteboard coffins. Laughable, but nobody laughed except one oversize gorilla with a permanent grin of fangs that were too even, hate-filled eyes flashing as they picked up the reflected neon flickerings.

The Ghost Train crashed its way back outside as though eager to cool off in the pouring rain, grinding to a standstill, the driver not even glancing back at his solitary child passenger, not missing the one who had remained behind.

Rowena ran down the slippery platform, pushed her way back into the fairground mêlée, her furtiveness instantly returning, scanning a sea of faces but seeing none she recognized. Somewhere Jane needed her. She had to find her.

Roy Catlin was surprised to see the yellow A.A. van within the hour. It drove slowly down the side-street, its driver checking the parked vehicles then reversing up when he spotted the one he was looking for.

'What's the trouble, mate?'

'Gearbox, I think,' Roy climbed out, not even bothering to pull his hood up against the rain. He didn't care whether he got wet or not, whether it was the gearbox. He'd given up, would just drift with the tide of ill-fortune until one day it would be Saturday and time to go home.

'I'll just have a quick check and then we'll make arrangements to have you towed to a garage,' the uniformed man climbed into the car, started it up, grated the gears twice and switched off the engine again. 'Looks like it is the gearbox.'

Oh Jesus Christ, things couldn't get any worse! Within half-an-hour Roy Catlin found himself back on the promenade, oblivious of the driving rain which had cleared the open spaces and filled the cafés and the funfair. The garage had given him an estimate for the repairs. £150. The car wouldn't be ready until Friday afternoon. Sorry mate, we'd like to do it sooner but it's a big job and we'll have to fit it in with everything else we've got on hand. Don't worry, though, we'll have it done by Saturday morning at the latest for you to go home.

He wasn't worried about not having the car for the rest of the week. Just about the hundred and fifty quid. That would be really crippling; they'd come on holiday on a Personal Loan. It was going to be their dearest holiday on record.

But it was an ill wind. Liz wasn't expecting to see him for hours yet, and he didn't really know where to find her. The harbour was a big place. A few hours of freedom, he could do just what he liked, go where his fancy took him. Not that there was really anywhere worth going. One either got crowded out or soaked in the rain, a clearcut choice.

'*Julie, Julie, do ya love me?*'

The tune and the words hit him, had him changing direction. Hurrying as though there was no time to be lost. Getting to Jacob Schaefer's fairground was the most important thing that could ever happen to him. And he didn't even ask himself why.

Perhaps it was the steady downpour which had blanketed

the noise. Or maybe Roy Catlin had other things on his mind so that he did not hear it. It seemed far away as he struggled to force his way along past the menagerie; the Punch and Judy theatre covered by a tarpaulin reminding him of a shroud. Even the wild beasts were subdued, not so much as a glint of resentment towards their onlookers as they sheltered in the covered compartments of their cages. Utter dejection, a depression that was deepening and closing in so that none might escape it. Except Roy Catlin.

He experienced a sense of euphoria at his unexpected freedom. And something else also which he could not quite place at first. A faint pleasant sensation spreading out from the lower half of his body, awareness slowly filtering into his confused brain. The Indian girl, Jane! The memory of her was coming back strong, a primitive call bringing with it a host of fantasies. He tried to tell himself that it was nonsense, just a jumble of sex-starved thoughts that were all Liz's fault. Women drove their menfolk into the arms of other women that way, a mixture of prudishness and nagging. He couldn't imagine himself with a mistress. Yes he could! The excitement of clandestine meetings, the blood coursing hotly through his veins, the fear of discovery adding its sprinkling of spice. A rejuvenation, the return to those halcyon courting days when love was uppermost in one's mind. It could all happen again.

Fantasy running riot; the feel of smooth dark hands caressing him, dark eyes that were fired with love, the voluminous blankets falling away to reveal . . . oh God, his erection was pushing hard now, growing by the second. He tugged his anorak down to cover the bulge which had to be showing. But he didn't want the feeling to stop.

A new sense of urgency. Almost running, seeing that colourful yet bedraggled tent ahead of him, seeing in his mind the girl again, the way she looked at *him*. He couldn't have been mistaken, almost a *pleading* expression. It had had the same effect on Rowena only for a different reason. Roy supposed it was logical. A woman took a liking to a feller so she liked his young daughter as well.

He stopped outside the entrance to the tent, not just

102

because of the way the flaps were fastened as surely as if a 'closed' sign had been hung on the outside. He stood there undecided, the sudden wave of nervousness taking him by surprise, like that long-ago evening when he had taken a bus across town to date Liz for the first time, seeing her standing there outside the gates of the Garden of Remembrance. Suddenly he was scared, would have turned back and gone home had he pandered to his innermost fears. It was like that now; he had to stand firm, gather his courage. It took some doing but he did it. Then he moved forward, starting untying the cords on the canvas with hands that shook visibly. A sudden shiver that left him as quickly as it came, to be replaced by a feeling of uneasiness.

Then despair as the flaps fell back revealing an empty tent. Staring at it in disbelief, the stark bareness of it seeming to leap at him, echoing his own feeling of hopelessness. Just a table and a chair, not even a half-finished carving lying on the table. Gone, as though she had no intention of returning.

'You lookin' for somebody, mister?'

Catlin turned slowly, saw the tall man with narrowed hostile eyes sucking a cigar stub, a belligerent pose, fists clenched, resting on his hips. Demanding an answer.

'I . . . I . . .' Roy swallowed, knowing that he was starting to blush, glancing down to make sure that his erection was screened by his anorak. 'I was looking for the fortune-teller.'

'Well she ain't here,' a leer that showered Havana ash. 'You can see that. The tent wouldn't be closed if she was.'

'Have you . . . have you any idea where she is?' hardly daring to ask the question but he had to know, holding his breath because he was frightened of the answer.

'She's busy. That any o' your business?'

'No. I . . . just wanted to talk to her.'

'Well you just fasten those bloody flaps up again. If you want to talk to her you'll have to wait until she opens up for business again.'

Roy Catlin retied the flaps, Schaefer watching his every move. But even as he tied the last knot Roy knew that he wasn't going to give up just like that. Schaefer was already moving away. Catlin began to follow at a distance. It was a reasonable assumption that Jane was engaged in some carving somewhere around the fair, and there was always the possibility that the boss might be going to her now. It was worth a chance anyway, particularly as he didn't have anywhere else to go.

Schaefer quickened his step, not once looking behind him; he had no reason to suspect that he was being followed. A detour that skirted the Hall of Mirrors. It was still cordoned off, a helmeted policeman on duty at the entrance. Maybe tomorrow it would be re-opened. Jacob Schaefer pursed his lips. Business might be very, *very* good, particularly if some of the bloodstains still remained. People were like that and you had to give them what they wanted. The sooner the police were off the premises, the better. Nobody liked the police around, it gave you a being-watched feeling.

Roy hung back, saw where the man was headed; the stretch of waste ground where the fairground people had their caravans. A feeling of hopelessness again because in all probability he was only going home. He'd never find Jane, mooch around for the rest of the day in the wet and eventually return to Liz so that the nagging could start all over again.

And then he saw the Indian girl! She was hurrying away from the caravans almost as though her intention was to escape from Jacob Schaefer. If the fairground boss saw her then he gave no sign of having done so. Every nerve in Roy's body tensed like high-tensile steel cable. He broke into a run, almost shouted for Jane to stop, but he didn't want to draw attention to either her or himself.

Breathlessly he closed in on her, afraid that the crowd milling around the merry-go-rounds and the bumper-cars might swallow her up, heedless of puddles which splashed up, saturating his socks and filling his shoes so that he squelched water with every step.

'Jane!' It was the first time he had used her name and the sound of it from his own lips gave him an inexplicable thrill.

'*Jane*!'

She stopped, whirled around. On her dark handsome features was an expression of terror. It died away as she recognized him, a slow smile filtering in to replace it. He thought she trembled slightly.

'Rowena's father!' she could just have been glad to see him or perhaps he was reading her thoughts as he wanted to.

Face to face now, Roy Catlin swallowing, his mouth dry, words evading him. He hadn't given any thought to what he was going to say and excuses eluded his confused mind.

'You were looking for me?' her eyes bored into him and he knew a lie would be futile.

'Yes, I was.'

'Let us go somewhere else to talk. We can't stand here in this heavy rain.'

He fell into step with her, heading away from the amusement arcades, aware that his arousement had not lessened any. She had pulled the blanket up to protect her head from the driving rain and all he could see was her face in profile. But it was enough. His fantasies had suddenly become reality. And he didn't know how to cope with them.

'I am glad you came,' she turned into an alleyway between two rows of sideshow tents, tossed the blanket back off her head. 'I am worried. More than that . . . I am *frightened*.'

'About what?'

'About a lot of things. Rowena for one.'

'Rowena!' Catlin felt a surge of panic. 'But she's all right. She's down by the harbour somewhere with my wife.'

'No,' Jane shook her head, anxiety flickering in her eyes. 'She is somewhere here. Alone!'

'Oh, God!' Roy glanced behind him, saw the milling people, the crowded alleyways where faces became one blur and remained unrecognizable. 'She . . . she can't be!'

'She is.' Jane was adamant. 'I have not seen her but I know. We must search for her!'

Roy nodded, swallowed. 'Have you any idea

where. . . ?'

'Unfortunately, no. She is not far away and I am sure we shall find her but. . . .'

'But what?'

'*There is danger everywhere. Forces which have been unleashed these past few days, some which even I cannot comprehend, powers which have lurked in waiting for years. We are, all of us, trapped here by circumstance. Myself, you, Rowena, and many others. A policeman died in the Hall of Mirrors. His killer will never be brought to justice. I knew it, I smelled death in the air that night.*'

Roy Catlin thought, this is madness. He wished he'd never come here. Yet if Rowena was wandering this terrible place unprotected then surely Providence had guided him here.

'Come, there is no time to waste,' Jane tugged at his arm. '*Just like the other night, I smell death in the air again.*'

6

LATE WEDNESDAY AFTERNOON

Rowena had tagged on to the queue outside the oblong-shaped tent which bore the crudely hand-painted sign 'HORRORS FROM THE DARK CONTINENT. Admission 25p.' People were filing in through the narrow entrance. It looked dark inside, just a dim blue bulb suspended by a single flex.

Rowena hesitated, remembered the Ghost Train, those inexplicable happenings still fresh in her mind. But this was different. There she had been alone except for her strange unwanted companion, here there were people all around. All she had to do was to go inside and remain there for as long as she wanted to. Then, later, she could come out and look for Jane again. By that time she would probably have returned to her fortune-telling tent.

It was stuffy in the tent, stale warm air tinged with an odour of sweat and damp clothing, mostly adults. The few children who had accompanied their parents clung to them with obvious dislike for this place. Rowena looked around her. It was difficult to see much or perhaps that was how it was meant to be, the shadows a cloak for yet another confidence trick. A series of glass cages set well back on long trestle tables, each one illuminated by a tiny length of strip lighting. She had to peer around the bodies of the audience, a glimpse here and there that was shut out when somebody moved. Not that she really wanted to see anyway. All she had to do was to pass the time in this tent. Nevertheless she was curious.

The exhibits reminded her of the waxworks she had seen in London the year before last, wax and paint gore that became exceedingly boring after a time. For a child, anyway. Not really frightening after you became used to it.

The whole show was a fake. Spears, assegais, their heads caked with what was supposed to be dried blood but in all probability was rust. Lobengula's mythical treasure, a model scene of massacre, the Indunas closing in for the kill to ensure that those who had buried the vast wealth never disclosed its whereabouts. Witch doctors' relics, bones and skulls that had a decidedly plastic look about them.

Somewhere at the other end of the tent a female voice said 'ugh, it's *horrible*!' A man's scathing reply, 'don't be bloody silly, they're all fakes. Mock-ups. Waste of 25p.' More murmurings of disgust. People were forcing their way out through the exit, others filling the vacant spaces. And all because of the pouring rain.

And then Rowena saw the jar. It was a big one, approximately the size of a two-gallon demijohn, raised a few inches above the level of the table by some wooden blocks, a tiny red bulb beneath it turning the liquid with which it was filled a claret colour right up to the sealed top. An object the size of a tennis ball floated in it, bobbing, turning. You see it, you don't see it. *Oh, Christ, nobody wanted to see that*!

The watchers hung back, wanting to turn and flee, run out into the sobering reality of grey wet daylight, forget that they had ever seen it. But they couldn't. They were held transfixed by a pair of tiny eyes in the miniature shaven skull with its dried and withered skin, eyes that glowed and flashed redly, hate reflected in every movement. *Seeing*.

'*He holds him with his glittering eye*.'

The nostrils breathed bubbles, just the odd one or two that soared up to the roof of the container and burst. Tiny mouth, lips that quivered as though they muttered some hateful incantations. Turning, coming back again. Always on the move. *Alive*.

A placard lay on the table in front of the jar, crudely printed with a felt pen, SHRUNKEN HEAD. BELIEVED TO HAVE COME FROM THE MAGATI PIGMY TRIBE.

The shaven skull came round again, touched the glass side and bounced off it. Vibrating. *Cursing*. Everybody backing away with gasps of horror and revulsion.

'It's made of fucking plastic,' somebody gave a laugh but it didn't sound convincing. 'There's air going in somewhere to make it bubble and move.'

But there wasn't. Just one small red bulb beneath a closed glass jar. *And the revolting head inside lived and breathed*.

Rowena backed away, would have fled except she found herself hemmed in by a tight circle of people who found it impossible to do anything except watch. Spinning, bobbing, suffused with red so that eyes, nose and mouth seemed to be filled with blood, drinking it with relish, an insatiable thirst that gave it life.

It's only plastic. A fake.

No, it's real; a pickled head with life still preserved in it.

You don't *have* to look.

Yes, you do, because it won't let you do anything else.

It was impossible to determine the colour of the skin beneath the red glow. Likewise there was no real way of deciding upon its racial origins. The process of shrinkage had destroyed everything of its former individuality. *Only the evil was left to fester and grow like a malignant cancer.*

A vibration tingled Rowena's hand, broke into the hypnotism like waves of dizziness. She looked down, stared into Doll's face, those wooden features starkly real. As real as the thing in the jar. *But there was no mistaking the expression of fear*!

The severed head was rotating, a full circle, bloodshot eyes missing nothing. Rowena felt them boring into her, almost as though they had singled her out of the crowd, settling on her. So *powerful.* She wilted, felt her strength, her willpower, being sapped. A scream penetrated her impaired hearing; it could have been her or one of the people around her, she couldn't be sure. Doll's voice hammering into her brain, fighting its way through the numbing haze of sheer terror. *Don't look into those eyes. It's after your soul*!

One half-moment when she feared everything was lost, when it felt as though something was being sucked out of her, a tearing force that racked her whole body. Then somehow she was looking away into the darkness, a welcoming cooling blackness which held no fears for her. Faintly somewhere Doll was speaking again. *Leave now whilst you still can.*

Rowena pushed and squeezed her way in the direction of the exit, gulping in the fresh air once she was outside, crying softly. She glanced down. Doll was just a lifeless chunk of wood again and that was the most frightening thing of all.

She walked aimlessly, wanting Jane but not knowing where to find her, afraid to venture away from the open spaces, looking to Doll for guidance but not finding it. It was as though the sheer effort of whatever he had had to do inside that place of horrors had exhausted him. Now she was alone again!

'*Rowena*!'

She sensed the cry rather than heard it, turning, seeing the blanket-clad figure hurrying across the open tract of ground behind the big-dipper. Jane . . . and her father! But not her mother.

'Rowena!' Relief in the Indian's expression. 'Are you all right?'

'Yes,' she nodded, wondered if she would be able to put into words all that had happened to her and if so whether she ought to recount it. Perhaps it would be better to forget it. So long as she did not go near either of those places again nothing could happen to her.

'Something's happened,' Jane glanced from Rowena to Roy. 'She's frightened. I think we found her just in time.'

'There,' Rowena pointed back in the direction of the tent of horrors. 'In there . . . head!'

'Oh!' Jane clasped her hands to her mouth. 'I should have guessed!'

'What is it?' Roy Catlin pulled Rowena to him.

'I . . . do not know really,' she glanced away, unwilling to meet his gaze. 'Something that has been brought into the fairground only recently. One of Mr Schaefer's purchases, a shrunken head that is supposed to have come from the descendants of a tribe of head-hunters in Africa. Most of the exhibits in the Horrors tent are plaster or wax models, fakes that are made to seem genuine by the dim lighting and the fact that they cannot be touched. I have seen the latest addition and it is no model. A genuine shrunken head, and so very old. It floats in a jar of liquid with red lighting beneath it so that a gruesome bloody effect is given. But, Roy . . . that head is still alive.'

'That's . . . that's utter rubbish!' Roy Catlin wanted to laugh but instead he found himself swallowing and a tiny shiver ran right the way up his spine and spread itself across his scalp. 'How on earth can a human head still be alive when it has been severed from the body years ago, then dried and shrunk and enclosed in a sealed jar filled with liquid? It's totally impossible!'

'I have come across many stranger things than that,' Jane spoke softly, turning her head so that there was no chance of Rowena lip-reading her. 'Things that defy every possible explanation. *Roy, would you believe me if I told you I was very, very frightened?*'

110

He watched her closely, saw a faint quiver of her lower lip. It was as though she had been close to tears and then fought them off with a mammoth effort. In a roundabout way she was asking his help, perhaps too proud to put it into words. Rowena had fallen silent, holding her doll, staring at it intently.

'Yes,' he scarcely recognized his own voice. 'Yes, I think I would. But I'm afraid I don't understand you.'

'I didn't expect you to,' Jane's hand found Rowena's, 'because I don't understand it myself. Things happen, terrible catastrophes all around me. The battle last Monday in which people were seriously hurt. That policeman's death in the Hall of Mirrors. And right now I sense the presence of death. I feared terribly for Rowena but she is all right. Something has happened somewhere, perhaps still undiscovered. *The most terrible thing of all is that I feel that somehow I am a part of it, that I am responsible*.'

'You can't be,' he didn't know what else to say.

'Nevertheless, I am terrified. I am so glad you came and that we found Rowena safe. I cannot tell you how much she means to me.' Jane glanced around, a flicker of nervous eyes. 'Is your wife not with you today?'

'No,' Catlin's relief was summed up in that one word, followed by a sudden fear that even at this moment Liz might be searching the fairground frantically for Rowena that she might come upon them and vent her spiteful wrath on himself. It was time he made some sort of a stand and this could be the time. All the same he would welcome a short while in Jane's company. It was a pity that Rowena had become involved. 'I don't really know where my wife is.' Nor do I care.

'Why did you come to the fair?' the Indian girl's voice was little louder than a whisper, almost lost in the noise of the grating music. 'Why did you come back?'

'I came because . . . I wanted to see *you*.' Roy knew he was blushing, didn't know what kind of reaction he might get. But Jane was somebody one could not lie to because she would guess the truth anyway. 'That is my only reason for being here. I had no idea that Rowena was not with her

111

mother.'

'I knew you would come,' it was a statement of fact without a hint of boasting in it. 'I would have waited at the tent except that Mr Schaefer insisted that I spent the morning repairing some of the carved horses' heads on one of the roundabouts. You're not happy with your wife, are you, Roy?'

'No,' again it was pointless to lie. She would know the truth anyway. 'Things have not been well between us for some time. This holiday seems to have brought everything to a head.'

'I am sorry.'

'You don't need to be. It's been boiling up so it had to happen some time.'

'I wish I could leave this place.'

'What's stopping you?'

'A lot of things,' her shoulders suddenly hunched in a posture of dejection. 'Jacob Schaefer is a hard master but without him I do not know what would happen to me. To tell fortunes one needs a fairground and they are not plentiful. Most of them have their own . . . *fakes*. It is not easy trying to survive in a foreign country.'

'What about your carving? You could sell your work for a lot of money and you work exceedingly fast.'

'*I am not doing any more carving!*' she spat the words out with a viciousness which took him aback. '*Not even for Jacob Schaefer. I never want to carve another piece of wood as long as I live.*'

Roy Catlin stared at her in sheer amazement. Rowena was clutching her carved doll as though she too had heard and understood and feared that her most cherished possession might suddenly be taken from her.

'Why ever not?' Roy saw that Jane was looking away from him again.

'I . . . don't know,' she seemed close to tears again. 'Only that I have come to hate everything I have fashioned out of wood. If I could somehow destroy them all I would do so. As with yourself, it is something that has been festering inside me for a long time and suddenly it has

112

burst and spread its poison into my system. *Oh, if only you knew how much I loathe the things I've created.* They're all around me mocking me everywhere I go in this place. I can't escape them, just as it is impossible for me to destroy them!'

When she looked up at him again she seemed to have aged a decade, crinkles in her face which he had not noticed before. And there was a deep sadness in her eyes, mingling with a hatred that smouldered there . . . a hatred for herself and that which she had done.

'What are we going to do then?' his voice sounded hollow, echoing her own feeling of helplessness.

'I wish I knew,' she wrung her hands together. 'I . . . just don't want to be left alone.'

They stood there looking at each other, Rowena between them. Words would have been inadequate; needing each other, Rowena needing them both.

'I'll be around,' Roy was the first to speak. 'I promise you that. You can rely on me.'

'Thank you,' Jane couldn't stop the tears from filling her eyes this time. 'I should tell you to leave now, pack your belongings and take your family well away from this place.'

'No. I'm not going. And I know Rowena wouldn't.'

'Your wife. . . .' hesitation, an obstacle temporarily forgotten.

'I'm staying, no matter what.'

Her fingers had found his, squeezing them softly. Right now Liz didn't matter one iota; he didn't give a damn for her.

'But *how* can I help?' a sense of inadequacy.

'I wish I could be more specific. Your presence is a great comfort to me. I don't know what will happen. When Jacob Schaefer knows that I will not do any more carving for him he may well order me to leave. There is no way of knowing, he is a man of many strange moods. But can you come and see me again? *Tonight.*'

'I'll be here,' he promised. He knew he was on course for a head-on collision with Liz and the sooner that was over the better. Rowena was his only worry.

113

The realization that Rowena was missing came as a mind-blowing shock to Liz. At first she could not believe that the child was not around somewhere. The ice-cream cornet in her hand dripped white sticky blobs down her kagoule and on to her damp jeans. She swivelled on her heels, looking up and down the street, across to the harbour. Children everywhere; she cursed them because none of them was her own. She opened her mouth to shout, closed it again. Rowena wouldn't hear her anyway.

Dizziness, like standing on the deck of a boat being tossed up and down by the waves. Steadying. Don't panic, she's probably not far away. The cornet plopped its contents into a puddle on the pavement but Liz Catlin didn't even notice.

It was ten minutes before she accepted the fact that Rowena was not in the immediate vicinity. Numbed, not knowing what to do. By this time Roy had probably been towed away to some garage out of town and there would be no chance of getting in touch with him. Maybe she should call the police. Have you got a photograph of your child, Madam? Or a detailed description? We'll do all we can, just leave it with us. Oh, God!

The blaring of a police siren had her whirling round, her heart starting to thump madly. A red and white patrol car with its beacon flashing, followed by two white-helmeted cyclists, forcing the crowds to push back on to the pavements, cutting a path to wherever police assistance was required. An accident?

Running futilely in the wake of the disappearing vehicles, shouting after them to stop, faces staring blankly after her. *My baby, what's happened to my baby*?

Liz couldn't hear the sirens any more, just the raucous blare of fairground music jarring her nerves and obliterating every other sound. Holding on to a wet railing trying to get her breath, oblivious of the seagull droppings which smeared her clothing. Not even able to cry, everything building up inside her, dry eyes that hurt so she could barely see. *Where's my baby*?

Walking again, lurching into a run, knowing that

Rowena would be somewhere inside the fairground. It was obvious, she couldn't understand why it hadn't occurred to her in the first place.

The enormity of Liz's task hit her like a physical blow. It seemed as though the entire holidaying population had congregated in this noisy sickly sweet-smelling place, huddling like sheep trying to escape the elements, jostling each other for places. A distraught bedraggled red-haired woman aroused no more than fleeting curiosity. It was none of their business. They didn't care.

Liz stopped, tried to think logically. As her thoughts collected they brought with them a feeling of anger. There was only once place Rowena would be, with that damned squaw! The thought gave her new strength, helped her to throw off the panic. Hell, that Indian was going to get a piece of her mind. She was a witch. Evil! You sensed it, the way she looked at you, contempt in those dark eyes. I'll poison your husband's mind against you. And your daughter's. I don't want either of them but I'll take them just the same. Because I hate you. Because you're *white*.

Fists clenched, Liz Catlin set off again. The fortune-teller's tent was on the other side of the fair. Two minutes' walk. Rowena would be there, but not for long.

She hadn't expected to see the police car here. It was parked sideways across the entrance to the Ghost Train, a motor cycle on either side. A barrier. A small crowd had gathered and a uniformed officer wearing a white crash helmet was shouting at them to stand back. They went into a huddle but didn't move.

The winking blue light jarred her brain like the beginning of a migraine, prevented clear thought. Panicking again. There *had* been an accident after all. Somewhere inside the tunnel. Someone had jumped or fallen off the train, someone young who was easily terrified. A child! Sobbing again now, running forward, heedless of everybody and everything. *I want to go to my baby*!

'I'm sorry, madam,' the constable stepped in front of her, arm upraised as though he was on point duty. 'You can't go in there.'

'I must!'

'Keep away please. There's been an accident.'

My baby! For God's sake let me go to my baby!

She was struggling, held by the wrists, trying to kick the policeman who had moved in on her, then sagging lifelessly against him. The tears which had held back for so long were suddenly released in a flood. 'My child!'

'Madam, it isn't a child in there. It's a man.'

A man . . . man . . . man. . . . The word flipped round her brain until it found the right slot, got its message through to her. *A man . . . not my baby . . . oh, merciful God, it's not my baby*!

'I'm sorry,' somehow she managed to pull herself together, found a sodden tissue in her pocket and blew her nose loudly into it. 'My little girl's gone missing. She's deaf, you know.'

'I'm sorry.' Everybody was apologizing to everybody else but it didn't alter the fact that Rowena was still missing. 'She may be around the amusements, quite safe. If you can't find her then go down to the police station and report it. They'll help you.'

She nodded, stopped herself from saying 'I'm sorry' again. 'Thank you. I'll go and look for her.'

That bloody squaw! Nothing but a whore. Roy would like to have it away with her, Liz could tell by the way he'd looked at her yesterday. Or was it the day before? She'd lost track of time. Well now she'd foul it up for both of them. This nonsense couldn't go on any longer.

The tent was closed, tied up in a way that almost said its occupant wasn't coming back any more. Liz trembled, wondered what to do next. If only it would stop raining. There were two courses of action open to her. She could take the policeman's advice and enlist the help of the law, or continue to look for Rowena herself. The latter seemed the simplest, no long complicated explanations.

She wandered aimlessly, not knowing where to start, scanning every child's face, hopes rising and being dashed like a ride on a switchback railway.

'All the threes, thirty-three.'

Rowena wouldn't be in the bingo hall. Neither would she be playing the pool tables. The menagerie maybe, she loved animals. Dismal depressing wet cages. Remus, the ageing lion, had ventured out of his roofed quarters to alleviate the boredom but it couldn't stop his yawning, huge jaws wide, pink tongue licking round his lips. His enclosure was littered with bones. Liz shuddered and remembered an old record they had at home, one her parents had bought her for her tenth birthday. 'Albert and the Lion.' The words started to come back to her but she shut them out, closed her eyes briefly. She must be in a bad state. Children didn't really get eaten by fairground lions.

It was strange that there was nobody else looking at the animals. They usually attracted a regular string of viewers. She supposed that the weather was to blame. The gorilla had his back turned, whilst the elephant's trunk could be seen waving above the high brick wall like some giant snake. Everybody and everything was in a state of black depression.

Liz did not know why she went round to the other side of the brick wall. Certainly she wasn't interested in looking at one scruffy African elephant. Possibly she though Rowena might be somewhere there. She came upon an untidy dumping ground for fairground waste and litter, rows of dustbins that had overflowed, their contents sodden and floating in large puddles, an odour of rotting foodstuff. It made her heave.

The elephant didn't move away. He was standing looking across to where a small man was busily tipping the contents of a broken bucket on to an already-spilling pile of rubbish. The man turned and Liz started, almost recoiled.

He was deformed, probably a polio victim. Wasted legs that struggled to support the gross body, arms that were excessively long yet bulged with a strength that the lower limbs lacked, resembling a gorilla in the way he moved. The face bore all the resentment of a social misfit, hating you because the revulsion showed on your features. Eyes that were not a matched pair, one lower and larger than the other, the nose little more than two ragged holes clogged with dried mucus, the mouth an angled slot with yellowed upper teeth protruding. There appeared to be no neck, the head growing directly out of the body. Smooth white skin, not fertile enough to grow hair, though on top of his skull a few hairs sprouted with difficulty, like strands of wheat in parched soil. He was dressed in second-hand clothes that had been hacked down to size with a pair of blunt scissors.

'I'm . . . looking for my . . . little girl,' Liz Catlin did not know why she said it. Maybe saying something was an attempt to temper the burning hatred in those eyes. She stepped back, contemplated running. There was nothing to keep her here.

'Lil' girl, uh!' the squat figure moved towards her, mouth widening in what could have been either an oblique smile or a snarl. 'Nice lil' girl, huh?'

Ugh! She thought she smelled vomit on him but it could have come from the piles of refuse. A lecherous dwarf, the kind they used to put in freak shows half-a-century ago.

'Yes, a nice little girl. Red hair. Hearing aids. She's deaf.'

'Deaf. Deaf. *Deaf*!' A shrill peel of laughter, insane enough to send icy trickles down her back, the hideous mouth foamed with spittle. 'Nice *deaf* girl.'

Liz's fury overcame her fear. How dare this mis-shapen monstrosity jeer at another's disability. He was laughing again, head back, cackling crazily. She thought, you're mad, you ought not to be allowed to roam loose in this place. A terrible thought that had her mind reeling. *Rowena — suppose this madman's done something to her*.

She felt physically sick, started to back away. He was coming after her with short shuffling steps. She glanced behind her, looking for help. There was nobody about except . . . to her right was another square of waste ground hemmed in by the rear of sideshows and the corrugated menagerie fence. A place she recognized, the box-like theatre with a tarpaulin that had been carelessly thrown over it and had slipped, probably due to the force of the rain. A face staring out at her, gaudy features, the large mouth permanently held in a malevolent grin.

Punch!

Her head jerked one way then the other as though pulled by an invisible wire. Punch. The dwarf. Punch again. A battle of wills, these two hideous beings fighting a hypnotic tug-of-war in an attempt to gain control of her mind.

A sudden wrench and she was free. Running, stumbling, splashing her way through deep puddles, not daring to glance behind her. She tried to scream but couldn't make it, just a gurgle that came to nothing, laughter echoing in her ears. Then she was out in the open, people all around. It hadn't happened, it was all in the mind. Sure, the dwarf and Punch had been there but she had interpreted their expressions as her frightened mind had wanted her to. Both were quite harmless. Nothing to worry about.

Sweating, trembling, the rain driving in from the sea and lashing her face, cooling her and bringing her gradually back to reality. She was overwrought and she still had not found Rowena. Oh, God!

The music taunting her: '*I'm nobody's child*. . . .'

Standing there looking about her, the people, the way they didn't care. Not even interested in the accident at the Ghost Train now. Because it didn't affect *them*. Another police car, escorting an ambulance. No flashing blue lights; which meant there was no hurry, nothing more could be done for whoever was the victim of yet another tragedy in this place.

'*Mummy . . . mummy!*'

A little girl in a blue anorak running towards her, damp chestnut hair awry, socks mudsplashed. Holding a tiny doll in one hand.

'*Rowena!*'

A reunion that had her sanity ricochetting like a ball in a squash court, struggling to get it under control. The embrace, the euphoria, then simmering back down to anger as she became aware of the two people standing watching her only a few yards away.

'What are you doing here?' her words were addressed to Roy, her narrowed eyes fixed on the Indian girl by his side.

'Looking for you,' Roy hoped that the lie sounded

119

convincing. 'And Rowena, of course. Jane helped me find her.' Something in Jane's favour anyway. Also it was true.

'I thought I said that none of us were coming to this dreadful place ever again!' Liz's words cut like a whiplash, powered by the memory of everything that had happened to her recently.

'We didn't have any choice, did we?' stating his own case, struggling to dominate in the presence of this girl who stood beside him, finding a pride he'd almost forgotten. 'Nothing to worry about. We found her and she's been with us most of the afternoon whilst we looked for you.'

'*Afternoon!*' Liz snapped. 'You're mad. I came straight here from the harbour. It couldn't be more than an hour ago. . . .'

Her words faded as she consulted her wristwatch, a flourish that sent rain droplets showering into the air.

The hands on her watch said five minutes past four. She shook it, placed it against her ear. It was ticking sweetly. And then Liz Catlin's mind was reeling again. She thought she heard the dwarf cackling somewhere. Or it might even have been Punch!

7
WEDNESDAY NIGHT

Chief Inspector Landenning had planned to take his wife out to dinner that evening. It was a longstanding twice-postponed engagement. Monday had been ruined by the Hell's Angels battle which had blended into P.C. Andrews's untimely death. Even with the whole force at full strength Landenning should have been able to get away for three hours on Wednesday night. Now he had to telephone his long-suffering spouse and try and explain that he wouldn't be home tonight because they had found a body in the Ghost Train tunnel. He wouldn't go into details; it wouldn't be fair to her and as likely as not he would throw up if he had to go over it all again. Certainly he didn't feel like eating.

He took the easy way out. The station sergeant could phone Patricia. That way she wouldn't get any details and in all probability the gory account would be in the following morning's papers. Exaggerated, of course. But it would save him having to tell her. By the time he got home she would have read all about it and might even understand, although that was doubtful.

There was no dodging the Press when he arrived at the station, three pairs of eyes that saw his pale and lined features and smelled a front-page feature. Unless they had the facts they'd substitute a string of wild guesses so it was better to tell them the truth. And that wasn't easy when you couldn't come up with any explanation yourself.

The press conference lasted twenty minutes. Landenning could have got it over in ten but reporters became suspicious if they thought you were rushing them.

'But *how* was this guy killed, inspector?'

Beaten. Strangled. Ripped apart so that all that was left was a pile of dismembered limbs. 'Mutilated. We haven't found the weapon yet. I'll let you have details when we do.'

'It was Arlett, wasn't it. The child-killer they thought was safe and let out after only seven years of a life sentence?'

Christ, they knew more than the police. There were some tattoos that tied up with Arlett's, other minor features, but they wouldn't know for sure until the experts had . . . pieced it all together. 'We can't be certain but it looks that way.'

'Any ideas on the killer?'

'None.'

'Could it be the same guy who killed P.C. Andrews?'

'It's possible, but the two killings were totally different. Andrews was bludgeoned to death. This chap was . . . *mutilated*.' You couldn't describe it any other way.

'Can you give us any details?'

121

Oh, Christ Almighty! They reminded him of the ravens sitting in the trees waiting for daybreak after the battle of Bannockburn. This was the part they really wanted to know. Sensationalism. But he wasn't going to give it to them. 'I can't release anything like that at the moment.'

'There's something . . . *funny* about this fairground, isn't there, inspector?'

Landenning's scalp tingled. They'd sensed it, too. An atmosphere that you couldn't describe. A kind of invisible evil. He was aware of it in the same way that he'd felt that those carvings and puppets were watching him. But that was ridiculous because they couldn't, because they were nothing more than grotesque wooden objects. It was probably all due to the weather and overwork, culminating in a deep depression. He'd have to go carefully otherwise he might have a breakdown. Maybe he should have gone out with his wife after all tonight. Just two or three hours away from it all. Therapy.

'Well, inspector, there *is* something odd about Schaefer's fair, isn't there?'

'Fairgrounds are funny places,' non-committal, relaxing a little now that there was a chance of a brief respite. 'Just a string of coincidences really, beginning with those bikers taking the place apart.'

Landenning didn't believe it and neither did the reporters. He shuffled some papers together, relieved that they took the hint, pocketed their notepads and stood up. But they'd be back. First thing tomorrow morning. Any ideas on the killer? Could it be the same guy who killed P.C. Andrews? Are you able to give us any *details* yet?

Oh, God, he'd seen some sights in his time, right from the period when he was a rookie on highway patrol – multiple crashes, bloody corpses scarcely recognizable as such, severed limbs. But nothing to compare with *that*.

He couldn't get it off his mind. Going down that tunnel in the dark because for some reason the lights had fused. Spooks and ghouls frozen in their last electric actions, a macabre world that wasn't artificial any more. You sensed a presence, something that danced just beyond the range of the torches, a flitting shadow that vanished into nothing. A smell that rasped your throat, a mixture of engine oil, hot rubber and a sour aroma that permeated everything. *The stench of death, once smelled never forgotten.*

Then they saw it. The C.I.D. sergeant gave a cry and almost dropped his torch. Hardened police officers stood back, hoping that somebody else would be the first to go forward into that clearing amidst the hardboard trees. A hag's face was turned towards them, blood oozing from her toothless mouth, blood that was warm and wet and sticky. The ghoul creature munched on a dismembered human body, soft spongy flesh gripped firmly between his huge fangs, a crimson fluid dripping steadily to the floor, like a Chinese water-torture if one stopped to listen. *Drip . . . drip . . . drip. . . .*

Pairs of luminous eyes mocked the intruders. Painted evil that was suddenly for real. It was the silence which got you when you stood still, the walls soundproofed against outside noise.

'*My God!*' the sergeant swung his torch in a shaky circle. Blood everywhere. His foot kicked against something and he stepped back, directed the beam downwards. A hand trailing bloody sinews, fingers clenched and clawing, re-membering the agony when it had been torn from the body. Shredded blood-soaked clothing everywhere, strips of flesh still adhering to the cloth.

One of the officers turned and vomited, spewing his breakfast over a mangled pulped human trunk. Everybody was retching. Including Landenning. *And then they saw the head!*

It sat there in the middle of the floor, held upright by the neck which acted as a suction-cap. Blood-filled, blood seeping from every orifice in the skull, mouth frozen into a crimson cry of terror, eyes redly reflecting the torchlight.

It saw them, cheeks ballooning out, vomiting a clot of congealed blood with a loud splat. Then it tottered and rolled over on to its side.

Six policemen, every one of them standing on the narrow brink which separated sanity and madness. Inspector

Landenning moved forward because he knew it was his duty, said 'somebody's carved this one up, all right' because he knew he was expected to say something. It sounded silly. The sergeant laughed, an eerie sound that echoed and mocked them from the surrounding shadows.

After that it was all routine. Somebody got the lights working again and then the photographers and fingerprint experts arrived. Landenning went back outside, sat in the patrol car and made some notes in a handwriting which was far removed from his usual confident scrawl. It would pose some problems for his typist but he couldn't help that.

Now he was trying to get it all out of his system. The police van had removed the jointed carcass and it was all back to paperwork. Reams of it. Worse because you *had* to keep remembering every bloody detail. And it would go on for weeks, maybe months, long after Schaefer's fair had closed down and moved on, taking the bloodstains with it, leaving behind the memories.

Yes, he would take his wife out tonight, that vegetarian restaurant on the Marine Drive. After that it would be back to work. There was no time for sleep, something for which he was grateful for once. He dreaded the subconscious, what it might bring. But he would face up to that when he was too exhausted to go on any longer.

Rowena was back in the big wood again. It was different though. Much darker, and the trees were flat and deadlooking, no rounded interesting trunks with leafy foliage forming a roof over her head, and the ground was hard and bare without any vegetation sprouting up out of it.

She came to the big clearing and that had changed, too. No bluebells, no sweet almost overpowering scent. She drew back, peering into the gloom. She knew she wasn't alone. Any moment those awful little goblins would spring out and take her captive. Frightening at the time, but she knew that Doll would come to her rescue and that they would go off somewhere together. Perhaps this time they would not go to that strange Indian encampment but instead back to his cottage. She was curious to find out what

124

his home was like.

She heard something beyond the nearest line of silhouette trees and tensed. This was it, they were coming! But there was no sudden rush of fairy feet, just slow dragging footsteps, much heavier than before, and slow laboured breathing.

A shape materialized out of the gloom, a squat form that walked with difficulty. A dwarf, and when he got close enough for her to be able to make out his features it would be Doll, bigger and alive, kindly. There was nothing to fear.

But it wasn't Doll! Even in his wooden form Doll did not have a face like that, ugly and deformed, a mouth that was horizontal instead of vertical, tiny eyes that narrowed when they saw her and had no kindness in them.

Rowena wanted to run, to flee from this place and the horrible little man who was advancing on her with long outstretched arms, but her feet refused to move.

'Lovely lil' girl,' he wheezed and gave a cough that reminded her of the way her mother's button box rattled when it was moved. 'Lovely lil' deaf girl!'

He stopped a yard or so from her and she caught the stench of his foul breath. His eyes seemed to enlarge, bulging out like growing air-bubbles until she thought they would burst. One was higher than the other, bigger too, and he didn't have a proper nose, just a couple of holes through which he seemed to have difficulty in breathing.

'Lovely lil' girl and all alone in the wood. Just you an' me, uh!'

And then she felt her limbs coming back to life as though they had recovered from the initial shock. And her one thought was to put as much distance between herself and this gremlin of evil as possible. She sprang away, felt the tips of his stretching fingers brush her shoulder. Running blindly, aware that she had the greater speed if only she knew in which direction to head; if only it wasn't for the shadows and encroaching darkness.

She hit something, felt it give and spring back into place, quivering like taut elastic. A tree but it wasn't growing out of the ground, just standing upright. So frightening. She

125

ran a few more yards, paused to listen. Silence at first, then she heard her pursuer's rasping breaths terminating in a shrill laugh. The sound almost paralysed her. Even though she was so young, she recognized madness.

He was moving again. No, the steps were too quick, too light for his heavy deformed body. *Somebody else. . . .*

A shadow that moved and was gone the instant she saw it. Rowena crouched down, prayed that the thumping of her heart wouldn't be heard. Where was she? Her surroundings were vaguely familiar, somewhere she had been recently, not the wood where Doll had grown to full size then come to her rescue. Realization jerked her lips wide in a mute cry. *She was in the Ghost Train wood and yet it was different.* There was no train, neither skeletons nor witches stirring their vile cauldron. Just herself and the dwarf and *somebody else!*

Time seemed to stand still; or maybe time did not exist and this was eternity, a terrifying situation which would never come to an end. She wanted to cry, release the tears which were bursting to escape from her eyes, but she dared not make a noise. She could not even hear the dwarf breathing now. Perhaps he had grown tired of chasing her and had gone away elsewhere.

A flash like summer lightning which momentarily lit up the whole scene. Tree shapes with twisted boughs, bare of leaves, grotesque in their weird unnatural outlines, nightmarish creatures poised to strike. Then came the scream, a cry that was suddenly cut off, the thud of something heavy falling to the ground. Rowena hid her face in her shaking hands and when she found the courage to peer through spread fingers she was amazed to see that it was much lighter; a kind of soft glow as though the sun had made an error of judgement and risen above the eastern horizon without waiting for the dawn to announce its coming. But there was neither horizon nor sun, just a never-ending forest of artificial tree shapes.

She saw the clearing; she hadn't ventured as far from it as she had thought, in fact she couldn't have run more than five or six yards although it had seemed like half a mile.

126

Maybe she had gone round in a circle and ended up almost where she had begun.

Her relief was short-lived. At first she could not make out what the spherical shape in the centre of the clearing was. It was like one of those cheap footballs that children kicked about on the beach yet not so regular in shape. Red, all sticky, as though a flagon of strawberry sauce had been poured over it and then a clump of seaweed stuck on the top. It didn't make sense. She took another step forward and even as she did so the crimson mass started to run down the object and ooze into a treacly pool around its base.

She saw and understood. *And this time she managed to scream.*

It was a human head, severed at the neck and stuck firmly upright on the ground, fresh blood running from it and revealing the features beneath it. Her first thought was that it was that revolting shrunken skull which had been floating in the jar, but as more blood drained away she could see that it wasn't. Recognition was instantaneous; the narrow hatchet-shaped face which if it had been covered with a dense growth of black hair would have belonged to the man roped to the sacrificial stake in the Indian village. Shaven, it represented her pursuer from the Ghost Train!

Rowena's screams died away to near-mute gasps of terror, her brain refusing to accept what her eyes saw, the scattered limbs and blood-splattered tree trunks, branches dripping steadily as though from a sudden thunderstorm, the heavy vile smell which caught the back of her throat.

And somewhere in the distance she heard laughter, maniacal peals that rose to a pitch and died slowly away. And she knew without any doubt who was responsible for this depraved act of carnage.

Rowena was hunting frantically for Doll. Her mind was confused, her thoughts erratic; she wasn't in the forest any more. She was back in her hotel bedroom, pulling open drawers, tipping clothing out on to the floor.

Doll had to be here somewhere, he couldn't have gone just like that, particularly now that he appeared to have lost his ability to grow almost to human size and walk. But he hadn't been the dwarf in the forest because that one was evil. And Doll was good.

She was crying softly, the light on so that there were no shadows for hideous things to lurk in. She couldn't get that awful scene out of her mind, the severed head which resembled the man who had tried to molest her on the Ghost Train and who had looked remarkably like the Indians' prisoner . . . *and both of them bore a resemblance to that awful shrunken head in the jar.*

It was too much for her to cope with, even thinking about it brought on a feeling of nausea. It had all been a dream, a nightmare. So real, but there couldn't be any other explanation. But she was back in her own room, the horrors gone. Almost. She could still hear that laughter, tried to shake her head but the sound wouldn't go. Afraid that at any second the door might fly open and that squat barely-human figure would shuffle in, reaching out for her. Cornering her, nowhere to run. Gloating.

A sudden draught that floated her nylon nightdress, fanned her face. She dared not look, dared not gaze upon that terrible face again. She screamed, started to struggle as fingers grasped her by the shoulders. *No! I'm not going to look at you. Let me go*!

'*Rowena! Wake up*!'

Slow realization that it wasn't the ogre who lived amongst the flat trees. Relief that weakened her, brought on the tears that had been held back for so long, her small body shuddering under the emotional impact.

'Rowena, wake up!' Liz Catlin shook her, pulled her round so they were looking into each other's face. 'You're sleep-walking again. And you've had a nightmare!'

'Doll,' Rowena muttered, the glazed expression returning to her wide eyes. 'I can't find Doll.'

'Well don't you worry about Doll now,' fleeting guilt in Liz's expression, glancing down at the floor for a second. 'Look, you'd better come and sleep in our. . . .'

She closed her eyes. Roy was missing. He'd gone out into the rainswept night just before ten o'clock. Liz had been furious when he hadn't returned by eleven. Towards midnight her anger had blended with apprehension. He'd never done anything like this before in the whole of their married life. But he'd been acting strangely this last couple of days. Things were getting on top of him and a wet holiday was worse than no holiday at all. Perhaps she ought to call the police; if he hadn't come back in another half-hour then that was exactly what she would do. But in the meantime Rowena couldn't be left alone.

'Doll. Must find Doll.'

'I expect he's around somewhere. You can look for him tomorrow.' A little shiver up and down her spine that submerged the guilt.

'No. I want him *now*!' Lip-reading, angry. And underneath it all so very frightened, seeing the dwarf again.

Liz Catlin sighed. Rowena could be extremely difficult when she got in one of her stubborn moods. And that hideous little carved doll wouldn't help her any. Which was why Liz had taken it and hidden it in their own room. Tomorrow she would find some way of getting rid of it, not even telling Roy. They would all be a lot better off without it.

'Look,' Liz was determined not to show sympathy; this was one time when firmness was called for. 'You've had a nightmare and you're going to spend the rest of the night with . . . with us. And you can look for that doll tomorrow. Come on!'

She grabbed Rowena by the wrist, pulled her towards the door. The child resisted, found herself being dragged along, sliding. 'No!' she screamed. 'I want Doll!' Fighting every inch of the way, kicking.

'*Shut up*!' Liz got her inside the adjoining double-bedroom, kicked the door shut behind her and shook her roughly. 'Stop it! You'll wake the whole hotel up.'

Rowena fell silent, sullen. I want Doll. I hate *you*! Her eyes flicked round the room, saw the bed with the covers thrown back, sheets rumpled on one side only. The fear began to creep back into her, the significance of the empty space, a foreboding.

'Where's Daddy?' she watched her mother's face closely, noting the distraught look in her eyes.

'He's . . . gone out.' That was true anyway.

'Where?'

Liz tightened her lips. Children had a habit of asking the most awkward questions. And they knew when you were lying, too. 'He . . . couldn't sleep. He's gone out to get some fresh air. I think he's got a headache.'

'It's raining. He'll get wet.'

The rain was lashing the window outside. The very idea of going outside, even for a breath of fresh air to clear a headache, was ridiculous.

'Well, that's *his* fault,' Liz pushed Rowena towards the bed. 'Now, get into bed with me and try and get some sleep. I expect Daddy will be back shortly.'

All lies and forlorn hopes. Rowena's perception was much more acute than that of a normal hearing child. There were more than just bad dreams abroad on this wild dark night. And yet again in the depths of her own silent world she heard those shrill peals of mad laughter.

Roy Catlin was sweating, a sinking feeling in his stomach as he hurried from the hotel across the promenade. He walked steadily in the opposite direction to the fairground until he was out of sight of the Beaumont Hotel. In all probability Liz was watching from their bedroom window, suspiciously following his progress across the puddle-strewn deserted seafront, the lines of multicoloured fairy-lights bravely trying to preserve some vestige of gaiety. Then he retraced his steps, almost running, until he reached the boundary of Schaefer's empire of make-believe.

The fair had closed down early tonight. Without its milling throngs it had an eeriness about it, a resentment towards intruders. Catlin found himself moving warily, keeping to the shadows, an intruder bent on some secret mission, flitting from cover to cover. He crouched down by the menagerie, watching and listening. A loud sniffing sound came from one of the closed cages, a rumbling throaty growl. Remus the lion resented human presence during the night hours. This was no place to hang about.

Then Roy saw the police cars, the lights of the Ghost Train enclosure and the rope cordon with a uniformed officer on duty at its entrance. A man had died in there today. The police were linking it with the Hall of Mirrors killing. This was no time to be found prowling about.

Again Roy Catlin took a circuitous route, losing his way once in the black maze of sideshow avenues, but eventually he saw the outlines of the caravans, Jane's to the right of Jacob Schaefer's. No lights showed in either window.

He was breathing heavily now, his mouth dry, almost wishing that he had not come. But there was no going back now.

A light tap on the door with his knuckles, an interminable wait; Jane wasn't home, he'd kept his word by coming and now he could leave with a clear conscience, go back to the hotel. No need ever to come here again. . . .

'I'm glad you came.'

He started, almost shouted out aloud. Vaguely he could make out a patch of darkness that moved, came closer. Only when she was a yard away from him could he discern Jane's silhouette, that same blanket covering her. She had come from somewhere behind the caravan, perhaps there was another door on the opposite side.

'We'd better go inside,' she whispered. 'It is as well not to show a light and we must keep our voices low. There are many eyes and ears in this place that are hostile to us.'

She pushed open the door and motioned him to step inside. Roy Catlin moved carefully in the blackness, fearful of falling over some unseen obstacle, afraid of the darkness itself. Jane followed him. He heard her close the door softly and guide him to some kind of settee, lowering herself down alongside him, knowing also that she had discarded her blanket. That thought in itself was exciting, even here.

'Terrible things have been happening,' he felt the warmth and fragrance of her breath, her lips brushing his ear. 'A terrible killing in the Ghost Train, even worse than

131

that of the police officer in the Hall of Mirrors. And Rowena was on the Ghost Train today!'

'How d'you know that?'

'Just a . . . feeling. Some things I know in advance, others when they are happening . . . but occasionally happenings are only made known to me afterwards. By then sometimes it is too late. Nevertheless, she came to no actual physical harm and we must be grateful for that. I am to blame, I encouraged her to come back here, gave her. . . .'

'Gave her *what*?'

'The doll. I should not have done that because it has created a relationship between us which it will not be easy to sever. It was wrong of me.'

'But what *is* going on in this place?'

'As I told you earlier today, I have no idea except that I feel that whatever it is centres on myself. Perhaps it has been here all along although I felt that it began with the battle between the motorbike gangs. *That is when my own shame and hate began.*'

'Whatever do you mean?' Roy slipped an arm around her, half expecting it to be pushed away, but it wasn't.

'One of the bikers took me,' there was a tremor in her voice. 'I was raped!'

'Oh, my God! I'm so sorry. . . .'

'What is done is done. But I can never forgive myself for my own part in it. . . .'

'Don't be stupid. There was nothing you could have done. You might be dead now if you'd tried to resist.'

'No, I didn't fight because it would have been useless. But within myself I didn't resist either. *I wanted him to do it. I enjoyed it although to all outward appearances I remained emotionless. I even orgasmed . . . Afterwards I cursed him with all the venom I could muster. But it was too late.*'

Roy Catlin felt his stomach churn again, followed by a wave of hate and jealousy towards the unknown Hell's Angel. And he was also aware that he was getting an erection.

'I have disgraced a noble race of people as well as the Cheyenne tribe,' Jane was speaking tonelessly, a kind of confessional recital addressed to the enshrouding darkness. 'The Cheyenne women are proud of their chastity, wearing their rope chastity belts until such time as they take a husband. So it would have been with myself but now I am unclean and no better than a whore who creeps into the lodges of young men after nightfall. *Worse, I am a murderer.*'

'No, you're not. You haven't killed anybody.'

'Indeed, I have. *I cursed him who lay with me and the one who aided him and they were dead before the sun set. I cursed the sun and the gaiety it gave people in this false place and by nightfall the rain had come. It has not ceased.*'

'That's all coincidence.'

'Perhaps. Perhaps not. But now forces are alive within this place against which I am powerless. I asked your help but that was selfish of me because nobody can help me. Except Manitou who gave me powers to unveil the future and even he has deserted me because I have betrayed my people. Perhaps if I flee then misfortune will accompany me and I shall free this place from the curse of the Indian gods.'

'No.' Roy Catlin sensed panic at the prospect of losing Jane and pulled her close to him. 'Don't go, Jane. Don't leave me!'

'I have given you bad thoughts,' her fingers brushed against the protruding hardness inside his trousers, 'but that is because I am a bad woman.'

Her mouth found his in the darkness, teeth biting tantalizingly, gently, on his lower lip, the feel of soft bare breasts against his chest. 'I am evil in that I asked you here tonight,' she murmured, 'because I knew from the first time I set eyes upon you that this would come about and even I cannot alter the course of Fate. But you must promise me that afterwards you will return to your wife. And Rowena, because she needs you.'

'I promise,' he knew there was no going back, that, as Jane had said, this was how it was meant to be.

He had to be dreaming, an erotic fantasy had come to torture him in his sleep and suddenly it would vanish like an autumnal mist dispersed by morning sunlight. But it didn't. Her naked body became part of his own, a gentle rhythm like the rocking of an infant's cradle, promises that came from the heart but could never be fulfilled. A slow escalation, savouring every second, holding back from the brink as long as possible, then being swept over and floating somewhere where only the two of them existed. Coming slowly back to reality, almost guiltily as though unseen eyes watched them. Dressing hurriedly.

'I cannot help being bad,' Jane drew back so that his pouted lips did not make contact with her own. 'I too am a victim of Fate. But what is done is done.'

'Don't go,' Roy pleaded.

'We shall see. But in the meantime both of us must guard Rowena. The future refuses to reveal what is in store for her. It is Salin I fear most.'

'Salin?'

'The hunchback who helps in the menagerie, the most despised man in the fairground. His very soul is festered with evil. He was watching the three of you as you walked away this afternoon and there was an expression on his face which frightened me. Even the lion and the gorilla cower in his presence.'

'I'll be back,' Roy Catlin stepped out into the wet night and heard the caravan door click shut behind him. Then he left, walking quickly, keeping to the shadows again and skirting that area where the police were still conducting their investigations.

It was as he passed close to the menagerie that a movement in the far shadows attracted his attention, had him crouching down, trying to pierce the darkness until his eyes ached under the strain. But all was still and by the time he reached the promenade he had convinced himself that it was all in his imagination. Maybe he had even imagined that guttural spine-chilling peal of laughter.

8

THURSDAY MORNING

Liz was still awake, as Roy had expected she would be, when he crept back into the bedroom. There was just enough light coming in through the open curtains for him to be able to make out his wife sitting straight and tense on the side of the bed, a smaller slumbering shape beside her. Rowena had probably had another nightmare but she was safe and that was all that mattered.

'Well,' Liz's tone was clipped, accusing, 'and where d'you think you've been until this hour?'

'I told you, I went out to get some fresh air.'

'So you've been walking the wet streets for two hours!' A sneer, switching on the light so that she could watch his expression. 'You've been up to something, Roy. I can tell.'

He felt his courage waning. It wasn't easy facing up to Liz when she was in one of her scathing moods. Only on rare occasions had he attempted to do so. That was the trouble, he should have taken a firm line with her early on in their marriage. Now it was an uphill battle. But he was determined to fight all the same.

'What d'you mean, "up to something"?' forcing the issue.

She caught her breath. Seething with anger, trying to hold it in check because she wasn't sure of herself, couldn't believe that this could actually happen to *her* husband. It was a shattering thought, the kind of thing one read about in women's magazines – the unfaithful husband returning home late at night, the wife suspecting that he'd been 'with another woman', the smell of unfamiliar perfume on his clothing, a strand or two of hair left from a clandestine embrace. Nothing more. Roy wouldn't do *that*! He wasn't the kind.

'I . . . I think. . . .' she didn't really know how to put it, 'that . . . that you've been seeing somebody else.'

He tried to laugh but that only made it worse. 'You're being stupid. I'd hardly go out there on a night like this looking for other women. I've been doing some . . . exploring.'

'Exploring? Where?'

'The fairground.'

'What on earth for?'

'Because there's a lot of strange things going on there. Apart from two killings.'

'It's none of your business and it's a place we should keep clear of. I thought we'd already agreed on that.'

'Perhaps. But Rowena was on the Ghost Train today.'

'How d'you know?'

'I . . . know.'

'*You've been talking to that Indian girl again, haven't you*?'

'Yes. Because it was necessary if I was to find anything out.'

'You're deceitful,' Liz's emotions were getting in a tangle. She wanted to be angry but instead she was on the verge of bursting into tears. 'I want to go home. Tomorrow we'll pack up and leave. Try to forget that we ever had a holiday this year.'

'We can't.' Smugness that he did his best to hide. 'We don't have a car. It won't be ready until Friday night, possibly Saturday morning, and by then it'll be time to go home anyway.'

'Oh, my God!' Liz buried her face in her hands, let the tears come. 'We're trapped!'

'Look,' Roy sat on the bed beside her, put an arm around her, felt guilty, 'we're here whether we like it or not. And there's something odd going on which we're caught up in.'

'Whatever do you mean?'

'I can't explain it exactly, but haven't you noticed anything about that fairground, the kind of eerie feeling you

136

get in there? Everything should be happy and carefree, instead it's like the whole place is brooding, angry. Waiting for something to happen.'

He had expected a denial, an outburst. Instead she remained silent. And when she looked up her tears had dried. The anger had disappeared and in its place was dejection. Hopelessness. 'Yes,' she said, 'I noticed it on the first night. The place is hateful, not like an ordinary fair. You can read it in the expressions of the stallholders, the way they look at you as though you shouldn't be there but they'll take your money just the same. And that dwarf is the worst of all.'

'Dwarf!' the arm encircling her trembled. '*You've met Salin?*'

'I don't know what his name is but when I was looking for Rowena he was hanging about behind the menagerie. God, he's awful. He shambled after me and I just ran. He's . . . I suppose he *is* human but he's more like a deformed ape!'

'He's evil.'

'But we don't *have* to go there, do we? This is all so stupid. If there is something odd about the fairground then all we have to do is to keep away from it.'

'We haven't been very successful so far.'

'No, but this time we'll. . . .'

Rowena was stirring, sitting up and rubbing her eyes. 'Doll,' she muttered. 'I want Doll.'

'She's had a nightmare,' Liz turned and placed a hand on Rowena's shoulder. 'She's lost that little doll of hers.'

'Lost it!' Roy was incredulous. 'But she hasn't been anywhere to lose it. She hasn't been outside the hotel.'

'Well it's disappeared,' Liz Catlin hoped she wasn't blushing, couldn't bring herself to look at either her husband or her daughter. 'Perhaps it'll turn up tomorrow.' She reached up, pulled the cord behind the bed and plunged the room into darkness.

She shuddered, moved up against Rowena as Roy climbed into bed. A feeling of revulsion mingled with hatred. She knew he'd done more than just talk to the Indian girl.

Jane made no move to climb back into her bunk after Roy Catlin had left. She sat there motionless, staring into the darkness. Afraid; not just for herself but for the man who had made love to her, and his deaf daughter. They were enmeshed in this web of evil as surely as she herself was. And the future eluded even her own clairvoyant powers as surely as if a mantle had been draped over her foresight.

Somewhere a clock struck. Three chimes. The night was well advanced but it was far from over yet. Her acute sense of hearing picked up noises outside. The steady beating of the rain against the caravan, a sheet of corrugated iron rattling somewhere. A scratching sound that could have been a rat foraging outside the door, but she knew it wasn't. Tensing. *Something against the window*. . . .

She couldn't hold back the single scream. A face squashed against the pane of glass but it wasn't just the pressure which caused the features outside to distort like some caricature of a monster in a horror cartoon. Then it was gone and she heard the door-handle turning and knew without any doubt that Salin was about to visit her, saw his ungainly squat shape framed in the dim light of the open door.

If there had been anywhere to run Jane would have fled. But there was nowhere. She shrank back, pulling the blanket tight around her body.

'What do you want, Salin?' she called out.

An animal-like grunt answered her. He was inside now, the door still open behind him, clutching something in one of his oversized hands, holding it up as though he wanted her to see it. She stared, could only make out the outline of the object but that was sufficient. There was no mistaking her own style of carving, the way the horse's head was thrown back, crude at first glance but almost alive if one inspected it closely. The neck tapered away in jagged spikes. Broken, wrenched from the body to which it had belonged.

She recognized it instantly, caught her breath in horror. She stared at it, her fury overcoming her fear at Salin's destruction of her work, the way he was trying to taunt her.

It was the head of one of the merry-go-round horses.

'You will pay for this,' she hissed. 'Jacob Schaefer will not let you get away with it!'

'You're a bad woman,' he was speaking coherently for once, frothing and spitting as he did so. 'You are responsible for all that has happened here. *You* brought evil to the fair.'

She swallowed, controlled her anger because she remembered that Salin had been to the Ghost Train and what had been found there later. His mind was deranged; he was as dangerous as the animals he helped to look after.

'Those carvings do not belong to me,' she spoke evenly. 'They are Mr Schaefer's property.'

'You made them. They are very bad. Dangerous. Must be destroyed.'

'They'll have the police after you if you damage any more.'

'Police!' he gave a snarling laugh. 'Even the police die in this place. You are trying to kill us all!' His eyes rolled and she saw the whites in the darkness. '*Maybe I should kill you*!'

She thought for a moment that he was about to attack her. He shuffled forward another few inches then stopped suddenly, his mis-shapen mouth twisting into a hideous grin. 'You fucked with that feller.'

His words cut into her, dazed her for a moment, and when her brain cleared her anger came surging back. 'You were spying on us through the window!'

He spat a blob of phlegm on to the floor. 'Squaw!' The hand holding the broken horse's head went back and up, a club poised to strike. Jane closed her eyes, prayed to Manitou that the end would be quick, that she would not be left to linger for years with a damaged brain, a disfigured babbling idiot like her attacker.

A scream, a tortured inhuman cry like a wounded wild beast, snarling and spitting, something falling heavily on the floor, writhing and kicking.

Jane, the Cheyenne, forced her eyes open, shied away at what she saw in the half-light of her caravan. Salin convulsed in a heap, cursing faintly through hideous lips that moved on one side only, blazed his hate from a single eye, the left dead and sightless. One arm clawed the air feebly, the other sagged lifeless over the damaged carving. One leg tried to kick and failed miserably whilst the second was twisted beneath him at an unnatural angle.

She backed away even though she knew he was helpless, that there was no way he could harm her, covered her ears in an attempt to shut out his foul mouthings.

Salin had been struck down as though a bolt of lightning going to earth had singled him out, paralysed his entire body on one side, but sadistically let him live so that he could suffer.

She turned away, closed her eyes. Didn't want to see. *And somewhere, faintly, she heard the neighing of a horse.*

Liz Catlin had never been an early riser. She hated the mornings, even on holiday. Especially pouring wet ones, and this morning was no exception.

She had awakened just after six o'clock, groaned into the pillow when she heard the rain still driving on to the window, not that she thought it might have stopped. The weather chart on the flickering old black and white television in the hotel lounge had shown an area of low pressure firmly ensconced over the British Isles; the satellite picture had revealed a depth of cloud stretching as far as the continent, and there was no way it was going to move at present. Even with freshening winds it would take a day or two to disperse. Roll on, Saturday. Everybody felt the same way, probably even the kids by now.

Liz slid out of bed and began to dress, moving quietly, glancing at Roy and Rowena. They hadn't even stirred. She might even be back before they awoke and then they would never know that she had been out.

Her last pair of dry jeans. It was impossible even to hang clothes out of the window. Later, perhaps, she would find a launderette somewhere and spin-dry all their clothes, otherwise after today they would be without any dry garments at all.

She pulled on a crumpled nylon sweater and reached for her anorak which was hanging behind the door, weighed down on one side because there was something in one of the pockets. A feeling of uneasiness, wishing she didn't have to do this. Maybe she didn't. That damned doll couldn't possibly have any bearing on what was happening all around them; that was just nonsense, fanciful thinking, giving way to one's fears. But it was certainly responsible for those vivid nightmares which Rowena had been having lately. There was no doubt about that. You'd only got to look at the thing to see why. Ugh, it was horrible! She glanced again to make sure that Rowena was still asleep and slipped the wooden doll out of the coat pocket. There was nothing very artistic about that sort of carving, a few grooves and bumps cut out of a chunk of wood, squat and ugly. And Jane had the nerve to sell this sort of rubbish for a quid a time!

Liz's anger had taken over by the time she reached the hall below. That Indian was a menace. She worked on folks, got them doing what she wanted them to. First Rowena, running off to her at every opportunity. Now Roy.

'Good morning, Mrs Catlin, you're up early this morning.'

Liz whirled, saw Mrs Hughes, the proprietor of the Beaumont Hotel, sorting residents' mail into a wooden rack by the front door. An aroma of frying came from the kitchen.

'Yes,' Liz felt suddenly guilty. Mr Hughes must think her highly eccentric, going out at this hour in this kind of weather. 'I . . . I've got a bit of a headache. I thought maybe a walk as far as the paper shop would help to clear it.'

'Oh, I'm sorry to hear that,' piercing grey eyes that could be searching out the real reason. 'I expect it's the weather, keeping everybody shut up indoors instead of getting plenty of fresh air. Let's just hope it changes today.'

Liar, you know it won't. It'll rain all day, and tomorrow, and the day after. You're another con-merchant, the same

141

as the Indian, filling people with false hope in case any of them might decide to pack up and go home early.

Outside, standing in the porch for a few seconds as though plucking up the necessary courage to splash out into the wet. Her fingers played with the doll in her pocket, hating it, wishing she didn't have to think about it. She saw a litter-bin across the road. She could just have dropped it in there, gone back to the dry hotel. No, somebody might find it, Rowena might be peeping down from behind the curtains. The doll had to be destroyed, disappear completely. There was a cliff-walk up on the headland above the town, a narrow footpath lined with stout steel railings on the seaward side. Beyond them was a sheer drop of two or three hundred feet down to the bay below, jagged rocks which over the centuries had claimed their share of unfortunate victims. Well, today they were going to claim yet another, one small grotesque wooden doll which would shatter on impact, the splinters floating out with the ebbing tide. And Rowena's connection with the fortune-teller would be severed. Liz Catlin laughed softly to herself.

Liz walked fast, not even noticing the rain now. But she could not get the Indian girl out of her mind. The bitch had seduced Roy last night and he was weak and stupid enough to let her. Liz could tell, had that feeling, an intuition that was rarely wrong. Most women sensed it when their husbands had been unfaithful to them. In the majority of cases they turned a blind eye and hoped that it wouldn't develop into anything serious, kidded themselves that it wasn't really going on. But not Liz. She wasn't going to let that squaw get away with it. Somehow she would have her revenge, and destroying the doll was as good a way as any to start.

The wind was stronger now than it had been all week, driving the rain horizontally, forcing Liz Catlin to walk with bowed head, her jeans already saturated from the knees downwards, feet squelching inside her shoes. She looked up, saw the towering cliffs above her, heard the waves beating on the rocks far below. It was impossible to see down to the cove below without clambering over the railings and crawling out to where the sheer drop began. That was how the accidents in recent years had happened, mostly young children. Liz felt sick at the thought.

She reached the top, paused to get her breath. *This was it, the end of the road for Rowena's Doll.*

Liz pulled it out of her pocket, weighed it in her hand. She did not want to look at it again but she felt her eyes being drawn down; she was forced to stare into those beady black eyes. Its expression had changed. No, it couldn't have, that was impossible because it was a wooden lifeless thing. *But it had*! The eyes . . . she read in them a fierce hate directed at herself and what she was about to do.

She closed her eyes, forced her arm up and back, balanced, tensed. *Now*! Hurling with every ounce of strength she could muster, opening her eyes, seeing the doll soaring upwards, twisting, turning, slowing until it reached its apex where it seemed to hover. Then falling, so gently, facing her so that once again she saw the eyes, *looking at her. A malevolence that had her stepping back, wanting to flee*.

Stationary, not falling anymore. One last hateful stare and then it was gone, plunging down beyond the cliff top, lost to view.

Liz turned, started to retrace her steps. A noise, she could not be certain where it came from; a scream, shrill and high-pitched so that it hurt and made her wince. Then cut off with a suddenness that was even more terrifying, leaving just the patter of driving rain.

And Liz Catlin was very frightened.

Rowena maintained a sullen silence throughout breakfast. Roy seemed more engrossed than usual in his morning newspaper and Liz stared down at her plate as she ate, not really wanting the food but feeling that she was obliged to eat it. Everybody wanted to say something but nobody did. Oh God, if only it was Saturday.

Guilt and anger. Rowena looked from her father to her mother. You've stolen Doll, I know it. And I hate you for it! Liz wilted beneath the stare, almost wished she had not taken such a drastic step. The doll couldn't really be all that bad; some parents bought their offsprings nightmarish luminous monsters that glowed in the dark. Then she remembered Doll's expression, the way his eyes had fixed on her, loathing and malevolent. That final scream had all been in her mind, her conscience crying out because she had deliberately thrown her daughter's favourite toy over the cliffs. Despicable. A tight knot in her stomach that was like the start of period pains. Scorned by her own husband who had forsaken her bed for a blanket and a Red Indian whore. *If* he had. Of course he had, you could tell by his face. He was feeling pretty bad about it now that his lust had been satisfied. But it was no good being soft with him. Let him suffer.

Roy knew that Liz knew. After that first accusation she had not raised the subject again which meant that he had been found guilty. All that remained now was for sentence to be passed. He wished she'd get it over with but knowing Liz's sulky moods it might go on for weeks and never be mentioned again. But she wouldn't forget and neither would she forgive. And he wouldn't keep away from the fair. Jane needed him, she was in some kind of deadly danger which even she couldn't explain. And that would undoubtedly lead to further conflict with Liz. Where the hell had his wife been this morning? She was missing when he woke up and she didn't return until just a few minutes before the breakfast bell. Judging by her saturated clothing she had been walking in the rain for some time which was totally out of character. At home if it was only raining lightly she refused to go as far as the corner shop. And there was also this business of Rowena's missing doll. Liz was responsible for its disappearance and you couldn't stoop much lower than that. Somehow, though, he had to see Jane again as soon as possible, if only to ascertain that no harm had befallen her.

There was no doubt in Rowena's mind that her mother had stolen Doll; not just hidden him but done something horrible to him . . . like burning him! It was jealousy, nothing else, because Jane had carved it. That was why

Mummy had gone out so early this morning. But she'd get her own back and in the meantime she wouldn't speak to her. She'd pretend her hearing-aid wasn't working properly and conveniently ignore everything her mother said.

'Well, we can't sit here all day,' Roy Catlin folded up his damp newspaper and pushed his chair back.

'Agreed,' Liz's voice was cold, still staring down at her plate. 'But where do you suggest we go? It's going to pour with rain non-stop and we don't have a car. And we're *not* going to the fair!'

Roy sighed, glanced at Rowena, but she apparently had not heard them speak, staring fixedly up at the ceiling. There was no way of engineering a trip to the fair at the moment. Perhaps an opportunity would present itself at a later stage.

'We haven't found Rowena's doll yet,' Roy Catlin watched his wife's face as he spoke. 'Perhaps we ought to go upstairs and have a good look for that before we do anything.'

'I've looked,' Liz raised her eyes, dropped them again. 'It isn't anywhere in either of the bedrooms.'

'It must be. She had it with her at bedtime.'

'*Well, it isn't!*' bordering on the hysterical. 'For God's sake don't keep on about it! Maybe she'll forget.'

She won't. And neither will any of us. 'Suppose we go out on a sea trip. They do have covered boats, you know.'

'Charming. In this weather? The sea's choppy and you know how easily Rowena gets sick.'

A sullen silence. It lasted maybe ten seconds before it was broken by a thunderous explosion that reverberated throughout the room and rattled a loose window pane. So close, blanketed by the sea fog that had thickened since daybreak, holding it in like a peal of overhead thunder.

'What's that?' Liz paled, turned towards the window. People were hurrying in the direction of the harbour.

'The maroon!' Roy was on his feet now. 'Somebody's in trouble out there. They've got to put the lifeboat out.'

Liz Catlin stood up, thought for one brief moment that she was going to faint as a wave of dizziness swept over her.

The echoes of the explosion were dying away when another sound jarred her brain. That shrill scream again, the one she'd heard earlier up on the cliffs, piercing, cut off suddenly.

'Let's go down to the harbour.' Roy was making a weak attempt at a smile. 'Maybe we'll see the lifeboat being launched.'

Liz Catlin found it difficult to walk; her legs wanted to crumple up under her. There was no logical explanation, but *somehow she felt she was responsible for whatever had happened at sea*.

But that was too ridiculous for words.

Stewart Middleton emerged somewhat reluctantly from his tent on the Sunview Camping Site soon after it began to get light. Clad in only a pair of bright blue bathing trunks he tried to convince himself of a number of things; that his skin was not a sickly office-pallid colour, nor did his spare roll of flesh spill over the elastic of his costume, that it wasn't raining any more or, if it was, that by the time he reached the tideline the early morning sun would be turning the large stretch of sand a deep golden colour, the sea would lose its cold metallic greyness and become sparkling mediterranean blue. He would swim to Beachy Head and back, then, glowing with health, he would return to his campsite and cook himself a hearty breakfast with total disregard for his calorie intake because of the energy he would have used up. He groaned, gave up trying to create illusions and padded along the wet sand. Damn it, he was going to make that swim this morning. He'd waited since Tuesday; another couple of mornings and it would be time to pack all his gear into the back of his old Morris 1000 Traveller and head homewards. And this rain wasn't going to let up. Ever!

The sand beneath his feet got soggier as he neared the edge of the tide. Damn this sea mist, you couldn't even make out the Head less than half-a-mile away. He waded in up to his thighs, shivered, his flesh goosepimpling. The water was as cold as it had been when he'd come down here on that day-trip in late April.

He lowered himself into the sea, struck out in a frenzied crawl, foaming the water all around him, trying to speed up his circulation. It wasn't too bad once you made the plunge and got going.

He must have been swimming for ten minutes before he sensed that something was wrong, trod water, trying to look around him. He had estimated that he was no more than thirty or forty yards from land but now all he saw was an expanse of grey, white-flecked sea on all sides, the mist hanging like a massive dirty curtain. Even at seventy or eighty yards he ought to have been able to discern the coastline. *There was nothing but an opaque greyness*.

He tried to stop himself from panicking. He couldn't be all that far out to sea. The problem was, a terrifying thought, in which direction did the land lie? Well, the tide was going out so if he swam against the current he should arrive on dry land within a relatively short time. There was nothing to worry about, people drowned because they panicked.

It was much harder going against the current than Stewart Middleton had anticipated. At one stage he thought that he wasn't making any progress at all. He tried to touch the bottom with his feet, submerged, came up again. Now he was really getting scared. The water here was *very* deep!

Something touched his leg, bobbed away again. He turned on his side, tried to see what it was, caught a glimpse of something small, floating. Driftwood, in all probability. It came in, hit him again, hard this time, a glancing blow on the ankle which had him crying out in pain, swallowing some water. Jesus Christ, it was as hard as metal but if that was the case it would sink. Ignoring it, and the throbbing ache, he tried to make out just one strip of welcoming land but there was only sea all around.

He saw it again, couldn't quite make out what it was, half-submerged in front of him, smaller than a beer can. Crazy, the tide should have swept it away from him!

A wave, bigger than the rest, submerging him. He raised

his head, spat sea-water, saw the object again. Rolling, spinning in the water; a tiny figure, features blending into a blur of living movement, flashing eyes, mouth twisted into a cruel grin. *Coming at him again.*

Stewart Middleton flipped over on to his back, kicking wildly with his legs, trying to drive the thing off. For a few moments it was screened by the splashes. Perhaps it had gone away, even sunk. A bone-jarring blow on his right shin was proof that it was still around, attacking him viciously, a little wooden figure gone berserk.

He drew up his legs in agony, went under yet again. It was dark below the surface, just a strange green glow like the inside of an aquarium. No fish, though, empty except for . . . *oh, Jesus God*!

Stewart Middleton saw it clearly now, bigger than before, definitely *alive*, features that had the stamp of evil on them, grinning its hate and knowing that it had him at its mercy, playing with him. He tried to strike upwards but it was too quick for him, diving in, slamming hard into his face. Dazed, feeling as though his lungs might explode at any second, a red haze before his eyes, streaked with crimson. Blood, claret turning to pink as it diluted. He tasted it in his mouth, a cut somewhere and his nose felt as though it might be broken.

Weakening. He couldn't see his attacker, it was somewhere behind him. The crushing blow on the back of his head blinded him temporarily. And again, this time on the side of the neck. Breathing in water, suffocating. Fighting.

Like an angry attacking hornet the thing came at him, each onslaught more vicious than the last, the water turning scarlet, foaming. Going down . . . down . . . taking in water now in quantity, consciousness beginning to slip away. One last moment of unrestricted vision, its face close to his own, magnified to human proportions, snarling like some ferocious predatory underwater creature sensing the helplessness of its prey. Coming in for the kill.

Stewart did not put up a fight this time. His body seemed to explode with the pressure of water inside it, agony that shattered his brain in a blinding flash of crimson. Then the blackness closed in on him, so soothing and comforting, as his senses slipped away from him, dulling the pain.

The *Catrona* had fished all night in the bay with mediocre success, a small privately-owned smack which relied upon a fair haul of mackerel merely to meet its running costs and the wages of a three-man crew. The previous week had shown a bonus but during these last three hours, usually the peak catching period of the day, it seemed as though for some inexplicable reason the shoals had moved on.

'Bloody queer,' Tom Lewins the skipper muttered as the last of the nets was hauled up on deck. 'The bay's virtually empty, as though some predatory fish has moved in and sent the mackerel scarpering. But we haven't had any sharks in these waters since '76. If this continues we'll all be broke. With the weather as it is we're not likely to take on much in the way of passengers.'

'It can't go on much longer,' an older man in oilskins leaning over the side of the vessel grimaced. 'Like bleedin' November.'

'Take it steady goin' back,' Lewins called to the third man at the helm. 'No way o' knowin' what's in these waters holiday times. Shouldn't think there'd be much traffic about with this weather, though.'

The engine chugged into life, groaning, vibrating. Foam churned sluggishly beyond the stern, gulls glided in and out of the fog, calling half-heartedly. One swooped, came up with an empty beak. Nobody was in luck this morning.

Down to three knots, it was impossible to go any faster. The crew sensed the silence beyond the engine noise. You could feel it. Even the wind had dropped, the rain falling vertically, the choppy waves reduced to a smooth swell. One had the feeling that at any moment the tide would stop, too.

Bloody creepy, Lewins thought, like everything was dead, just left to float on a barren sea, going nowhere, just drifting forever.

And just as suddenly as that background silence had descended it lifted. Wild mournful calling escalating to a shrill viciousness. Sea birds beyond the fishermen's range of vision. The boat going closer as though drawn by the cries. Vague shapes, outstretched wings, swooping, jinking, going up and round again. Mobbing something.

A small object, the waves gently lapping over it, submerging it, surfacing again.

'What the fuck is it?' Lewins strained his eyes.

'Food o' some sort. Gotta be else all them birds wouldn't be goin' crazy over it.'

'Don't look like it to me. We'll soon see, though.'

The wash from the *Catrona* caught whatever it was in the water, pushed it away then brought it back in closer. Eyes strained; a kid's doll of some sort, couldn't be sure though. The birds wheeled, came back in. A herring gull dived, stabbed with a wicked beak, hit something solid. Shied off, a long wail that had every element of terror in it, disappearing into the fog.

Then it happened, so suddenly that everybody on board had no forewarning of impending danger. A huge looming shape, bows that came right up out of the water, the noise of the smooth running engines drowned by those of the chugging idling fishing boat, steel grey so that it blended with the background of fog and seascape, a steel battering-ram.

A crunching noise, an efficient demolition job of the small craft by the larger one, timber spliced and splintered, instant flotsam. Bodies, bloody and broken, the living attempting to swim, caught by the swell of the collision and going under.

A duel that was over within seconds. The victor, a coastguard patrol boat, circling awkwardly liked a winged duck, water pouring in through the hole in its bows, two men hastily unfastening a life-raft.

A monster in its death throes, rearing up, gurgling its agony, shuddering, sliding, settling. Sliding again. The raft bobbed up and down, spun round. The men paddled frantically, desperate to be clear of the suction of a sinking ship, just making it but being drawn back nevertheless. The men in the raft, white-faced, looking around them, saw a bloody arm raised above the surface in a gesture of despair but it was gone before they could get to it.

They stared at each other in blank shocked silence, pulled in their paddles. Their S.O.S. had got through and now there was nothing to do except wait until help arrived, sit here on a grey fog-shrouded mill-pond and stare at the floating debris which the tide did not seem to want. Except for one tiny chunky piece of wood that found a current, sped away as though on some urgent task.

A carved doll, almost swimming, seeming to turn and look back for a second, features bland except for the eyes; twin wooden orbs that seemed to see and laugh malevolently at what they saw.

And somewhere far away a deep boom echoed along the rocky coastline.

9

THURSDAY AFTERNOON

The rain had eased, almost died away. Just a fine drizzle, perhaps it was the mist coming in off the bay if one could only tell the difference. Grey skies overhead but the clouds were higher than they had been all week. Depressing, but at least one was not forced to remain indoors for the rest of the day.

Scattered holidaymakers dotted the wet sands, the hardier ones in bathing costumes, but most in waterproofs. Beach balls were kicked by wellington boots; children dug mud as though it was fine powdery sand; everyone needed to expend their pent-up energy.

Rowena Catlin walked on sullenly ahead of her parents; dissent in her posture, contempt almost.

'She's in one of her moods,' Liz commented.

'Apparently,' Roy sighed. And no bloody wonder considering you've done something to her doll!

'She'll snap out of it, she usually does. We should've waited for the lifeboat to come back.'

'You're just morbid, like these people who congregate at road accidents,' Roy could not resist a sneer.

'That's ridiculous. We don't even know that anybody was hurt.'

'They reckon a fishing-boat and a coastguard patrol had a head-on in the fog. Somebody's sure to have been pretty badly smashed up. Or drowned.'

'You're the one who's morbid. I don't expect we'll hear another word about it apart from a brief paragraph in tomorrow morning's paper.'

'They've gone to town on those fairground killings,' Roy replied. 'They're calling it "The Phantom of the Fairground" according to one placard I saw on the promenade this morning. Well, *I* certainly don't want to read about it. Roll on Saturday morning and back to our lovely old humdrum boring life at home. Hey, Rowena's getting too far ahead.'

Roy quickened his step, subconsciously glad of the excuse to leave Liz behind. Rowena had her shoes and socks off and was splashing in the edge of the tide, jumping back every time a sizeable wave came her way.

'Rowena, don't go too far.' She wouldn't hear but maybe Liz would think he was doing his best and she'd stop nagging. Rowena frisked on, almost as though she had heard and was deliberately defying her parents. She hadn't spoken to them all morning but Roy didn't blame her for that. She was silently blaming both of them for Doll's disappearance.

Suddenly she gave a cry, a shrill shriek of delight, dashing forward into the sea until the water was almost up to her waist, reaching out for something. Almost losing her balance and falling. Frantically grabbing at whatever it was, pulling it clear of the water, leaping back on to the sand.

'Rowena, how dare you go in the water fully dressed!'

152

Liz's shout sounded a long way off. Roy broke into a run; he didn't want her to catch him up. Yet. A feeling of uneasiness. Children often collected bits of wreckage on the beach but there was something significant in the way Rowena was holding it to her as though unwilling to let anybody else see it.

'Rowena, what's that you've got?'

She turned, a triumphant expression on her features, deliberated a moment as to whether to disclose her find, then held something aloft. Something draped in seaweed and dripping water but recognizable nonetheless.

Doll!

'Liz recoiled, unable to take her eyes off the small saturated figurine. Even at that distance there could be no possibility of mistaken identity. She closed her eyes, heard that scream again, cutting out just the way it had before. Oh God, it wasn't possible! The sea had thwarted her, returned that grotesque doll within a matter of hours. She looked again, deathly pale, met those eyes. They couldn't see, it was impossible. The thing was nothing more than a crudely carved chunk of wood. Yet. . . .

'My doll . . . doll . . . *Doll!*' Rowena was dancing like a saturated ballerina, unaware of the incoming tide which reached out and touched her feet as if paying homage to the doll she held.

'Are you all right, Liz?' Roy turned and there was genuine concern in his expression.

'Yes . . . I'm . . . all right.'

'Well, you don't look it. Perhaps we'd better go back to the hotel and you can lie down for a bit.'

'No, I'll be O.K.' I don't want to go anywhere except home and away from here, and *that. But you won't escape by going home because Rowena will take it with her.*

I'll get rid of it somehow. No you won't because you've already tried and failed. Even the oceans of the world refuse to accept it into their domain because it's so evil.

'Well, at least we've found that damned Doll,' Roy dropped back to walk with Liz, watching Rowena skipping on ahead, singing out loud in her own special tuneless way, reflecting a world where music had no place. He glanced at Liz, noted her tenseness, how she bit her lower lip the way she always did when she was uncertain of herself. He thought, you know more about this than you're letting on but, whatever you've been up to, that doll's scared the living daylights out of you.

Maybe Jane would be able to throw some light on the mystery. And Roy Catlin began trying to work out some way by which he might be able to see Jane again.

Inspector Landenning had not enjoyed his brief break from the murder hunt. He could not even remember what he had eaten at the vegetarian restaurant, only that his wife had nagged him throughout the meal. 'You're day-dreaming again. You can't think about anything except work. It makes me wonder why we bother to go out.'

And how the hell could anyone who had seen that body in the Ghost Train tunnel think of anything except 'work'. It would take years to forget that; he probably never would.

And now Fate had dealt the investigating detectives a cruel blow and put them right back to square one. That hunchbacked dwarf, typecast for the part of murderer, was *dead*. Suspect number one; they'd been watching him closely, nothing concrete but policemen had intuitions. Two men assigned to keep him under surveillance night and day. They'd followed him, seen him go to the fortune-teller's caravan just after that other guy (he was staying at the Beaumont Hotel and within a few hours they'd have a dossier on him) had left. The scream. Salin writhing on the floor of the caravan. A massive stroke. And then he'd snuffed it with a detective at his hospital bedside. Of all the fucking rotten luck!

Now he'd have to go right back to Jacob Schaefer's fairground, virtually start all over again. This time it was going to be tough and he wasn't going to pull any punches. That Indian girl knew something, he was certain of that. And if she did then he was going to damned well drag it out of her.

154

Landenning got that same creepy feeling the moment he got out of his car by the Hall of Mirrors. He stood there looking about him. *Stop watching me for Christ's sake!* Fine driving drizzle, dripping from canvas canopies. Faces, staring. Those damned horses on the merry-go-round seemed to single him out. One was missing, jagged slivers of wood where it had been. Somehow it must have got broken. He wished the whole bloody lot would get wrecked!

An incoherent chattering made him whirl round, a sound like a children's record of animated voices. He tensed, then the music started up again and drowned it. Suddenly he knew what it was; there was a Punch and Judy performance just beginning. His scalp started to prickle. Jesus Christ, he really was overworking to let things like that get on his nerves.

The uniformed constable on duty at the murder scene was looking at him, signs of nervousness in the presence of a senior officer. When Landenning had first earned his promotion he used to get his kicks from seeing subordinates shuffle their feet and pull their shoulders back. But he'd got over that. One cop was much the same as another, all working for the same end; a team, not stacked up in tiers.

'I'll be in in a minute, constable,' he called out. 'Just want to take a look around first.'

'Very good, sir.' Visibly relaxing, you could almost hear the sigh of relief.

Landenning walked slowly in the direction of the fortune-telling tent. The flaps hung loosely so there was somebody inside, and as he got closer he heard voices. 'You'll bloody well do as I tell you or else you can pack your things and get out.'

'I am doing no more carving.' A woman's voice, husky, sullen.

'But why not?'

'Because I cannot. Not at present, anyway. Please leave me alone.'

'I can't have broken and smashed figures on the round-abouts. There's been some more vandalism in the night, one of the horses has had its head smashed off. I'll pay you a bonus to get all this damage repaired.'

'*No*!' Almost a scream.

Then Landenning was pushing his way into the tent, meeting Jacob Schaefer's angry glare, seeing the frightened expression on the Indian's face, both of them startled by his appearance. 'I'm sorry to intrude.' I'm not really sorry, but I'm not likely to get the information I'm seeking by bulldozing them at the start.

'Ah, inspector,' a smile on the craggy face but the eyes were piercing and hostile. 'What can we do for you?'

'I'd like to talk to Miss. . . .' Oh Christ, what the hell was her name?

'Please carry on.' Schaefer stood back, made no move to leave, his expression hardening, eyes flicking from one to the other.

'I want to talk to her alone. I will probably come and see you later.'

'Very well,' the fairground owner let out his pent-up breath, stepped slowly towards the exit. 'I would not wish to hinder you in your enquiries, inspector.'

'Thank you, Mr Schaefer,' waiting until the other was out of earshot before turning to Jane, noting at once how distraught she was. 'You're upset . . . Jane.'

'It is nothing,' she dropped her gaze. 'Just a small disagreement with Mr. Schaefer.'

'About what? You don't want to do any more carving?' And I don't bloody well blame you.

'You are right, I will not carve for him again.'

A pause to see if any further information was forthcoming but when it wasn't, 'Why?'

She started, looked away. 'I . . . do not know.'

'Is it because . . . there's something *odd* about your carvings?'

'I do not understand you.'

'All right,' there was nothing to be gained by becoming angry. 'You're fed up with carving and that's that. Now, why did this guy Salin come to see you in the early hours of this morning?'

Again she looked uncomfortable, pulled the blanket even tighter around her slim body as though subconsciously she was trying to build a cocoon. 'He was a strange man. There was no accounting for his comings and goings or his moods. I did not like him. Perhaps he wanted somebody to talk to, but he collapsed before we had a chance to speak.'

'Who was he, where did he come from?'

'Just a fairground drifter like myself, here today gone tomorrow. Nobody liked him, not even the animals he looked after.'

'*And what about the guy who left your caravan just before Salin arrived*?'

Jane stiffened. 'You know about that, too?'

'We do. And I'm afraid you'll have to tell me all about it.'

'He's . . . just a friend.'

'What's his name?'

'Roy,' she paused, managed to remember the surname. 'Catlin. He is holidaying here. His young daughter is deaf. She sometimes comes and talks to me.'

'But what did *he* come for?' steel-grey eyes.

'For the same reason that most men visit women secretly in the dead of night.' Relief now that she had told him but not a trace of guilt.

'I see. You're having an affair with him?'

'No! I may not even see him again.'

'All right, we'll have to check on him. I just wish that dwarf hadn't died. I feel he could have told us a lot.'

'Inspector,' she hesitated, half changed her mind then decided to speak after all, 'I wish I could leave this place. But it is not easy and as a result I shall probably be forced to carry on carving for Mr Schaefer. But . . . *I don't know what is happening here but whatever it is, it is something so evil, so powerful, that even you are helpless to fight against it*!'

'I know,' he nodded, suddenly saw her in a different light, no longer as one of those who were placing every possible obstacle in his way. She wanted to co-operate but did not know how to. 'I got that feeling myself. I still have it, sensed it the moment I got out of the car. I'm just hoping

157

we'll be able to get to the bottom of it.'

'I hope so, too.' She watched him step out into the rain through eyes that had suddenly misted up.

Then she came to a decision, picked up her small ornate knife which lay on the table. She had no alternative other than to carry out Jacob Schaefer's orders. And the very thought of it terrified her. Her fingers would work as though they had a will of their own.

Billy Freeman had been trying to work out some way he could get rid of Sylvia. She was a real pain in the arse but he'd been too blind to see it in the beginning and had let their relationship grow until now it was almost impossible to extricate himself from it. Her folks had earmarked him as a future son-in-law from the very first time she had taken him home. Looking at her now he could understand their attitude: at twenty-three she was going to have difficulty in getting anybody else. Her adolescent spots had returned with a look of permanency about them, she'd put on at least a stone this year (she didn't even hint at going on a diet these days), and it was now necessary for her to wear glasses the whole time instead of just for work. Rapid deterioration. And they weren't even married yet.

Last year he had taken a tough line and told her they were through. She'd gone into hysterics and threatened suicide but he'd stood firm . . . until she'd taken those aspirins, just enough to give everybody a scare and get them back together again. He'd weakened, bought her an engagement ring. Playing for time whilst he tried to think of something else. But there wasn't anything else; he was hooked and the sooner he accepted the fact, the better. Eventually it would have to come to marriage.

He glanced sideways at her as he played the fruit machines in the amusement arcade. She was watching him like she always did, as though he might suddenly dash outside and disappear. He would have done just that if he'd had somewhere to go. A sort of adoration in her expression. It gave him the creeps. Jesus, what a bloody fool he'd been! His mother had said he'd come to regret it some day if he kept dating her. For the first few months of their courtship she'd played hard to get but that had all changed after he'd screwed her. She'd taken on a new personality the moment she'd lost her virginity, wanting to be fucked every night and always hinting that she *might* just be pregnant. Jesus, she'd got her talons into him, had him eating out of her hand and hating himself for it. One determined effort to free himself (the aspirin business) and now he was back to square one, with nightmares about wedding bells waking him up in a cold sweat every night.

Finally, he had resigned himself to his fate, but he despised every ounce of her overweight body for the way it clung to him like a limpet-mine. There wasn't anything he could do about it, except. . . .

Through the wide rain-splashed windows he saw the big-dipper, crazy hurtling cars that careered up steep slopes and came headlong down one-in-four gradients, their passengers clinging desperately to the safety bars, girls screaming. Some passengers looking as though they were puking, but they were going so fast you couldn't be sure. Now that was something that ought to happen to Sylvia. Give her a rough ride, shake that self-satisfied smirk off her pimply face. She wouldn't want to fuck for a week after that!

'Now that's something I've always wanted to do,' he pulled out a comb and ran it through his thick tawny hair, something he did about every ten minutes throughout the day.

'What's that?' Nervousness in her tone, anticipating his reply.

'The big-dipper. Like motorbike scrambling only you don't have to do anything except hang on.' Biking was something his parents had deprived him of throughout his youth, and since he'd got tied up with Syliva he'd never had enough money to fulfil this longing.

'That's ridiculous,' she wasn't smirking anymore.

'No, it isn't. It's good for you to get shaken up occasionally. You don't have to come along, though. You can stop right here in the dry and watch. Look at those girls queueing up for the next trip; looks like a party of camping sixth-formers. They're not scared. I reckon I might go and join 'em.'

'*No!*' it was almost a scream of jealousy. 'You know I don't like you chatting to other girls, Billy.'

'I won't be chatting to them. You couldn't hear what anybody said up there, anyway. I'll just be squashed in one of those cars nice and tight with 'em.'

'You're mad,' her lips tightened, the lenses of her glasses magnifying the expression of fear in her eyes. 'Why don't we go on the bumper-cars instead?'

'Because I want to go on the big-dipper!' Petulant, determined to have his own way this time, contemptuous of her cowardice but enjoying every second of it. 'I'll see you in a bit, *darling*.'

Billy Freeman turned towards the door, jangling some small change in the pockets of his jeans, seeing Sylvia's reflection in the window, her despairing, futile grab to hold him back. 'Wait. I'll come with you.'

She caught him up by the swing doors, linking an arm inside his, running along to keep up with him.

'Like I said, you're welcome to come,' he grunted, '*if* you've got the nerve!'

She didn't answer, splashing through puddles, soaking her splayed gawky plimsolled feet. Those girls were staring at them, stupid stuck-up bitches. There was a knot in Sylvia's stomach; she felt as though she could have thrown up right then. But she was going to have to go through with this.

Following blindly, holding on to Billy's belt now. Two tickets, joining the queue. Schoolgirls giggling but you couldn't hear their silly childish chatter. Two of them were staring at Billy, eyes agog. Sylvia clenched her fists, wished she had the courage to go and punch their faces. How dare they! Flaunting themselves, prostitutes in the making but they weren't going to get any joy out of Billy Freeman whilst *she* was around. The cars were slowing now, stopping. People getting out, having difficulty in standing upright. A young boy was heaving. Sylvia turned her head away because if she saw him throw up then she'd be sick, too.

Those schoolgirls were staring again. No, not just them . . . a strange feeling that she was suddenly the centre of attraction, like some actress who had forgotten her lines and made a fool of herself. Catching her breath, seeing a pair of fixed orbs, unblinking, meeting her gaze. She wanted to laugh out loud but couldn't. *Because the eyes belonged to a gargoyle-like carving, a masthead on the nearest dipper car.*

A face like a devil, an intensity of evil reflected in its squat flat features, mouth curved in a leer, broken teeth from which one almost caught the foul odour of decay. It was watching her, making her step back a pace.

'What's the matter with you now?' Billy caught her wrist and pulled her on. 'You're not backing out now that I've paid for your ticket.' Shouting in an attempt to make himself heard, dragging her bodily along. Closer to that awful carving. . . .

She didn't know whether she had screamed or not. If she had then nobody heard her. Feeling giddy, wishing she could faint then Billy wouldn't be able to go on the big-dipper. The sensation passed, they were headed towards the cars.

No, not that one. I don't want to go in the one with that awful carved head on the front. Any one, but not that one!

Billy twisted her wrist until it hurt. She tried to dig her heels in, slid along on the loose gravel. Struggling, being pulled into the car, sprawling on a seat that immediately wet her right through to her pants. Eyes closed, open again, now seeing the back of that head. Forced relief; only a lump of wood, not even a proper finish at the rear. Pull yourself together, Sylvia. It's your nerves, worrying about Billy and that he might try to jilt you again. And this damned weather isn't helping. It's too late to get off now so you'll have to sit tight and pray that it'll be over quick.

Nobody seemed in any hurry. The cars were crowded, the fine driving drizzle almost forgotten. Yet there was an atmosphere of tension. You only became aware of it if you looked at the person seated opposite you, reflecting your own subconscious fears, escalating them.

Strained faces glanced at each other, looking away in embarrassment when they saw terror, felt it themselves. It was going to be a fast hair-raising ride, no time to get your breath as you were hurled mercilessly up and down on this miniature switchback railway. Faster, faster, screaming because you were terrified; wanting to get off but you had to stick it out. Masochism, because you had got on willingly, knowing. Sadism on the part of the operators because they got their kicks from doing this to you, and charging you 50p for the privilege of trying to make you throw up.

Still waiting. The man in the tattered jacket who was taking the money had gone across to the small generator hut. Maybe he operated the big-dipper as well. If so, he was taking his time about it.

Sylvia was biting her fingernails, a habit she had kicked when she was thirteen. If there had been a cigarette handy she would have smoked it. She stole a glance at Billy, saw how the colour had drained from his features, wondered if she was doing the right thing by hounding him like this. Mum and Dad had reservations about him now, they hadn't wanted her to go back to him after her suicide attempt. He's no good, you'll be well rid of him. But she was determined to have him at any cost and not just because she needed a man to satisfy her sexual cravings. It was a question of pride now, she'd gone too far to give up, couldn't face the other girls in the supermarket where she worked if she let him escape now. If he got away this time she would do the aspirin job properly, make everybody sorry. You'll cry when I'm dead and wish you could get me back but I'll be somewhere up there laughing at you.

Oh God, somebody start this thing up and let's get it over. Let's all be sick and get it out of our system. But the motors inside that shed were silent, the little man still hidden from view. A problem of some kind, maybe a technical fault. Sod it, let's get off and demand our money back; a let-out, we don't have to have our guts churned up and we don't have to lose any face over it either. But nobody moved, fifty people who might have been chained and manacled to their seats. The depression had grown and spread like some contagious disease, ravaging its victims, rendering them helpless.

Billy Freeman unfurled a sliver of chewing gum and slid it almost furtively between his lips. His mouth was so dry that he had to champ hard on the wafer in order to get some saliva flowing. His last piece of gum and no way was he going to share it with Sylvia. Sod it, he'd never realized until now just how much he hated that fat stuck-up pimply cow. His parents didn't like her but that didn't count for much because they were social-climbers and would never accept anybody so lowly as a shop-assistant. Maybe that was the reason he had stuck to her, to get back at them; what they called cutting off your nose to spite your face.

He looked at her again. Christ, she was shit-scared, clutching at the bar already. He laughed silently. Maybe when they got to the very top she'd jump out! No, she wouldn't have the nerve, no more than she had had with those aspirins. All the same it was an intriguing idea. . . .

Billy felt his muscles tensing, his heartbeat starting to speed up. Just *suppose* Sylvia *did* fall out of the car. It had happened before on big-dippers, accidents that hit the headlines and were forgotten in a few days. Damn it, it was a pity that there were two of those wet giggling schoolgirls in the same truck. On his own with Sylvia it would have been no problem, timed right when the car was at the apex of the track, the others temporarily screened from view. Sylvia panicking, himself trying to calm her, unable to hold her back. Did she fall or was she pushed? The question might never arise. His blood coursed hotly through his veins.

The man was coming back out of the generator hut and you could tell by his walk that everything was OK, whatever had been the problem was sorted out. Any second now. . . .

A feeling of inferiority engulfed Billy Freeman, fanned the flames of anger inside him, not just towards Sylvia, her parents and his own parents, but towards *everybody*. They'd made him like he was, a nobody, never given him a chance. He worked at the sawmill, loading off-cuts for firewood, because he'd never had the chance to do anything else and never would have. Because he'd been sent to a school with one of the worst academic records in the country. His teacher at the primary school had thought that he might be a 'gifted child' but nobody had done anything about it, least of all himself. Learning had come easily in those days but it had slowed up once he'd gone to the comprehensive. Nobody was interested in his ability. In fact, they did their best to stamp on it. They'd pushed him under, deliberately put obstacles in the path of his progress, relegated him to a labouring job at the sawmill instead of an office job with a future. But he'd make 'em pay!

A jerk, rolling, thrown forward and then hurled back as the line of cars started to pick up speed. Sylvia closed her eyes, her stomach already starting to protest. She saw that carved face again, the mouth wider than before, laughing. *You're going to die.*

'*No!*' she screamed, opened her eyes, saw only the back of its head. Her imagination was running wild; she was frightened, gripping the steel bar in front of her. The younger girls were screaming, wasting their breath yelling for the truck to stop.

Going up; then down without any warning. Sylvia groped for Billy's arm, found it and clung to it hard. He moved, trying to shake her off. 'No, *please*, Billy. Hold me tight.'

His face was turned towards her and there was no mistaking the expression; eyes narrowed to mere slits, lips compressed. Hate steamed from him. She let go instinctively, gripped the safety bar again. Sheer terror engulfed her. Frightened to look in any direction, frightened to shut her eyes in case she saw . . . *that!*

Billy Freeman laughed out loud at the way she recoiled from him. They were being thrown backwards and forwards alternately, everybody wishing they had not come along. Except himself. Oh God, he was enjoying every second knowing that she *knew* and she could do fuck all

164

about it.

He waited his chance, anticipated the next roll, seemed to lose his balance and rolled right over on to Sylvia, straddling her almost in a coital position. She tensed, yelled something which he didn't catch but didn't let go of the bar. A sudden downward plunge almost dislodged him but he managed to keep his balance. This was really great, the ride exhilarating, exciting him, lust and anger combining into almost a feeling of omnipotency.

'Look at me, you bitch. Look at me!'

Maybe she heard him and was too scared to do anything except obey. Her eyes uplifted, her features white and trembling, suddenly terrified of the closeness of his body. She didn't like the look in his eyes, the way he was laughing, the feeling of a growing erection pushing at her as though at any second it would burst its way to freedom and bore its way into her. That's rape, Billy, and you never had to rape me before because I always let you. Not here, though, not with these young girls watching.

They aren't watching, you conceited cow. They're leaning over the side spewing their guts up with their eyes shut tight. But I couldn't care less because now I'm going to pay you back for all the agony you've caused me. You used every trick in the book to get Billy Freeman but now you'll wish you'd never set eyes on him.

His thick fingers gripped her blouse, tore it asunder in one movement, ripping her bra away with it. She'd given up struggling, lying back and feeling the rain driving on to her bared breasts. Now his hands were going lower down, forcing their way in between her thighs. This was no sensuous titillation but a vicious hurtful assault, making her jerk and cry out with pain. His lips chased hers, caught them, his tongue forcing an entrance.

One last act of retaliation: she bit hard, held on, tasted his blood. The lower half of his body reared up and a knee came crushing into her abdomen. Her teeth clamped tightly and she was aware of something soft and loose like a sliver of raw liver in her mouth. And Billy was free, clinging desperately to the rail, blood pouring down his chin, spouting as he tried to curse.

Her knees came up as she writhed in agony on the seat, spitting out the tip of severed tongue, seeing it hit him like an arrogantly spat plum stone, bloodied and sticking to his shirt. Everything inside her stomach seemed to come up at once, a mixture of fish and chips, hotdogs and ice-cream, a fountain of vomit that caught the wind and came back at her.

Going up, almost vertical. Billy Freeman lost his balance, came down hard on her. *Oh God, don't kiss me, Billy*! His crimson frothing mouth found hers again in a vile nightmarish vampire-like kiss, forcing her to take his pumping blood, his erection pushing wildly, suddenly freed from its imprisonment and demanding satisfaction.

Billy Freeman almost got what his maddened body desired most. *Almost*! Suddenly a forest of hands attacked him from the rear, beating sharply on the back of his skull, tugging at his hair, somehow dragging him clear of the girl on the seat beneath him. Blows rained from all directions, the car swerved and he felt himself falling. A heap of bodies; he tried to see, attempted to throw his attackers off. Two schoolgirls, their young faces aghast with horror, yelling at him, kicking, punching.

He tried to yell at them but all that came out was a gush of blood and a series of four-lettered grunts. Fuck them, it was nothing to do with them so why didn't they mind their own bloody business? Kicking out, catching one of them in the side and seeing her go slithering across the floor. Turning for the other, being pulled back by the hair.

You fucking bitch, Sylvia! She had him so he couldn't reach her, dragging him up on to the seat, head over the side. Swallowing blood, nearly choking. You bastard! Fingers that had to be Sylvia's delving deep into his open vent, closing over his testicles, crushing them with devastating force.

Billy Freeman was screaming with an agony to which death would have been a welcome end, hanging out of the careering truck, seeing a strange face through pain-blurred vision. The eyes picked out his own, got their message through. That grotesque figurehead. *You're all going to die*!

For a moment his excruciating pain was forgotten. A new fear, one that struck at his heart like an ice-cold rapier. The wide mouth laughing just as he had been laughing a few moments ago; leering, hating.

Something gave, a tearing sensation that ripped right up into the pit of his stomach. Freed, falling, gushing blood. A shuddering impact. One huddled bleeding body caught up on the track, razor sharp wheels ploughing through flesh and bone, a mighty mincing machine that threw its fodder in all directions.

Resonant clangs of metal on metal, a medley of screams, bodies airborne like sky-divers except that no parachutes opened; plummeting, hitting concrete and gravel far below with sickening thuds. Cars snaking up like two giant serpents in deadly combat. Blow for blow, collapsing.

Slow motion now, everything grinding to a halt. A battlefield with the dead and the dying strewn amidst smoking twisted metal, surrounded by a sea of faces. Humanity delighting in the misfortunes of humanity, mentally drinking the blood and savouring the distinctive aroma of death. None coming forward to help because it would spoil it all, just a few belated shocked screams that petered out into silence.

All staring. Not just at the corpses and twitching wounded but at one small face that seemed to fix every one of them with its tiny black eyes. A wooden carving, a monument to death, a victor gloating over the vanquished. Crowds moving back, hearing its laughter in the air, each and every one of them held by its glittering eye.

Bee-bor, bee-bor.

The shrill sound of approaching sirens breaking the spell, freeing them from a sensation of timeless terror. Now seeing that carved head for what it was: a lifeless object, blood-splattered because everything was blood-splattered, the eyes nothing more than two tiny lumps of wood.

A girl's crushed body hung suspended over a horizontal steel girder twenty feet from the ground, naked except for a few shreds of clothing clinging to her. Swinging gently, outstretched arms rotating and seeming to point with broken fingers.

Look . . . there . . . mangled torso, the head crushed, mouth wide, a stub of crimson severed tongue jutting out in one last act of defiance.

Pointing again, this time coming to rest, aligned on the masthead of a crumpled dipper car. Accusing.

That is the fiend who killed us!

But those who stared up at the overweight pimpled body did not understand. Sylvia lost her point of balance, slid slowly, slipped. With a dull crunch she sprawled headlong amidst the last remains of Billy Freeman, his tongue seeming to stretch out in an attempt to reach her.

10

THURSDAY EVENING

Rowena had run on along the beach, deliberately keeping fifty yards or so ahead of her parents. Along with her sense of relief at being reunited with Doll was a longing for independence; not so much from her father (he was a friend of Jane's) but from her mother. Her mother in some way was responsible for Doll's disappearance and the child could tell from Liz's expression that she was furious that the small wooden figure had been found. *And also she was frightened.*

But now all that Rowena wanted was to be with Doll on this rain-soaked beach. Perhaps if she gradually increased the distance between herself and her parents she would be able to shake them off. Two or three hundred yards ahead the beach cut sharply back towards the headland, screened by an outcrop of rock. For a few moments then her parents would not be able to see her. She resisted the temptation to break into a sprint.

Glancing back once. Roy and Liz Catlin seemed to be arguing over something, their attention distracted for a few seconds. She seized her chance, ducked down behind a long stretch of rock and made it round the bend. The beach narrowed here, curved again. Hidden by the first line of cliffs Rowena slowed, looked about her. A deserted cove, the tide further in here, a sudden feeling of loneliness as though she had stepped into an empty world, a place where life was extinct.

Then she saw the caves, jagged holes in the rockface, dark and mysterious, seaweed piled up at the entrances as though Nature was attempting to guard her secrets from Man and his destructive instincts. Welcoming, she didn't know why. She was walking towards them before she realized it.

Hurry, they will be here soon.

Doll's voice. She looked down at him but his features were impassive, black eyes expressionless. Running again, not knowing why, clambering over slippery rocks, looking back guiltily the way she had come but there was still no sign of her parents.

She stood in the mouth of the nearest cave, peering in but only able to see a few yards inside. The floor was sandy, the walls slimy with some kind of green fungus. She hesitated, fearful of what might lie within its deep shadows.

Go inside. Do not be afraid.

Just a couple of yards, no more. A roaring sound as though this tunnel might wind back on itself and go right down into the deepest ocean, a multitude of sounds like sea creatures roaring their wrath at having their secret domain discovered. Rowena drew back, on the point of fleeing outside into the daylight.

Wait. Hide me here before I am stolen again.

This time it seemed that Doll's eyes glittered, one brief movement, a sensation of vibration in Rowena's hand. Then he was still and lifeless again. Her mother had been responsible for his disappearance last night, there was no doubt in her mind now. Liz Catlin had tried to destroy him but he was too clever for her and had come back on the waves. But now he needed a hiding place, somewhere safe like this cave where he wouldn't be found. Oh, but I don't want to leave you. I need you. I love you, Doll.

You must. Hide me and leave me here!

This time it was an order, harsh and commanding. The voice which rasped inside her brain was becoming angry and impatient. Frightening. No longer that of Doll who had led her to safety out of the deep woods.

'Rowena, Rowena, where *are* you?' Her mother's voice, somewhere out on the beach, frantic.

Hide me, child. Do not disobey me!

She glanced around. The sandy floor was strewn with chunks of rock draped with rotting marine vegetation that gave off a pungent nauseating smell. There were plenty of hiding places for her doll, one as good as another.

Rowena was trembling violently, almost on the verge of tears. Doll had never spoken to her in this way before, not a trace of kindness in his tone, vibrating again as though he was shaking with anger. She stooped down, set him gently upright with his back to a large rock. Here he wouldn't be seen from the entrance and the tide could not reach him to wash him away.

Go quickly!

So terse. Nasty. He didn't want her any more, he wanted his freedom. But I love you and we've been such good friends.

Leave, at once!

Backing away, the tears starting to come. Doll was lost in the shadows now, hidden the way he wanted to be, left in the solitude of a beach tomb, rejecting her. Perhaps she could return tomorrow. . . .

Crying, she emerged into the open, had to shield her eyes against the grey brightness of watery daylight.

'Rowena!' Relief in Roy Catlin's voice, his arms going around her and pulling her close. 'Whatever were you doing in there?'

But Rowena was already pulling him away, fearful lest

he might enter the cave and discover Doll.

'You really are a naughty girl!' Liz caught up with them, breathless and angry. 'How stupid of you to go off like that. You must never go in caves. They're dangerous, they might fall in and bury you or else you'd get lost and wander about in the dark until you died. I've a good mind to take you back to the hotel and put you straight to bed!'

Rowena met her mother's hostile stare through her own tears. It's all your fault, if you hadn't tried to get rid of Doll I wouldn't have gone in there. But you've got what you wanted, you've turned him against me, made him hate me because he thinks it's all my fault. Oh, how I hate you!

'She's had a bad scare,' Roy said. 'And, anyway, I think we'd better be getting back. It's only an hour till dinner.'

A watery golden haze started to spread across the sand, the incoming waves looking less grey and forbidding. Something shiny, possibly a sailing boat, glinted out at sea.

'Look,' Roy pointed towards the sky where a glowing orb could just be discerned behind the thinning low cloud, 'I do believe the sun's trying to come out!'

A few minutes of wan sunlight, a promise that was never going to be fulfilled, the mischievous sun deliberately raising the spirits of damp holidaymakers only to dash them almost immediately. Before the Catlins had rounded the bend the clouds had knitted together again, a grey depressing blanket that shut out the golden rays and began to thicken again.

It was 5.45 by the clock in the hallway when Roy, Liz and Rowena entered the Beaumont Hotel. A trail of damp footprints on the Marley tiles leading to the stairway was evidence that most of the dejected residents had already returned.

'We'll have to get a move on,' Liz snapped. 'We've only got a quarter of an hour to get changed for dinner and you know Mrs Hughes doesn't like people being late. Goodness knows how I'm going to get all these clothes dry. . . .'

Her words died away as she noticed the man in the dark blue raincoat. He was standing by the notice board, studying the leaflets offering day-trips by coach and rail to places of interest in the locality. But he was no tourist, and neither was he trying to smile and make believe that it did not matter whether the sun shone or not. His bearing was one of confident authority, and there was a disconcerting gleam in his steely eyes.

'Mr Catlin.' A plain statement of fact, leaving no room for denial.

'Yes,' Roy stopped in mid-stride, uneasiness flooding over him. 'That's me.'

'Inspector Landenning,' a card was shown briefly but there was no friendly handshake. 'I'd like a word with you, please. Alone.'

Liz was staring, suddenly frightened. Rowena, too, turned her tear-stained face in the direction of the two men, tried to lip-read the stranger but it wasn't easy; his thick lips barely moved when he spoke.

'Is . . . is there anything *I* can do?' Liz didn't know what to say, what this policeman wanted, but she was determined to find out.

'I'm afraid not,' Landenning's expression was unreadable. 'I have to talk to your husband alone.'

'Oh . . . I see.' Dragging herself away towards the stairs, eyes glued to those muddy footmarks, pulling Rowena along by the wrist, suddenly not wanting to hear what Inspector Landenning had to say.

When they reached the first landing Liz turned and glanced back. Roy and the inspector had gone out to the porch, the heavy glass door still swinging behind them, conversing in low tones.

And suddenly Liz Catlin began to cry.

Paul Stott had only one ambition in life; to fish. He did not mind where or how he fished so long as he was constantly in pursuit of underwater life. He had spent the last thirty of his forty-five years dreaming of an idyllic existence: enough money to satisfy his basic needs and those of his long-suffering wife Margaret, leaving sufficient time for him to indulge in his favourite pastime without the restrictions of a conventional routine. It was no easier now than it had been when he was twenty. Giving up his office job, he had attempted to establish himself in the widely popular and supposedly profitable business of fish farming. Somehow it had not worked out, probably because he was short of business acumen; several thousand trout fingerlings will not bring in an income if their market has not been fully explored. A man cannot live by fish alone and within two years, an undischarged bankrupt, Paul was endeavouring to improve his business education by selling chemical fertilizers to farmers in mid-Wales. He took orders for consignments which he was never likely to see (nor wished to), and chased up non-deliveries following complaints from customers. He was the meat in the sandwich, buffeted one way by irate farmers, thrown another by unsympathetic employers who were experts at passing the buck. And in the end he discovered that he had less free time than when he was in the office, his evenings spent amidst a deluge of paperwork and computer print-outs, chasing mythical loads of fertilizer which constantly went astray.

Even Paul's weekend fishing on the local river was curtailed by this backlog of work and his own failure to master the mysteries of repping. Traditionally, in the lives of the Stotts, Sundays were reserved exclusively for the local river bank. After a year this was reduced to Sunday afternoons (the mornings having to be devoted to the sending out of the previous week's invoices), and when finally that narrow stretch of water suffered pollution from a nearby factory, Paul was deprived of his favourite sport.

Somehow Paul battled through, still hoping for better times. Their annual holiday, at least, would mean a week devoted to fishing. The resort offered the best prospects on that particular stretch of coastline. Sea-fishing; there were trips to be had day and night, well-stocked rivers beyond the estuary even if the price of daily tickets was extortionate. But, it seemed, Fate was an ardent campaigner for the league against cruel sports, and had called upon the weather to aid her in her cause.

All sea-fishing was cancelled until further notice by order of the harbour master. The fog had reduced visibility, and he could not risk another tragedy at sea. He was already being blamed for not having imposed restrictions earlier, and there would be a lot of awkward questions asked at the inquest. The missing swimmer . . . well, the sea accounted for a few every year even in the most perfect of conditions. Nevertheless, all sea-going craft were grounded and the ban on off-shore fishing would not be lifted until the weather improved which, according to the meteorological office, would not be for the next couple of days at least.

'It's a pig!' Paul Stott sweated inside his oilskins and wellington boots, scuffing the wet sand with his toes as he walked, a flimsy-looking fishing net draped over one shoulder. Kids bought scores of these nets to fish the rock pools along the shore, and that was exactly what he was going to do. He didn't need the oilskins, the setting sun was trying to break through, but he derived some satisfaction from the discomfort they caused. If he wasn't allowed to go out to sea to fish, then at least he would wear his gear.

'Where's a pig?' Margaret's voice was dreamy, bored, stifling a yawn. She threw back the hood of her anorak exposing short dark hair. Attractive, her placid nature showing in her frequent smiles, she was determined not to let the depression which hovered in the background move in on her. Any holiday was a gamble and by the law of averages you had to have bad weather sometime. She wasn't really bothered herself but she felt sorry for Paul. This week meant so much to him.

'I don't mean a *real* pig,' irritation in his tone. 'I mean the *weather's* a pig.'

'Oh, I see,' noting the creases on his broad face, his unhealthy pallor, a look of almost desperation on his features, the stamp of failure.

'It's like somebody's put a curse on this place,' he grunted. 'The week starts off blazing hot, then everything collapses when these Hell's Angels idiots smash the fair-ground up, not that I've got much time for fairs. A couple of murders, a swimmer lost in the bay, a collision at sea with

174

five drowned, and all the time the rain pissing down.'

'Paul!' exaggerated shock, an inbred prudery.

'Well, when you've had three days of solid downpour and it doesn't look like letting up for the rest of the week there's no room for niceties,' he managed a grin all the same. 'I haven't cast a line since we've been here and with the rivers in full spate and no fishing boats allowed out of harbour it doesn't look like I'm going to get a chance. So I'll do the next best thing, a pretty poor second all the same, but I'll have me a few crabs and shrimps out of the rock pools.'

'All right,' at least it would give him the opportunity to work off some of his frustration, 'but how much farther up the beach are we going?'

'I reckon we'll find what we're looking for beneath those cliffs round the bend. We'll give it an hour, anyway.'

'We'll have to watch the tide, it's coming in fast now.'

'I doubt whether it comes right up to the rock face except at spring tides,' he fumbled to try and light a well-burned briar pipe, his constant companion on fishing trips. 'One thing about self-catering holiday accommodation is that you don't have to be back for meals at any set time.'

Which means, Margaret Stott thought, that we'll probably be eating a late supper tonight.

They rounded the bend, made their way along the shingle below the towering cliffs, gulls perched on the rocks looking remarkably like waiting vultures from a distance. Margaret shivered; this place had a forbidding look about it, so far removed from the wide beach they had just left, the sort of place where eighteenth-century smugglers would unload their illicit cargo.

Paul clambered over the rocks with surprising agility in spite of his cumbersome gear, peering into pools, dipping his net here and there. Margaret remained on the shingle, wishing it had been a warm sunny evening when she could have found some sheltered spot and passed the time reading a book. This evening it was going to be a long drawn-out session. Selfishly she reminded herself that it would be darker much earlier than usual with all this low cloud.

She busied herself hunting for shells, found a couple that interested her and would make nice ornaments for the living-room at home, and slipped them into her pocket. Wandering aimlessly, day-dreaming, relishing the prospect of the day after tomorrow. Home – and it didn't matter all that much if it rained because one was in familiar surroundings, constructive things to do rather than just passing the time.

Back to reality with a feeling of uneasiness. Something was wrong; it took her several seconds to fathom out what it was. Two things – the darkness and the tide. Both had moved faster than she had anticipated, a deep dusk glinted on a shining expanse of water that rippled against the bottom of the cliffs. *The tide had come right in, cut off their retreat.*

Panic. Turning, running, kicking up a shower of small stones. Shouting. '*Paul . . . for God's sake . . . the tide!*'

Stark silhouettes, jagged upright rocks, every one of them seeming human. '*Paul . . . Paul!*'

No answer, just an echo that came back off the cliffs to mock her. Paul . . . Paul . . . Pa . . . ul. She fell, grazed her leg and cried out, picked herself up, looked wildly about her. The light was dwindling fast, not just thickening rain clouds as she had thought at first. She looked at her wristwatch, had to hold it close up to her face to make out the tiny hands. 9.10. It couldn't be; it had only been seven o'clock when they had come down to the beach. But the incoming tide was her greatest concern, a soft swishing noise as it lapped against the rocks on either side of this narrow peninsula, sinister in its relentless assault on the coastline.

Paul *had* to be somewhere around. Absent-mindedness was his trouble, a total obsession with fishing to the exclusion of everything else. More than likely he was engrossed in chasing some elusive shrimps in a wide rock pool. But it was too dark for him to see.

'*Paul . . . Paul . . . for God's sake. We're trapped by the tide!*'

No answer. Looking frantically in every direction. Then

she heard something, a movement that slithered pebbles and crunched shingle.

'Oh, thank God! Paul, whatever are we going to do?'

She had expected him to emerge out of the shadows, puffing away unconcernedly at his pipe, muttering that it was nothing to get all het-up about. *But he didn't come.* The footsteps stopped, just the noise of the tide as it continued its relentless progress.

She tried to shout again but this time only a hoarse whisper came out. Why didn't her husband answer? Surely he had heard her.

It was almost too dark to see now, the shadows of the cliffs reaching right out across the water, turning it to an inky forbidding black so that it was difficult to discern where the rocky shelf ended. Something had happened to Paul otherwise he would have been here by now. Possibly he had daydreamed back the way they had come and she hadn't noticed, and even now he wasn't aware that she wasn't following him.

Margaret Stott stood there weak and frightened, the full realization of her own helplessness sweeping over her like electric shock waves. She was all alone, the tide might rise and cover this outcrop of rock, sweeping her out to sea, drown her!

But she wasn't alone. Somebody was here because she'd heard them. It had to be Paul because it couldn't be anybody else.

'*Paul!*' this time she managed a cry, a shrill scream that sapped her remaining strength. Then she sank down slowly on to a flat slab of rock, sobs beginning to shake her body, head buried in her spread hands.

Then the noise came again. Like footsteps in a way, as though whoever it was wore wooden clogs that clacked together clumsily, scraping on rock and stone. She stiffened, turned and tried to peer into the blackness, thought she saw something but it was impossible to be sure.

'Who's . . . there?' she barely recognized her own voice, now certain that it was not her husband back there and that whoever it was might be alien to her. There had been murders at the fair and the papers had sensationalized them; a homicidal maniac who was still at large!

Water lapped at her feet and she drew them up, knew she was being forced back towards the cliffs, back there where . . . *something lurked in the darkness*. She began to drag herself over the rocks, grazing her legs, once falling almost waist-deep in a pool, her groping splashing fingers coming into contact with some form of underwater life that *moved*. Ugh! She stopped to listen every few seconds; just the waves, nothing else. She tried to tell herself that she had imagined it all, that there wasn't anybody else here.

Crawling, groping her way, fearful of falling into a deeper pool. Oh God, what a fool she was to have spurned swimming lessons in her youth.

Her fingers touched something that wasn't rock, something big and soft lying across her path, material that crinkled and rustled as she ran her hands over it. Then she screamed loudly, a piercing yell that disturbed a roosting cormorant on the cliff high above and sent it flapping away in search of more peaceful surroundings.

It took Margaret Stott some seconds to realize that the object barring her path was a human body clad in waterproof clothing. *Her husband's body*. Sheer terror at the thought that he might be injured or ill (he couldn't be dead because that was an idea her mind refused to accept; Paul would never die). Fingers examining him with urgency, smoothing up over the shoulders . . . *a warm, sticky morass, a pulp that felt like the offal which the butcher left for the cat on Fridays. Jagged spinters of bone that pierced the palms of her hands. . . . Her scream rent the stillness of the empty cove. She knew beyond any doubt that her husband was dead, his skull pounded and crushed beyond recognition, only the darkness sparing her the horror of seeing what she had touched.*

Almost fainting, not caring whether she lived or drowned, she drew back. A wave washed gently against her and went unnoticed; far off a curlew was warbling its mournful lonely cry as though in sympathy.

And even as Margaret knelt there dazed and trembling,

the noise which she had heard a few minutes earlier came again; faster this time like the clicking of castanets. She straightened up, stumbled against the corpse, stepped over it, tried to run and fell heavily. A low groan escaped her lips but the pain could not overcome her terror. Her ankle felt as though it might be broken but she didn't care. She dragged herself along, through a shallow pool, fighting to clamber out at the other end; slimy rock denied her a firm hold but she made it in the end. She was up against the cliff face now. *Trapped! Whatever it was that followed her was only yards away, slowing down now like some giant crab that realized its prey was cornered.*

No longer was Margaret capable of clear thinking, clawing at the overhanging cliff until her fingernails were broken and bleeding. If there was any way upwards she had no chance of making it. To her left was deep water, to her right a jumble of rocks maybe ten or twenty yards wide, disappearing into the tide. She began to edge her way along, sobbing her grief and terror, hearing her pursuer easing his way after her.

Then, suddenly, the rock face disappeared and she fell headlong into a narrow opening, felt soft sand and pebbles beneath her. A cave of some kind, probably just a niche in the cliffs above high-water mark. Even in her state of hopelessness she crawled on. So dark and cold, water dripping all around her. Keep going, you'll die in the end, but you have to keep going.

Behind her Margaret heard the shuffling sounds of the one who hunted her. It was no good looking back because she would not be able to see him.

It was a kind of passage she was in, rough rock on either side, barely room for her to squeeze through. Once she lifted a hand and felt the roof less than a foot above her head.

The tunnel was becoming narrower, the rock scraping her head so that she was forced to drag herself along with one cheek on the floor. The air, too, was becoming stale, had a cloying unpleasant odour about it reminding her of a damp cellar that had been shut up for decades.

Her strength would not last much longer. She could not understand why her pursuer did not take her. She could not even hear him now but she knew he was close, perhaps only a few yards away, gloating over her desperate efforts to escape him. *Oh, kill me, damn you, like you killed those people in the fairground.*

Then, without warning, she was stuck, her body wedged firmly in the tapering tunnel, one of those childhood nightmares where the walls came in at you, threatening to crush you. In the nightmares they . . . receded. These didn't, they stayed.

Now she was fighting for breath, this awful place almost airless, the darkness and the silence terrifying. She had no idea how far she had come or how long she had been burrowing into the hillside. Even had the face of her watch been luminous she could not have moved her arm or her head to check the time. No sound, neither the dripping of water nor the swish of the incoming tide. A voice, imprisoned with only her mounting terror for a companion.

She attempted to go back, fought with all her waning strength, but her shoulders were jammed in such a way that she could not free them. Becoming weaker with every passing moment, she lay still, her heartbeat vibrating, shaking her whole body. *I'm going to die here. He was too big to follow me in here but I'll die just the same.*

Buried alive, the air thinning and petering out, her brain refusing to acknowledge the pain in her leg because it did not matter anymore.

A noise, faint and scraping, so close that her body went rigid. Perhaps this was a labyrinth inhabited by vermin, rats that would gnaw the living flesh from her bones or sea snakes which would slime all over her body before sinking their poisonous fangs into her. Or insects that swarmed and suffocated, stinging and feasting.

Seconds became hours. Which would come first, the welcome oblivion of death or some hideous nightmare out of the blackness? She began to scream, a wheezing whine that was using up the last of the oxygen so that when finally she felt a hard object brushing against her shaking legs it was almost a relief to know that the suspense was over.

Feet moved over her buttocks, tiny jerking movements like a clockwork soldier striding rampantly into battle, kicking viciously. Somehow it squeezed past her, and she felt it turning to confront her, could almost make out its silhouette, blacker than the surrounding blackness, mocking her with laughter that rang through her brain until she, too, began to laugh.

Insane mirth, so violent that she scarcely felt the devastating blows as tiny feet and hands lacerated her skull unmercifully.

'Well?' Liz Catlin's features were lined with strain and she seemed to have aged a decade as Roy entered the hotel bedroom. He had half-hoped that his wife and daughter might have gone down to the dining-room but he knew Liz would wait for him. Worried, accusing. Damn that bloody inspector coming here with his damn-fool questions.

Rowena was sitting on a chair by the window staring sullenly out into the bay, possibly not even aware that her father had returned.

'Nothing to worry about,' Roy tried to smile and failed; just as he had failed to think up some reasonably plausible explanation for the police wishing to question him.

'What d'you mean, nothing to worry about? Can't you see I'm almost out of my mind?'

'You're worrying yourself unnecessarily. He was just making a few enquiries, checking out everybody who had been at the fair last night.'

'I might have known!' her lips curled in contempt. 'You sneaked off to see that damned squaw and somebody spotted you. So now you're one of their suspects for these murders!'

'Don't jump to conclusions. The police want me to help them,' a sudden brainwave, a white lie that he was going to use to his advantage.

'Whatever do you mean?' She stared at him in amazement.

'They think possibly that I may have noticed something

which might be a valuable clue leading them to the killer. You know how it is, that murder case a year or two ago where they used hypnotism so that one of the witnesses was able to give them a car number which his subconscious had retained whilst he wasn't even aware of having noticed it.'

'You mean they're going to *hypnotize* you?' incredulity.

'No, I'm merely making comparisons. Like they sometimes get a policewoman to dress identically to a murdered girl and walk the same route on which the victim was killed in the hope that people might remember something, the face of a bystander maybe.'

'You're talking in riddles.'

'All right,' sudden elation because he sensed that his idea was working, 'let me put it to you in words of one syllable. The inspector wants me to go back to the fair, *alone*, and mooch about, take note of things. All very vague, I know, but they haven't much to work on.'

'You mean,' Liz's lips tightened, 'you've got to go back *there, to the fair?*'

'That's right.' His pulses were pounding. This was his only chance of getting to see Jane again.

Her eyes bored into his, suspecting a lie but there was no way of proving it except by checking with the police – and she wasn't going to do that.

Rowena glanced round, eyes red-rimmed, tear stains still showing on her freckled cheeks. Roy Catlin looked, turned away quickly because there was no way her thoughts could have been misinterpreted. You're telling lies, Daddy, and I hate you for it!

'We'd better go and get some dinner,' he said.

'I'm not hungry,' Liz was angry, defiant.

'Well *I* am and so is Rowena. If you want to stay here, please feel free.' He tugged open a drawer in the dressing-table and pulled out his last clean shirt.

Five minutes later Liz and Rowena were following him downstairs.

Roy Catlin tried to shake off the feeling of guilt as he entered the fairground by the menagerie entrance, tried to convince himself that it wasn't just because of the way he felt about Jane that he was going in search of her. He failed miserably on both counts.

Then he saw the debris, the smashed dipper cars beneath the twisted length of track, crowds standing staring. And the drizzle had turned back to rain.

He didn't need to ask what had happened; the wreckage told its own horrific story, patches of fresh sand scattered on the shale to hide. . . . . A mounting terror that had every nerve trembling in his body. These gloating people saw it as just another accident, something that had happened because it was meant to happen. But he *knew*. Not how or why, but that whatever evil existed here had brought it about and that this latest disaster would not be the last.

A length of rope cordoned off the remnants of the big-dipper (probably the same rope that had been around the Hall of Mirrors) and a group of plain-clothes policemen were sifting through the wreckage. But they wouldn't find anything! Queues had formed outside the re-opened Hall of Mirrors; human vultures eager to feast their eyes on anything that might be a bloodstain.

Catlin hurried on, glancing neither to the right nor the left, knowing just how a fugitive from the law felt. An old saying, one he'd read frequently in detective stories, that a murderer always returns to the scene of his crime, hammered at him. Christ, if Landenning got to know that he'd been back here then that really would start the inspector thinking. But Roy had to go on, there was no turning back.

Dusk already and the rain pelting down, invisible fairies dancing in the puddles, as his mother used to tell him when he stared morosely out of the window on wet Sundays. Now he almost started believing her. Here, on Jacob Schaefer's fairground, *anything* was possible.

He sprinted the last twenty yards to the Indian girl's caravan, his mouth dry with a foul taste in it. *Fear*. A kind of premonition that he did not understand.

His fist hammered on the door, vibrating the whole caravan. Tensing, impatient, hand raised to strike again, vaguely aware of the darkness which was falling fast, when the door was suddenly thrown open.

Jane stood there, this time dressed in brown fringed garments, trousers and shirt that were frayed with wear, snugly fitting her body and showing it off with a sensuous shapeliness, small firm breasts and slim hips, an inch or so of ankle displayed above her dark crimson moccasins.

'I. . . .' Roy thought for one moment that she was about to slam the door in his face. 'I said . . . promised I would come.'

She stared at him, a blank expression that took a second or so to clear, the vagueness being replaced by shock and horror.

'You have seen?' she made no move to stand back so that he could step inside.

'Yes . . . the accident. What happened?'

'They have become more angry and more powerful than even I imagined. This place smells of death and they are not finished with us yet!'

He swallowed, words eluding him.

'You must not stay,' she snapped.

'I will. I want to help.'

'Nobody can help, it is too late. Save yourself and your family. Flee this place now. *Tonight.*'

'No, no. I won't. I won't leave you.' Despair and desperation, sick with fear.

'For Rowena's sake,' a hoarse whisper that was almost a shout. 'Roy, forget that you ever saw me. And destroy that doll which I foolishly gave to Rowena. *Please, for my sake!*'

And then she flung the door closed and left him standing there in the torrrential rain, the gathering darkness around him seeming to echo with shrill mocking laughter.

11
THURSDAY NIGHT

Jane squatted on the floor of her caravan in the darkness, not moving, not knowing how long it was since Roy Catlin had come and gone. It was Rowena she feared for most; she cursed herself for her foolishness in carving that doll and giving it to the child. But at that time she didn't know; even now she wasn't absolutely sure.

Outside in the fairground music had faded, the hubbub of voices had died down to a few late-night revellers. Soon all would be quiet and that was the time she feared most.

The night passed slowly.

Eyes all around her, pinpoints in the darkness like glow-worms. All her own making. They were all in here as though they had congregated by some pre-arranged signal, combining their hate for the one who had created them and made them what they were. The horse's head which Salin had ripped from its body, now repaired, wilder than ever, a spectral stallion with flying mane. Grotesque faces that grinned evilly, Punch in full regalia dominating them all, his baton poised to strike at any second. Judy cowered in the background with her baby, the policeman standing by her in a protective stance; both of them hated Jane, too, because she had made Punch, their perpetual tormentor.

And the latest . . . almost finished, a replica of the doll she had given to Rowena. Jane hadn't meant it to be like that but the knife had carved it so, her slender fingers just holding it, doing as they were commanded. The hawk face, eyes that saw; *Okeepa, the torture symbol of the Plains Indians, a god manifested in many shapes across the ancient land, feared by every tribe*. They made sacrifices to him and he provided crops and buffalo; but if they angered he brought death. The whites had destroyed the buffalo, imprisoned the redman on reservations where the land was so poor that the crops withered and died. And Okeepa demanded revenge in a battle where he would never surrender.

He was here now in everything that Jane had carved, Punch, the horses, dolls that had been sold for a pittance so that Okeepa would be spread across the land of the white man, latent vengeance, awaiting the day when the old tribes would rise up again.

She trembled, bowed her head, felt the evil presence, the damp cold that penetrated her bones. I am your humble servant, Okeepa, doing your bidding, but please spare the deaf child in her innocence and the man who is her father.

I shall be the judge, Mistai, the last of a line who carved and preserved my image. Yet you have much to answer for, your treacherous betrayal of our race, mating with one whose skin is white. Your ancestors cover their faces in shame at what you have done, moaning their grief in the land of the Wise One.

I did not understand, I did not know that I was the chosen one, your servant sent to this land. Already I am in repentance for what I have done, hoping that my mother and her mother who were both called Mistai will forgive me.

Forgiveness is no more plentiful than the rain in the desert lands. It has to be earned. Come with me!

The darkness was fading slowly, a grey creeping light dispelling it, revealing not the interior of her cramped caravan but a wide landscape where a dried-up watercourse led down to a grove of cottonwood trees. She smelled the sour aroma of dead campfires in the air, the undergrowth all around trampled flat as though a herd of stampeding buffalo had fled before the unscrupulous white hunters.

The half-light was deceiving; at first she thought that dawn was breaking but then she realized that it was a dying light that spread from the west. Sunset in a desolate place, all alone yet being drawn irresistibly down to those trees,

186

frightened and confused.

As she got nearer she heard the screams, cries of agony that hung in the still atmosphere. She wanted to flee but was unable, forced to go forward by some invisible power.

Go forward, Mistai, and be cleansed of your sins so that your people may forgive you.

Glancing around but seeing nobody. She reached the trees and started to follow a well-beaten track into the interior. Screams and curses becoming louder all the time, souls in torment that were denied the peace of death.

A wide clearing, the remnants of what had once been an Indian encampment. But now the tipis were flattened, the fires doused, some still smouldering. Only the central totem remained, its carved face as she knew it would be, Okeepa looking down in anger, features contorted with hate for the dozen or so white men in blue uniforms who crowded beneath it. Bodies lay on the ground all around, dark-skinned Cheyenne women mostly, the older squaws still fully clothed, the young ones stripped of their garments and bearing evidence of their fate. Glazed eyes stared upwards as though even in death they called upon Okeepa to take their souls safely to the land of the Wise One. Bloody disfigurations where final sabre thrusts had ended their physical and mental sufferings, rape terminating in death.

Jane stood inside the clearing but none appeared to see her; they had eyes only for the handsome naked girl who sprawled on the grass at the foot of the totem, still alive, her body shaking with pain and anguish. The last survivor.

A soldier stepped forward, pulled her roughly into a sitting position, the long dark hair falling away from her face to reveal puffed and bruised features, dark eyes that mirrored her refusal to concede willingly.

Jane swayed on her feet, almost fell, but the sensation of dizziness passed and was replaced by one of numbed shock; not disbelief, for Okeepa would not have summoned her here to witness a lie. She saw herself, began to experience the pain. And then she was lying there on the ground staring up into those lusting contemptuous faces, wincing at the spittle

which hit her flesh like thunder raindrops, being racked by
the ache of blows she could not remember and the burning
inside her from the ultimate in degradation. And she knew
now that she was Mistai!

The end was near. They had all taken her and now there
was nothing left but death. She raised her eyes, looked
beyond her torturers and into the face of Okeepa, flinched
beneath his gaze. *You have betrayed your people.*

No, it was forced upon me, I was powerless to resist the
matings.

All but one. To him you gave yourself willingly.

Her eyes dropped again, singled out a soldier standing
well back from the group as though he was trying to hide
from her. He flinched, met her gaze. Compassion, apologizing silently, trying to make her understand. Her body
went cold, the pain and suffering momentarily forgotten
for what Okeepa said was true . . . *she had mated willingly
in the guise of rape with this horse soldier who was Rowena's
father.*

Far away thunder was rolling angrily and a flash of
lightning heralded the coming of a storm. White man's
spittle or raindrops, there was no difference. Okeepa's
voice blended with the rumbling of the elements.

*You have conceded the superiority of the redman, Mistai.
By this one act of willing copulation you have given more
than the lands of your ancestors and the buffalo by which
they lived. You have traded not only your body but the
heritage of your people. You shall not die, your crime will
not be erased so easily. I shall give you life, a burden of
shame to bear so that in generations hence you shall avenge
this day and right your wrong with this soldier's death and
the death of his children's children. Go forth and carry my
image with you!*

The storm came with unbelievable rapidity, lashing rain
that drove the taunting soldiers back to the shelter of the
cottonwoods. Jane lay there, letting her aching body be
washed but she knew it could not be cleansed. The lightning came and went, and left only empty darkness in its
wake, the soldiers gone in search of yet another defenceless

village, this one forgotten except by one man whose conscience would torture him until the end of his days.

And then came the bearded man in all his vileness, impregnated with the stench of his own evil, lowering himself on to her and despising her as he took her. Beating her when he was finished.

When he, too, had left she remained there alone with Okeepa, sobbing her shame, frightened by his silence; vowing to do as he had commanded.

Then she was back in the caravan, the dawn light filtering in through the windows, surrounded by her carvings, looking from one to another and seeing the likeness of Okeepa in each one, acknowledging her promise; knowing there was no other way. She, Mistai, must destroy one whom she had loved briefly because it was the will of her people in the land of the Wise One whom some called Manitou. She clasped her hands to her eyes at the terrible thought, heard the figures around her laughing at her. This time there was no doubt in her mind; Okeepa had guided her carving in his own silent mysterious way and now she had received a direct command, the minions of her own making rising up like ghouls from their graves to take control of her.

And Roy Catlin must die.

Roy Catlin's first reaction on turning away from Jane's caravan was one of utter dejection, a depression which had been hovering over him all week now suddenly descending upon him, cloaking his life just as surely as the rain clouds overhead did. He walked away aimlessly, his thoughts jumbled, unable to come to any decision.

Then came anger, a slow fury building up inside him. For some reason Jane had succumbed to the evil of this place, didn't want to fight against it anymore, had lost the will to live.

He wanted to help her, but without her co-operation that was impossible. He thought about going back to the caravan and demanding that she listened to him, but he knew she wouldn't. The day after tomorrow he would be away from this place, probably would never see her again nor learn of her fate.

Voices. Harsh angry chattering. He turned, knew instinctively whence they came. The Punch and Judy Show was giving its last performance of the evening. Before he realized it he was heading towards the small theatre in its dowdy setting behind the menagerie, jangling coins in his pocket, aware that he was going to join the audience. I'm crazy, he told himself, I don't want to see that disgusting show again. But he knew for some reason that he had to.

Within minutes he was inside the enclosure, huddling with a group of people, silent watchers who seemed transfixed by what was taking place on the stage. The same scenery, the room with that ridiculous moon peeping in through the latticed window.

But something had changed. It took him only a few seconds to realize it. Punch was his usual evil self, if anything more malevolent, but no longer were Judy and the policeman cowering before his vicious onslaught. Their rage was unbelievable, a determination reflected in their expressions as they retaliated, the policeman's truncheon and Judy's rolling-pin battering away at the maniacal elongated face, driving him back.

Roy tensed, a strange elation at this turn of events. It was stupid, puppets that were controlled by concealed humans generating an atmosphere such as this, the age-old battle of good versus evil being enacted in yet another form, affecting him in this way.

A cheering, shouting audience, noticeably few children amongst them. It could have been the lateness of the hour; one always tried to settle for a logical explanation. Punch had been driven off stage, came back again with a demoniacal expression on his face, swinging his club and trying to pierce the barricade of weapons that defended the cradle.

Roy's mouth was dry. Of course, they wouldn't work to any kind of script on these shows. Those behind the scenes just provided incoherent chatter and violence, kept up the action. *But suddenly it seemed as though they had lost control of the puppets.* The policeman swung wildly, connected with a resounding bang, and Punch fell, a crumpled

190

heap that became the target for a flurry of blows. But, as invincible as ever, he was back on his feet.

A gasp of amazement from the audience. The grotesque figure's right arm dangled loosely, club trailing on the stage floor. Disbelief in those eyes which should have been fixed and expressionless. Fear! The left arm was thrown up in an attempt to ward off the renewed battering from his assailants, backing away, screeching insanely. Off the stage, necks craned in an attempt to see what was happening behind the scenes. The voices rose to a pitch, maybe it was all part of the act – an attempt to convince the few juvenile watchers that the battle was not yet over. A scream; Punch's. A thud. Everybody waiting breathlessly.

Then silence, the striped curtains snagging their way to a closed position. Groans of disappointment came from the crowd; an inconclusive ending.

Dissatisfied customers filed out, turning up already damp coat collars. Roy Catlin mingled with them, then hung back, sheltering beneath the canopy of a closed sideshow. Watching, not knowing why; not wanting to return to his hotel.

The fairground was empty except for a few stall-holders packing up. Roy pressed himself back into the shadows, undecided. Perhaps he should go back to the hotel, make a determined effort to forget this place and everything that had happened. It was none of his business.

Then he saw a man leaving the miniature theatre, scurrying, carrying something beneath his arm. Roy stared, tensed, felt that all-too-familiar tingling going up his spine and spreading into his scalp. The theatre puppets; all four of them, including the infant which one never saw properly.

They seemed to be struggling in the man's grasp, hands groping, pummelling, Punch turning and twisting as though to escape the others, his broken limb hanging lifeless. Screeches of rage and fear that might have been the echoes of his own imagination but Roy knew they weren't. Punch and his fellow puppets had somehow got out of control, their evil taking over and defying those who sought to work them with strings and wires.

191

Roy Catlin moved out from his hiding place and began to follow at a discreet distance. He knew where the man was headed, there could be no doubt about that. The Punch and Judy characters were being taken back to their Indian maker. Jane's words came back to him – *'they have become more angry and more powerful than even I imagined.'*

And then he remembered Rowena's doll, and a sliver of sheer terror stabbed at his heart.

12

FRIDAY MORNING

Roy Catlin tried to calm himself as he entered the Beaumont Hotel. There was no point in alarming Liz. Now he thought about it he did not remember having seen Rowena's doll since their return from the beach but in all probability she had kept it in her pocket for fear that they might try to take it from her. That was what worried him most.

When he entered the bedroom Liz was still fully dressed, sitting on the edge of the bed. She looked up, gave a loud sigh. 'I trust your night has been a fruitful one as well as a wet one!'

'Where's Rowena?'

'In her bedroom, of course.'

'I thought she was going to sleep in here with us.'

'She insisted on going back to her own room.'

'I'll check on her,' he turned back towards the door. 'By the way, where's that doll got to?'

'She hasn't got it. And neither is she making the fuss about looking for it like she did before. As though . . . she's thrown it away!'

'She wouldn't do that,' Roy pursed his lips. 'And if she

hasn't got it then there's something drastically odd going on.'

'Why worry? If Rowena isn't bothered about the damned thing why should we be?'

'Because it's *evil*, that's why,' his eyes narrowed. '*Oh God, Liz, you've no idea what's going on out there. All these carved figures are taking over!*'

He had expected a contemptuous retort but none was forthcoming. Instead she buried her face in her hands, shoulders slumping. A feeling of sympathy flooded over him but this was swamped by his fear for Rowena's safety. Turning away he left the room.

Rowena was sleeping soundly, her face turned to the wall. He glanced at her, let his gaze rove around the room. There was no sign of Doll. He moved quietly, not wanting to switch the light on, easing open drawers that creaked and stuck, rummaged amongst clothing, a pile of books. But there was no sign of the gruesome little figure.

He stood there undecided. In some ways it was a relief not to find it. But where was it? That was what worried him most. Finally he stepped back out on to the landing, closing the door softly behind him.

Rowena stirred restlessly. This time it was a dream and she was aware of it, the vivid scenes that had existed in her slumber already beginning to fade as she opened her eyes. Daylight crept in through the gap in the curtains, cold and grey, and she wondered if it was still raining. It had to be, really, because she could not imagine it doing anything else.

The cave; she had dreamed she was back in that damp dark place, Doll lying behind the pile of rocks. No longer angry. He hadn't meant what he had said yesterday; it was her mother he hated, not herself. Come back to me, Rowena, I'm so sorry.

She sat up, flung back the sheets, wondered what time it was. She crossed to the window and pulled back the curtains. It was early, not long after dawn. The sky was grey and a thin drizzle made a film on the outside of the glass.

193

Doll wanted her. Even if it was only a dream she knew that he needed to be reunited with her. The promenade below was deserted except for a milkman delivering from an electric cart that whined its way between stops, splashing through the puddles.

She came to an instant decision. She would go and find Doll, bring him back here. It wouldn't take long, her parents need not even know she had been out.

Within five minutes she was dressed and creeping downstairs. The front door lock was stiff and it took all her strength to press it back. She left it ajar, moved outside. The drizzle was coming fast, bringing with it a sea mist, the mountains shrouded by low cloud.

Rowena walked quickly, crossed the promenade, ran until she reached the sands. She turned and looked back, saw that the curtains of her parents' bedroom window were still closed. It wouldn't take long, there and back inside half-an-hour, and back in bed with Doll hidden by the time anybody was thinking about getting up.

Uneasy, a premonition that all was not well. Even the seagulls seemed to have deserted this stretch of coastline, the distant tide the only sound to be heard. She began wishing she had not come. It was that cave which worried her most, not knowing where it led to, what lay within its dark recesses. But she didn't have to go *right* inside, just a yard or two; Doll would be where she had left him and she could grab him and *run*.

It seemed an eternity before she reached the lonely cave hidden by the protruding cliffs, saw the sticky wet sand leading up to the shingle and rocks. The tide had been right in but it hadn't reached the cave. At least she hoped it hadn't because it might have washed Doll away with it.

Clambering over the rocks, going on all fours because they were slippery with a fresh coating of wet weed, seeing the cave staring at her like a single black eye. She shuddered, forced herself to go on. Almost there.

She paused in the entrance, her keen eyes picking out footprints leading inside. She thought at first they were her own from yesterday but they were too big. Apprehensive now. Who else had been here? Had they found Doll and taken him. . . ? She drew back, studied the footmarks again. *One set going in, none coming out. It was simple logic that whoever had entered was still inside*!

Staring hard, trying to pierce the blackness, almost seeing a crouching shape waiting to pounce on her; remembering those dreams of the forest and the dwarf, the Ghost Train and all its nightmares. But she wasn't giving up now. One sudden rush, trembling in the darkness, groping amongst sharp rocks that stabbed at her fingers, trying not to think about the small creatures which might live in places like this.

Then she touched something hard and light which rolled away as though it was trying to escape her. She was grabbing for it, catching it and turning to run in the same movement. Angry whispers behind her, cries of rage from deep in the hillside that this child had ventured inside and escaped. Not daring to look back, holding a tiny wooden figure to her, fearful that it might slip from her grasp.

Take me back, child!

She heard Doll's voice the same as it always was, a whispering sound somewhere inside her, his body vibrating with a terrible anger. Shocked, a puppy that has gone to its master to be fondled and been chastised instead.

How dare you take me away!

Rowena almost returned to the cave, replaced him where she had found him, the tears building up behind her eyes. But no, he was *hers* and a damp smelly cave was no place to leave him. Determination, the kind which she had to use to overcome her disability in class at the PHU, a continual fight against all odds. No, I'm not taking you back, Doll. You're coming with me and I'm never going to let you out of my sight again.

It was as though he was fighting her, struggling, trembling with rage, but she wasn't even going to look at him. She stuffed him into the pocket of her anorak and concentrated on picking her way across the treacherous mounds of rock. The sea mist had come in closer, a grey blanket cast from the skies to shield her activities. *Or to trap her here in this brooding place.*

Suddenly she saw the man. She might have passed by without noticing him had she not slipped and in regaining her balance glanced across to her left. First the horror, the shock; then the shrill scream. She wanted to look away but her gaze was riveted on the awful scene.

The body was lying across a rock, clad in oilskins, head downwards in a deep pool . . . except that he didn't have a head, just a mulch like pulped over-ripe fruit that oozed its juices into the water and turned it scarlet! Something was swimming just below the surface, sending out ripples that widened and spread, finally disintegrating when they reached the sides.

Rowena didn't want to look but she could not tear her gaze away, saw the way a white hand bobbed in the water as though feebly signalling for help even after death. And Doll was shrieking angrily, more muffled because he was in her pocket.

This is a place of death. Flee, and leave me behind.

Terror constricted her usually clear thinking. Scrambling backwards like a rock crab, transfixed by the sight of death and blood, her limbs responding weakly. She had no idea who the dead man was, it was just the fact that he was *dead*.

Shingle crunched beneath her, another yard and the awful sight was hidden from her. Walking because she did not have the strength to run, wanting to be sick, retching on an empty stomach. Her anorak swung back and forth as she moved, propelled by the weight in her pocket.

Only when she was back on the long straight beach did her reasoning return. A man was dead. The police and an ambulance usually came when that happened, like they had done at the fair, but they could not get a vehicle to that cove through the soft sand and over the rocks. She wondered how they would take the dead man away. But they wouldn't be able to if they didn't know he was there.

A sudden realization of her own responsibility; it was up to *her* to disclose his whereabouts! She would have to tell *somebody*. In some ways this prospect was even more terrifying than her actual discovery. Her mother would be

196

furious with her for having gone to the cave. If she told her father it would be the same as telling her mother, because daddy couldn't do anything without asking her first, or so it had been until recently.

Standing there on a wet misty beach trying to work out a solution. She was reluctant to speak to strangers; they didn't understand her impaired speech, thought she was an idiot. But she couldn't just leave that man there for the gulls (if they returned) and the rock creatures to feed on. Whom then should she tell?

She couldn't understand why she had not thought of *Jane* in the first place. The Indian girl was the obvious answer! She understood, would know what to do. Rowena's strength seemed to return and Doll was much quieter now, lying still and silent in her pocket. She started off at a fast walk then broke into a run.

People were already up around the fair, men in overalls and raincoats opening up stalls, moving with an air of boredom as they went about their daily routine, not even turning to glance at the small girl who hurried across the open space behind the remnants of the big-dipper. In the distance she saw a policeman but he had his back towards her. Then, finally, she was pounding on the door of Jane's caravan. Open up, oh please, Jane, open up. I need your help!

Rowena trembled with relief when she heard a sound within, slow footsteps, hesitant. Then Jane's voice. 'Who's there?'

'Rowena.'

A bolt was shot, the door dragged open, Jane's dark features framed in the gap, tired and dishevelled, eyes wide with amazement.

'Whatever are you doing here at this hour, Rowena?'

'Please. . . .' the words did not come as easily as her brain commanded, 'help me . . . dead man. . . .'

The door was dragged wide for the child to enter, slammed shut after her.

'You should not be here, Rowena!' Concern rather than a reprimand. 'Now, tell me what it is all about.'

197

With some difficulty Rowena recounted her story, the way Doll had insisted on being left in the cave, how she had gone back to fetch him and what she had found there. Jane paled, did her utmost to conceal the terror which widened her dark eyes.

'Where is your doll?' she asked at length.

Rowena tugged at her pocket, brought out Doll, could almost feel a throbbing coming from him.

'Give him to me,' the Indian tried to speak kindly.

'*No!*' Shocked, Rowena stepped back, half-turned away, determined not to hand over her most precious belonging . . . not even to Jane.

Jane tensed, made as though to grab the wooden figure, somehow managed to stop herself, closed her eyes momentarily. 'Rowena . . . please give me the doll. It is very important.'

Silence. They eyed each other, conflicting wills, neither giving way.

'All right,' Jane's voice was low when she spoke again, sounding very tired. 'I will not take him from you against your will. But come with me. I want to show you something.'

Rowena followed her through the doorway into the main living area, the uneasiness returning, the same feeling she had experienced in the cave, a living force in the atmosphere . . . something *malevolent*.

On the shelves and table were the carved figures, rows of painted faces that stared with eyes that saw, a flickering that could have been the light shining on new paint. Rowena halted, almost turned and ran. Punch, with a new arm that was thicker, stronger, wielding his baton. Judy, so frightened, turning away as though to shield her baby. The policeman, hopelessness, defeat in his expression. A horse's head, wild and dangerous. More faces, Indian totems, angered gods determined to wreak their vengeance on the mortals in their midst. And lastly, one half-finished figurine which might have been Doll's twin, turned so that he, too, saw. They were all looking.

And Rowena, the girl whose hearing had been impaired

since birth, heard their vile laughter ringing deafeningly inside her head.

'Perhaps now you understand,' Jane turned as though deliberately trying to shield Rowena from them. 'I cannot explain, at least not so that you would understand, Rowena. Once they were just wooden figures; at least that is what I thought in my foolish innocence. I made one, then another, without realizing. I created an army of evil and now I am powerless to stop them, and even when I knew, Mr Schaefer demanded that I carve and carve and repair the damaged ones. Even now I am forced to work on them. The one I gave you, the one you call Doll, he is *very* powerful. So cunning that he made his escape from this haven of death so that he could carry his evil into the outside world. Now you have brought him back. Give him to me so that at least they will all be confined in this one place.'

Rowena gave up her doll, watched Jane place him on the table.

'I do not want you to come here again,' Jane's lips quivered, she was very close to breaking down. 'Or your father. Ever. Once I thought that you could help me, now I know that is impossible. I shall only be sentencing you to my fate. Go from here and forget Jane who carved you a doll and took it back from you.'

Rowena hung her head. 'The man . . . cave. . . .'

'Whoever he is, we cannot help him. It is too late. Try to forget that also. Tomorrow you will be going home, away from all this. Last night I prayed to my god, the Wise One. Only he can save me and destroy these terrible things that I have created.'

Only the driving rain reminded Rowena that she was no longer back in Jane's caravan, that the fairground lay behind her. The promenade around her was no longer deserted: people were hurrying to buy an habitual morning newspaper so that they could read of tragedies and economic recessions over breakfast; those who had already eaten were once again being lured by the diesel odours and blaring music of the fair, a steady stream of worshippers going to pay homage in their hardboard temple, jangling their offerings in their pockets.

As Rowena approached the Beaumont Hotel she saw that the curtains of her parents' bedroom were still closed. And the front door was still open, just the way she had left it. Her legs were suddenly weak, bending under her. Then came a falling sensation, a desperate grab for the stair-rail, brushing it. Slipping, somersaulting down into a black abyss, a feeling of weightlessness. Somebody calling her out of the darkness, a voice that might have belonged to Jane.

13

FRIDAY AFTERNOON

'I can't for the life of me imagine what Rowena was doing out at that hour,' Liz Catlin made a valiant effort to swallow a mouthful of leather-like kipper. Some of her anger had subsided but she could not hide her concern. 'She's absolutely flaked out. Exhaustion. She'll have to stop in bed today. Thank God we're going home tomorrow! But if she shows any signs of running a temperature I'm going to call a doctor.'

'One of us will have to stay with her,' Roy did not lift his eyes, sensed his wife's sudden suspicion. Of course it'll be me that stays in because that way I won't be able to sneak off to the fairground.

'I want to do some shopping this morning. We'll need to take some food home with us, and I've one or two small presents to buy as well,' Liz spoke quickly. Too quickly. 'You never know, Rowena might be well enough for us all to go out this afternoon.' You're not going anywhere on your own again this holiday! 'The weathermen seem to think this low's going to move away and there's a high following it in.'

Bloody typical, Roy groaned. It'll be back to blazing hot tomorrow, an official drought declared after a fortnight. Back to Balfour and Wren's, all nice and peaceful and boring.

'And how's the little girl now?' Mrs Hughes appeared from the kitchen door, a hint that late breakfasters weren't expected to linger after 9.30.

'She'll be all right,' Liz tried to smile. 'It's been a big week for her. And the weather hasn't helped.'

'They say it's going to clear up. Thank goodness. It's the people camping I feel sorry for.' Serves 'em bloody well right, they should support hard-working hoteliers.

Liz lowered her voice as Mrs Hughes moved away to another table. 'You'd better stop in with Rowena, Roy. I'll pop out for an hour or two.'

He nodded. That was what he'd expected. Friday would slip away and tomorrow it would all be over. Perhaps it was as well. All the same, it left him with a feeling of dissatisfaction, even guilt. Now he would never know.

Inspector Landenning hated the seaside. In his younger days he had day-dreamed of a coastal posting. Blue skies reflected in a shimmering sea, continual heatwaves, the only crimes an occasional pickpocket on the promenade or a theft on the beach. But it wasn't like that at all. Rain and more bloody rain, a mist that hid the sea, and enough gruesome murders to make the Rue Morgue seem like a holiday camp.

He turned seawards and took a deep breath to steady himself. Foul damp air, the only resort where the seagulls coughed; except that there weren't any gulls. Not a sign or a sound of birdlife. This cove was deserted except for himself and the four C.I.D. officers who had examined the body and now gone into the cave. Landenning didn't want to go in there. Jesus Christ, no! He'd had nightmares about tunnels ever since the Ghost Train killing.

Somewhere a dangerous killer was at large, killing wantonly, mutilating the bodies of his victims. After this one they'd have to call in the Yard. Quite frankly he'd welcome a few London coppers around because this maniac would strike again for sure; this kind always did.

'We'll have to try and enlist the help of some local pot-holers if there are any, inspector.' Landenning jumped. He hadn't heard the young sergeant approaching. Everybody's nerves were stretched.

'What's the trouble then, sergeant?'

'There's a woman stuck fast in a narrow passage leading off the cave. Christ knows how she managed to get as far as she did. You can just see her feet if you shine your torch down the tunnel.'

Bloody hell, no, I don't want to see any more! 'And what the devil's she doing down there, sergeant?'

'Search me, sir. Maybe a lovers' quarrel, she killed the bloke over there and thought she could hide in the caves. Crazy, I know. By the way, there's been a child in the cave as well. It's been and gone . . . twice!'

Landenning turned back towards the sea, wished this damned mist would clear. It was like a bad dream. Maybe if he rubbed his eyes he would wake up and find that it wasn't really happening after all.

'Organize it, will you, sergeant,' so tired he almost didn't care whether they got the bastard or not. 'I'll go back and get the experts out. They'll really love this one.'

He didn't take the Land Rover because he needed the walk, the damp cold air. Most of all he needed time, because at his stage in life he had to learn to pace himself whether he liked it or not.

He glanced at his watch as he climbed the stone steps which led from the beach up to the promenade. 1.45. Two whole hours since that youth had discovered the body; the *first* one. Nowadays one almost expected a second. They didn't come singly here!

The mist had almost gone. Landenning stared in disbelief. Away on the horizon between grey sky and an even greyer sea was a golden line with patches of blue in it. It might just

202

be that area of high pressure which was supposed to be moving in. Funny the way the weather dominated your life, if you stopped to think about it. More so than the moon and the stars.

A lifting of the spirits that took some of the tiredness away. But something was still wrong. Of course, the gulls. They should have been lining the harbour rails, wheeling, diving, an incessant hunt for food whether it was stale bread thrown by the holidaymakers or mackerel from the fishing boats.

There wasn't a bird in sight. And that was when Inspector Landenning sensed the real extent of the evil which hung over this place.

Liz Catlin had not intended to go to the fairground. Indeed, it was the last place she would have chosen to visit. Yet long before she reached the shops in the busy main street she knew that was where she was going.

As she retraced her steps she shivered at the thought of visiting the very cancer which had spread its vile tentacles into their holiday. She didn't *want* to go there but there were a number of reasons why she had to. Jealousy for a start. She wanted to look upon the girl with whom her husband had been unfaithful, a kind of projected hate, a burning desire to get some of it out of her system. Not just that, looking for *signs*, a gleam in the eyes that meant her husband was likely to go there again, or, hopefully, an expression of disappointment. Liz could barely remember what the Indian girl looked like, a bundle of blankets with a dark face. The fortune-teller hadn't just cast her spell over Roy. Rowena was affected too, a lure of some kind that drew them back again and again.

Even that was not sufficient to take Liz Catlin back to Jacob Schaefer's domain. The evil that Roy had spoken of, she knew it was *real*, something about the place that brought about murders, accidents, tragedies. She'd felt it herself, especially that night of the Punch and Judy Show. Now she just wanted to walk there, look around her, be able to tell herself that it was a figment of the imagination, a kind of living bad dream that stemmed from the weather. An hour, maybe less, and she'd know, be able to wipe some of it out of her memory, go home and start all over again.

It had stopped raining and a brightness behind the clouds hinted that the sun might break through. Probably it would disappear again in a few minutes but it would be nice to catch a glimpse of it.

There seemed more people about than ever today, anoraks and raincoats carried over arms or shoulders. But even now an air of gaiety was lacking. Liz almost changed her mind. But it wouldn't take long.

'*I can see clearly now the rain has gone. . . .*'

Deliberate optimism on the part of the fairground's disc jockey. She doubted it. These people didn't think that way and, anyway, they welcomed the rain because it drove the people in here off the beaches. She wandered aimlessly along the sideshows, not really seeing. Thinking about Rowena. Maybe she had come here early this morning.

She arrived at the menagerie, found herself making a detour, seeing that dwarf again, a cretin with mad eyes shuffling after her. He'd died, a stroke or something like that. Too many people had died lately.

The fortune-teller's tent. Liz hesitated, didn't really want to go inside now that she was faced with it, but her dilemma was solved for her when she saw the ropes tied across the entrance. Jane wasn't here, perhaps she had left the fair altogether. No, Roy wouldn't really have done *that* with her; he'd just gone to see her because she had some kind of affinity with Rowena.

If you tried hard enough you could convince yourself of anything. There was nothing strange going on here, just the usual type of fair. It had only seemed worse because of the pouring rain. You paid through the nose to avoid getting depressed on a wet holiday, but in the end it got you. You couldn't win.

She felt suddenly selfconscious, as though everybody was watching her, but when she turned round nobody was. Nobody was interested in Liz Catlin. Except those awful carved and painted horses' heads on the merry-go-round, wild eyes that picked her out. One passed, the next fixed her with its steely glare. And the next . . . and the one after that.

Trying to look away but there was nowhere you could escape them. Snow White and the Seven Dwarfs carved into a fairyland scene with coloured lights flashing on and off. A witch and seven evil gnomes, leering. *Oh God, she could even hear them laughing at her*!

Turning, running crazily one way then another, but they were everywhere. Screeching. *This is a place of death from which there is no escape*!

I'm going mad, she thought. I must be because there are crowds of people here and nobody else seems to notice. *And they're running the Ghost Train again even after what happened*. . . .

She stared, almost hypnotized, at the small red engine, its driver leaning on the cab, a cigarette cupped between his hands as though he had developed a habit of shielding it from the rain. Three full cars, a waiting queue of people.

Liz walked slowly towards them, found herself standing behind a tall man with a balding head. Next trip in ten minutes, all the horrors of the fair. Rowena had been in there all alone, maybe this was where it had all begun, her nightmares and strange behaviour. Liz was scared, scared to hell, but she had to go in there and see, discover what her daughter had been through.

Mechanical movements and confused thoughts, handing over a coin and getting a small green ticket in return, not knowing or caring whether she should have had any change. Seeing the train clattering the tunnel doors on its return, passengers alighting. Vague expressions. Numbed shock that hadn't filtered through yet.

She found a seat, pushed right up against the side so that a man and a youth could squeeze in alongside her, got the feeling again that she ought not to be here. There was still time to get off and run, escape from this place and try to erase the memory. But that was impossible. She had to see it through, go all the way. *Because this was what had happened to Rowena*.

The driver came down the platform, seemingly in slow motion, scanning the faces of his passengers but not really seeing them. A sort of check that had no purpose. Going back again, kicking an empty cigarette packet that went skimming under the train, climbing back into his cab with an air of reluctance. Just a job, the same as any other.

A juddering vibration, jerking forward, buffers clanging. Then picking up speed, everybody wincing as the engine struck the blood-red double doors, throwing them back, going through.

It's too late now, there's no going back!

A rush of air that stank of diesel fumes, something brushing against Liz Catlin's face, bringing the first scream, destroying that sense of apathy. Now it was for real! Luminous figures, a hideous ghoul munching on a bloody human limb, eyes turning to follow the progress of the train, stepping forward, reaching out as though for the next course of succulent flesh. Piercing screams, some from hidden tapes, mostly from the crouching frightened passengers. Parents attempted to comfort their offspring with words that were drowned in the din.

A forest, trees that were flat and cast no shadows, twisted branches that bent and touched the floor, shapes moving amongst them. A gorilla-like creature with eyes that glowed redly, beating its chest, roaring. But its face . . . *oh, God, its face*. Liz saw it as more than just a ferocious animal, the fangs and nose like those of some carved pagan god, tall and terrible, seeing her and . . . She recognized the features, there could be no mistake. *Rowena's doll had grown bigger than lifesize and was alive. Here in this place!*

The train slowed, it might even have stopped; she couldn't drag her eyes away from that thing. Laughing at her, mocking her. Then another figure cut into the scene, a man who would have been huge had he not been dwarfed by this beast. Wild eyes, a flowing black beard that was matted by some kind of congealed dull red fluid, clothes tattered so that they were unrecognizable. Shouting, cursing; afraid! In his hands he wielded an axe, the blade

206

wet and crimson. Threatening, holding back because he was afraid, the god-thing contemptuous, unwilling to move in and end it all because it was enjoying it.

Liz recoiled, her limbs frozen, trying to scream but failing. Then she saw the child crouched on the other side of this cardboard clearing, face hidden by tiny splayed hands. But she didn't need to see the freckled features to recognize her, to know who it was wearing that crumpled dusty blue anorak. *It was Rowena.*

Still she could not move, held there as though invisible manacles secured her to the truck; forced to watch. *Oh God, they're fighting over my baby, one of them's going to kill her!*

Axeman and god circling each other, roaring their hate. A wild swing but it fell inches short of the taller one, bringing a snarl of contempt from the twisted mouth. Rowena had turned as though to flee but still she stayed.

Run! Hide!

Then the axe found its mark, a deep gash on the broad chest, like a split in a gnarled tree trunk, opening but not bleeding. Solid. And with a screech that jarred the brain the monster closed in, one blow sending the axe spinning, tearing at the body of its opponent with sharp claws, ripping the flesh, blood pouring out of the wounds, a frenzy of laceration and mutilation.

All over so quickly. Liz was screaming, or perhaps it was all inside her head, the noises coming from this hideous forest of terror. Now began a game of hide-and-seek, the child flitting from one tree to another, crouching, moving on, her pursuer tearing a path in her wake, toppling trees but always there were more.

A never-ending chase, the terrified child always seeming to find another hiding place. Going further and further away into the forest until finally the bestial roaring was almost inaudible.

Vibrations again, a sensation of movement, blackness and trailing things that brushed your face. Liz stared straight ahead of her then flinched as she saw the face in front, the ape god's head magnified out of all proportion, the mouth a yawning red cavern, coming at her fast. She felt its hot foul breath, managed to close her eyes so that she would not see.

Impact! A clattering sound like an iron bar being trailed along a length of railings. Dazzling brightness that hurt the eyes and blinded. Not moving anymore. People, voices, music. Wan sunlight.

Alone on the train. The forest had gone, the screams just echoes in her brain. She found that she could move, somehow dragged herself on to the raised wooden platform, walking unsteadily. *My baby's back in there with that . . . that fiend! I've got to go back in there, find her.* She glanced behind her, the tunnel doors still swinging gently, the painted final horror quivering in the darkness of its own domain.

Shaken and trembling, Liz Catlin hurried across the open fairground, head bowed, looking neither to right nor left. Crowds around but she saw nobody, that same feeling of being watched but no longer caring. Starting to hurry once she reached the promenade, an urgency that was overwhelming, almost forcing her into a run.

Through the hall of the Beaumont Hotel, up the stairs. Breathless. Bursting into Rowena's bedroom.

'Oh, thank God!' Relief at finding the child still there in bed, sleeping.

'What's the matter with you?' Liz jumped, unaware that Roy had heard her and followed her in.

'I . . . I. . . .' she tried to find words and failed. 'Nothing.'

'Yes, there is,' he was commanding suddenly, the way he used to be years ago. It was time for honesty all round. 'Come on, let's hear it. You've been to the fair, haven't you?'

'Yes,' she couldn't help a shudder. 'I just . . . *had to*. There's something there that's affecting all our lives. I thought maybe if I went and found nothing I'd be able to forget it and go home. Put it all down to a bad holiday and hope for something better next year.'

'But it wasn't like that, was it? It's like I've been telling

208

you all along, an evil that gets you, soaks into you. That doll of Rowena's was part of it but maybe it's gone now. And tomorrow we'll be gone.'

'And in the meantime . . . you won't go there again, will you, Roy?'

'No,' he shook his head, didn't flinch beneath her gaze. 'I don't want to go there again. Ever!'

Jane had carved diligently all morning, her attractive face tense with fear and revulsion, loathing every groove, every chip of wood which fell to the floor of her caravan. Occasionally she glanced up, checked that the figure she had almost completed resembled Rowena's doll. Her skill had not failed her, even in this terrible hour. Soon she would be finished. *And then it would all begin.*

The shelves around her were empty, the puppets repaired and returned. Just these two, the final link in the chain of evil, Okeepa and his brother who were one and the same. She could feel their presence, a living power that commanded her and despised her. Then sun had gone in again as though these devils controlled even day and night, calling upon the shadows and the darkness.

Soft footsteps outside, the door being pushed open, somebody entering. Jane did not turn her head because she knew it would be Jacob Schaefer; she had been expecting him at any time during the last hour.

'You have done well,' his guttural voice had a note of satisfaction in it. 'All is now complete, as it was before Monday. Now go back to your tent and continue telling the people that which they wish to hear.'

'You do not understand,' she muttered. 'You have no idea what you have done to me.'

'Perhaps, perhaps not,' he laughed. 'Only that my fair shall one day be the most colourful in the whole of Europe, its figures and carvings equal to even those of the Swiss craftsmen. Because I have *you*.'

'You do not even *realize* what is happening here?'

'*I know*,' a hoarse, almost frightened whisper, 'but *they* will not hurt us, not you and me. It is their home, we provide for them, mend them when they are broken.'

'*They have not yet begun*,' she turned, stared up into his cragged lined face through the wispy growth of grey beard. 'You have compelled me to complete a cycle of evil and now they need us no longer. We are *their* puppets now!'

He started, the length of cigar almost falling from his thin lips. 'It cannot be.'

'It is.' Jane's eyes reflected an inner terror, near panic. From the beginning of this week it has been so. They have wrought death in their own way, claiming this place for their own domain and slaying within its surrounds.'

'Then we will move on.'

'It will make no difference. It is too late.'

'*Then destroy them*!' A shrill screech.

'And if we fail then their revenge will be a thousand times more terrible.'

Schaefer's eyes were riveted on the two totem dolls, their eyes picked him out, bored into him. Ashen-faced, he backed away, veins standing out on his forehead. Then he turned, shambled out through the doorway.

Jane sat there, a blank expression on her features, knowing that what Jacob Schaefer had said was right. Her conscience told her so. *She had created these fiends and she must be responsible for destroying them. If that was possible.*

Somewhere she heard shrill laughter in the wind, taunting, contemptuous.

14

FRIDAY NIGHT

Rowena was still sleeping at a quarter to six when Roy and Liz looked into her room.

'What d'you think?' there was concern in Liz Catlin's voice.

'She's slept virtually all day. But she hasn't got a temperature. It can't be anything other than exhaustion.'

'I don't like it. She's so still, her breathing so shallow. Perhaps we ought to get a doctor to look at her.'

'You know how reluctant doctors are to come out, especially to strangers, and most of them are so bloody-minded. Let's have dinner first and afterwards we'll decide what to do.'

Liz nodded. For once in her life she was going to enjoy packing the suitcases to go home. They'd all feel better when they got away from this place. They might even be able to pick up the car tonight.

Rowena sensed the door closing, then her eyes opened. She saw the room was empty and sat up, stretched. She felt better, relaxed and refreshed after a long sleep. But she could not stop here. Once before she had sensed that Jane was in trouble, now she was sure of it. She had to go to her; it was a matter of life and death!

She dressed quickly, then opened the door and looked furtively out on to the landing. There was nobody about; a muffled hubbub of conversation came from the dining-room downstairs. She went downstairs, ran across the hall and out into the porch, hesitated. The sky had clouded over and it was starting to rain again, a persistent heavy drizzle with a look of permanency about it.

She could hear the fair, louder than usual as though Jacob Schaefer had ordered the records to be played at full volume to attract the crowds on a wet evening.

'*Don't go out tonight. . . .*'

Rowena mingled with the people; it appeared that everybody was going to the fair tonight. One last fling before the great homeward trek tomorrow. Go home broke because you haven't had a good holiday if you don't.

She went in by the menagerie entrance because it was the nearest, a long dingy avenue in which the puddles were starting to fill up again. Her feeling of tension became stronger almost at once, her nagging concern for Jane

211

developing into a slight headache that might get worse. But she had to go on, find Jane quickly before her parents missed her and came looking for her.

A sudden roar that vibrated inside her head. People moving back, staring at the line of animal cages, expressions of smug horror on their faces. You can't get at us, get as angry as you like.

And it was quite obvious that Remus the ageing lion was very angry. He stood on his hind legs, front paws resting on the bars, jaws wide in preparation for another roar, displaying all the gaps where once strong teeth had gleamed. He still had his claws though, three or four inches of razor-sharp nail that were capable of terrible lacerations on the body of any foe. He dropped down, sprang up again, his weight shaking the bars, the golden-maned beast sensing that a continued assault on the steel strips might give him his freedom.

'I don't like the look of 'im.' A woman's voice.

'Don't worry, 'e can't get out. 'E's too old anyway,' somebody hastily reassured her. 'Sommat's upset 'im, all the same.'

Remus lowered himself down, crouched motionless as though debating whether to make his escape bid now or later. He turned and stood with his back to his audience, but one had the impression that he had not abandoned the idea. Those muscles had not softened up during the years of captivity.

A drumming like a distant tomtom, getting louder and louder. And louder. Remus was forgotten as all eyes were switched to George the gorilla. So huge, you didn't really appreciate his size until he stretched up to his full height, fists pounding on the hairy chest. His lips were drawn back exposing a full set of powerful teeth. But it was his silence which was most terrifying, as though he was mulling over some deep plot to take his revenge on Man. Gorillas were supposed to be simple creatures who required only food and shelter. They were supposed to enjoy human company. But it was quite obvious that George did not think like that.

A harsh trumpeting, Attila the elephant pacing restlessly around his small enclosure, tiny eyes almost closed, just a couple of black evil slits. Normally placid, occasionally used for giving rides to children, something was troubling him. His trunk snaked out, was held erect as though pointing accusingly at the sea of faces. Then, without warning, a jet of water that had been sucked in and stored for this very purpose hit the crowd with force, saturating the nearest, driving everybody back out of range. A shrill noise, a kind of elephantine laugh, but tonight there was no humour in Attila, dropping dung with loud splats as though in deliberate insult.

The crowd swelled, taunting the animals with whistles and cat-calls, so that Rowena had to push her way through a forest of bodies. Nobody glanced down at one small girl because there were far more interesting things to watch.

And by the time Rowena reached the main fairground she was very frightened. *Something was happening here tonight, the malevolence which had been steadily escalating all week was suddenly reaching its peak.*

Rowena had hung about outside Jane's caravan for some time, her courage failing her now that at last she had reached her destination. Her Indian friend would be angry that she had come here, would in all probability order her to return straight away to her parents; in which case it would all have been a waste of time and effort, her only reward a double scolding. Even now there was still time to return to her bedroom before her parents realized that she was missing. But no! Jane needed her, this time more than ever. Rowena would not be sent away. If necessary she would sit on those caravan steps and refuse to move. This renewed determination had her stepping forward, reaching up for the handle and pushing the door open.

'Rowena, you should not have come but I knew that you would,' Jane's voice was soft, no trace of reprimand in it, more a deep sadness in her eyes. She was sitting on the floor, wearing her suit of brown animal skins, the two dolls propped up on the table in the centre.

213

Rowena felt her gaze being drawn towards Doll. She started when she saw the other one, but dragged her eyes back to meet Jane's. 'I came because you need me and I will not be sent away.'

Jane closed her eyes, her face lined, breathing in deeply, silent for a moment with her own troubled thoughts. 'Yes, I need you, my child, but it is wrong of me to ask your help. Yet only you can help me.'

The child's eyes widened, she wanted to ask why and how but she remained silent, sensing once again Doll's influence, so much more powerful now. That was because there were two of them, projecting themselves into her mind. *You cannot help her. Go away.* I can and I will. I hate you, Doll, because you're not like you used to be, no longer kind and loving. And I hate your brother, too!

'Before long it will be dark,' Jane was desperately trying not to look at the two carvings. 'And that is when it will all begin, Rowena. I made these fiends in my innocence, guided by the spirit of my ancestor, Mistai the Cheyenne. She came to hate the white race so fiercely that she handed her hatred on to her daughter who was also called Mistai, and who was my mother. Oh, I have become their tool of vengeance, sent unknowingly across the great waters so that I might bring about destruction with magic that comes from the dark lands where Okeepa lives. My hands were guided, I fashioned his image whom you call Doll and then made his brother who is also called Okeepa, a magic so powerful that I am helpless to fight against it. Only during the daylight hours am I safe. Tonight when it is dark I shall be helpless and will do their bidding. Except for you, Rowena. You are my only hope. But it is wrong of me to ask you to do these things because I put you in danger, a danger so great that I try not to think about it.'

'I will help you,' Rowena's features were taut and determined. '*They* will not stop me.'

Fury vibrated from the two totem dolls, a force that Rowena felt, the atmosphere cold and damp, their shrill voices screaming in her brain. *Remember the forest . . . the forest!*

She resisted it, flung it back at them. *You were unable to harm me in the forest just as you are unable to harm me now. You deceived me, pretended to be my friend. I will help Jane to fight against you.*

'It is so,' it was as if the fortune-teller had read the child's thoughts, was aware of the struggle of wills. 'You, Rowena, are far stronger than I. Why, I am not sure. Perhaps, you have taken on the good in me and strengthened it. I could not have brought back Doll from the cave as you did. His evil was so powerful that it caused disasters at sea, drownings, only the beginning of his devilish plot to exterminate the hated white race. Yet you returned him here against his will where he forced me to create his evil brother, the second Okeepa who is also part of himself, so' that his power would be complete. Perhaps my prayers to Manitou, the Wise One, have not gone unanswered and in his mysterious wisdom he has sent you to help me.'

'Then you won't send me away?' Rowena was close to tears.

'No. It is selfish of me but perhaps that is how it is meant to be. But until it is dark we must hide elsewhere, for surely your parents will come searching for you. One word of warning, once darkness falls I shall not be strong, my instinct will be to give way to Okeepa. You must keep close to me and give me your strength. Okeepa will strive to win this night and if that happens his evil will be unleashed on your race and none will be powerful enough to stop it. Foolish as I am, I mended the broken Punch, restored them all to their former strength and gave them back whence they came. Tonight when the fair has closed we must bring them all together so that they may be destroyed forever. I pray to Manitou that he will guide us, for we shall have but one chance.'

Liz Catlin was on the verge of hysteria. Only three quarters of an hour ago it had seemed that Rowena was too exhausted to leave her bed; now the child was gone, and all her clothes too.

'*She's gone to the fairground!*' Liz shrieked. 'I know it.

That witch of an Indian has lured her back.' Remembering her mother's tales of kidnapping by roving bands of gypsies, children disappearing never to be seen again. And the Ghost Train, that awful monster in the guise of a painted cut-out gorilla, and the child which could have been none other than Rowena. 'Oh, Roy, however are we going to find her. You know as well as I do that it's no ordinary place.'

Roy was white-faced, shaking. Jane wasn't evil but she was caught up in it just like everybody else. And that damned doll, that was what was worrying him most.

'I'm going to the police,' he said. 'Maybe there's no need to panic. Rowena may be perfectly OK but we can't take any chances. I'll go and telephone Inspector Landenning. I think he's the one guy who understands that something out of the ordinary is happening at that fair.'

'I'm not letting you out of my sight,' Liz was adamant. She had visions of Roy sneaking back to the fairground on his own. And this time it wasn't just the Indian fortune-teller of whom she was afraid but something far more insidious.

'We'll go round to the station,' Roy turned towards the door. 'It's only a couple of streets away and it'll be easier than trying to explain on the telephone.' He wasn't going to be able to shake off Liz this time.

Liz followed him down the stairs and out into the street. It was raining again, heavily, and there were more people about than usual, all of them seeming to head towards the dazzling lights of Jacob Schaefer's fair.

Away to the west that streak of gold and blue which had promised so much earlier had been obliterated by a heavy cloud formation, the sky seeming to frown and brood. Night itself was eager to take over.

The police station was empty when they arrived, a sombre Victorian building with a black and white marble floor and a carved mahogany enquiry counter, a series of hatches that reminded Roy of hen-coops. Posters every-where, duplications of colorado beetle and don't-drink-and-drive warnings as though every area of vacant wall-space had to be covered, perhaps to hide peeling paintwork or crumbling plaster.

He pressed a bell which rang somewhere reluctantly as though its battery was flat. A long wait; somebody somewhere was shuffling papers. A match rasped. Liz wanted to scream. 'For Jesus Christ's sake doesn't anybody care that my baby's missing?'

Then one of the trapdoors was lifted, a young constable regarding them questioningly as though it was too much of an effort to ask 'can I help you?' There were dark rings beneath his eyes as though he was short of sleep.

'I'd like to see Inspector Landenning,' Roy said and sensed immediately that somehow that wasn't going to be possible.

'I'm sorry, sir,' a momentary drooping of heavy eyelids, 'but I'm afraid the inspector isn't in.'

'When *will* he be in?'

'Your guess is as good as mine, sir. We're stretched on manpower at present with all that's happened this week. He could be back in five minutes, it might be five hours. More likely five hours, I'd say. Is it a personal matter or can I help you?'

'Our daughter's gone missing. She's *deaf*,' Liz cut in. For once she was deliberately invoking sympathy, mentally reprimanding herself for not saying 'partially-hearing'. But this was no time for trivial details. 'We think she's in the fairground and could be in danger.'

'I'd better have your names and the address of where you're staying,' one learned to recognize holidaymakers, 'and also a description of your child which we'll circulate to all officers on duty in the area. It may take some time, though. Loads of kids wander off like yours has done and then just turn up again. I'd suggest, madam, that you both go and have a real good look for her in the fairground.'

Liz Catlin suddenly wanted to scream; anger, fear, frustration. That fairground, the one place both she and Roy had vowed never to set foot in again, and now they were going right back there.

She tensed. The policeman was speaking again but it was

217

not his words she heard, nor his face into which she was staring vacantly. She saw elongated hideous grinning features, a bent conical hat perched on the head, a permanent mischievous grin to match the nonsensical chatter. It was as though Punch was challenging her to find Rowena, mocking her, trying to push her beyond the brink of sanity.

And Roy was saying, 'Thank you, officer, if we don't have any luck we'll come back. But first we'll try the fairground.'

Jacob Schaefer was on his way back to Jane's caravan when he spied the Indian girl walking in front of him with a small child. He quickened his step, opened his mouth to call her name, then changed his mind and dropped back. Perhaps it was better if that damned Cheyenne squaw had no part in this and he did things his own way. Yes, he reflected, it was probably much better.

He knew the caravan door would not be locked. And even if it had been the lock was only too simple to open with a length of wire. It smelled musty inside, like a tomb that had been shut up for centuries, the air stale and heavy . . . and so *cold*.

He had not realized that it was almost dark. There was no time to be lost, just enough light to see by, vague outlines in the shadowy recesses of the caravan . . . the two figures which Jane insisted on calling Okeepa. *Their eyes alive and watching him. . . .*

It is almost dark.

Reaching at arms' length, revulsion churning the bile in his stomach, wanting to snatch his hands away and run from this place screaming insanely but somehow forcing himself to go through with it. Droplets of cold sweat stood out like icicles on Schaefer's forehead, the eternal dead cigar dislodged itself from his dry lower lip and bounced away unnoticed. Fingers closing over something cold-blooded, hideous toads that writhed and fought in his grasp; slimy evil creatures of the darkness.

Turning, almost dropping one but grabbing it again, a torch-bearer with flames aloft staggering out into the wet

218

dusk, heedless of a multitude of eyes that followed his progress across to his own caravan. Shouldering open the door, throwing his double burden on to the littered table, wiping his hands on his soiled trousers. Retching. It had gone so cold in here, too, and he knew only too well why.

Trying not to look at them, shielding his face with one hand as he groped blindly on the floor, knew that what he was seeking was somewhere down there. Mocking laughter rang in his ears. Panicking, it might be too late; he should have heeded Jane's warning earlier, done this whilst there was still time.

His fingers found the axe, closed over the short wooden handle, reassurance surging back. It would not be long now, so simple to one who had chopped sticks for a living in his youth, in a country where poverty was rife and one was content with the basic things in life; food, warmth and shelter.

The chopper seemed so very heavy, the weight of a woodman's axe. It was all he could do to lift it, swinging it up, catching it against something which shattered and fell to the floor. It did not matter, nothing mattered except the extermination of these creatures which had no right to life.

Still trying not to look, but catching a faint glimpse of his own reflection in a dusty mirror. He gasped aloud, it had to be a trick of the failing light. The man he saw was big and dark, only a faint resemblance to his own features beneath the jet black mane of hair and flowing beard. Clothed in filthy rags, the muscles seeming to grow even as he watched. A cry of fear, backing away, pleading for that reflected strength which mocked him with his own weakness. Seeing shapes that grew like weird inflating balloons, their huge shadows blocking the last of the light.

Total darkness. All he could see were the eyes, two pairs of glowing red orbs that burned brighter and brighter, scorching into his own so that . . . he saw only a shimmering red haze. He tried to flee but all sense of direction had gone and he stumbled and fell, covering his eyes. But he could not shut those carvings out.

Waiting for the end, his body burned as though a thousand gamma rays were directed at him, fire that was consuming his brain, the heat convulsing him so that he kicked and flayed wildly.

And then the inferno cooled and he was left staring blankly, eyes that saw but did not understand; two shapes that watched him but he did not know what they were. Once he experienced a faint glimmering of fear but it was beyond his comprehension and then that, too, died.

Jacob Schaefer lived but he was nothing. He did not move because his body had no reason to. Sounds came and went but they were only sounds. He was quite content because he did not know otherwise and sometime later he discovered that he could make strange noises with his mouth.

And the tiny wooden figures on the table just sat and watched him. Only their expressions had changed but even that depended upon from which angle they were viewed, whether or not one was able to see the eyes. The hate which had glowed there had simmered and died away, the slit mouths widened to a bland smile. Smug satisfaction. Gloating.

Then those mouths widened still further and they were laughing.

15

EARLY SATURDAY MORNING

The fair should have closed down by 11.30. A bye-law of 1872 required that 'all noisy frivolities must cease within half an hour of midnight'. But for some reason tonight was an exception. The customers were plentiful and the fairground people were greedy. And the police were nowhere to be seen. It was a carnival atmosphere that never materialized, activity without gaiety.

'It's just a waste of time,' Liz Catlin groaned. 'We'll never find her in this crowd. She might not even be here, she could've gone down on the beach. Anywhere.'

'She's here,' Roy said. 'I know she is.'

'Well, there's no sign of your Indian . . . friend,' a hint of bitter jealousy, 'neither in her tent nor in her caravan.'

'We'll try the Punch and Judy.'

Oh, no! Liz slowed, remembered that awful blood, the disgusting performance. 'She wouldn't go there, I'm sure.'

'We've got to search thoroughly. We needn't stop once we've made sure she's not there.'

A crowded theatre space, all the seats taken and as many people standing. Roy and Liz squeezed into the rear of the enclosure, tried to peer round those in front of them but it was impossible to tell whether Rowena was there or not. The stage lit, everywhere else in darkness.

Punch was in full command, a harsh chattering sound coming from his cruel mouth that could only be interpreted as obscenities, the other figures cowering before him. More evil than ever, raining blows with stunning force.

'Ugh!' Liz turned her head away. 'Do we *have* to stay here, Roy?'

'Well there's no point in going until the end of the performance because otherwise we'll never know whether or not Rowena's here. It won't be long now, looks like Punch is winding it all up.'

Punch had Judy and the policeman in a corner, taking his time, playing with them, savouring the climax to this last bout of violence. Suddenly his words were drowned by a roar that vibrated the corrugated sheeting which separated the theatre from the menagerie, a noise that hit you with the force of a physical blow. And again, before the first one had died away; an orchestra of wild jungle sounds, native war drums beating with venom, a bull elephant trumpeting his own contribution, combining in their hatred of mankind.

Punch stiffened, baton half-raised, as though he, too, heard. *And was afraid*!

221

'It's only the animals,' Roy shouted in Liz's ear. 'They're restless tonight.'

Then came the silence as though all the fairground noises had been perfectly synchronized; a record ending, the next reluctant to start up straightaway. Merry-go-rounds, bumper-cars, waltzers, everything at a standstill. Seconds, minutes, it seemed an eternity, claustrophobic as though some malevolent force had thrown a dark mantle over Jacob Schaefer's fairground.

Then the music came back, another oldie so scratched that the words were barely discernible.

'. . . .the night . . . has a thousand eyes. . . .'

Punch jerked into action with a devastating over-arm blow, a sickening thud like the cracking of bone. Judy fell, lay insert. Horrified gasps came from the watchers, a child in the front row was screaming.

Judy's head was split wide open, the bonnet crushed right into the gaping crack, white material slowly turning crimson, saturated until it could absorb no more and the bright fluid spilled out in a thick slow trickle. Blood, it couldn't be anything else, no simulation could be so real.

Punch was laughing insanely, a windmill of blows bringing the figure in blue to its knees, a battered helmet rolling away exposing a bald pate and a spreading purple bruise. A dent that was filling up fast like some mountain rock-pool in a thunderstorm, the liquid gushing down the agonized face below, bloodied so that it was unrecognizable. One last despairing gesture from the policeman before he was finally felled, a bundle of blue turning to red.

Only the infant was left, a squawking swathed pitiful little form, flaying its limbs frantically. The crazed psychopath stood over it, laughing harshly, kicking it with oversize boots so that it screamed with pain. Angry shouts came from the audience mingled with cries of revulsion.

Punch stopped, turned to face them; evil incarnate, his features seemingly no longer fixed and wooden, lashing them with a piercing babble of rage and hate that was only cut short when Remus, the lion, began to voice his own fury again, joined by the torso-thumping gorilla and the trumpeting elephant.

Punch turned back, began battering the baby, crimson spottling the tiny stage and its scenery. Somebody threw an empty beer can; it bounced back off the side of the painted room and struck Punch with a metallic clang.

Once again the arch-villain of puppet shows whirled, crazed by this intrusion of his tiny domain, swinging his club in the direction from which the attack had come, his spate of maniacal insults unheard in the bestial roaring from the menagerie, almost flinging himself forward in a frenzied attack on the audience.

The striped curtains jerked their way across the bowed and rusty wires, billowing outwards as the murderous assault continued, just one last glimpse of that awful face before they met; lips curled and moving, eyes narrowed, nostrils flared, blood dripping everywhere.

Roy Catlin held Liz to him, felt her trembling. Chairs were being overturned and kicked aside in the rush to leave, angry mutterings, another object striking the small elevated theatre. Roy tried to check the faces of the children who shoved their way past him in a stampede of fear but nowhere did he find what he was looking for. Then just he and Liz were left standing there amidst the overturned chairs and benches, sweet-papers and empty crisp packets floating in the puddles.

'Well, she's not here,' he muttered, 'which is just as well after *that*.'

'Look!' Liz pointed back over his shoulder at the square frame of lighted curtain.

Roy turned, felt instant nausea at what he saw, a rivulet, like thick claret wine, crept beneath the material, formed into a blob on the edge of the overhanging woodwork, then dripped down slowly to the ground.

'There's only one way to find out for sure,' he disengaged himself from her clutching hands.

'No, Roy. *Don't!*'

But he was gone, striding forward the six or seven yards which took him directly below stage. He reached up a trembling hand, felt the warm sticky fluid on his finger-tips.

223

He closed his eyes, brought his fingers slowly to his mouth and licked them. . . . He retched. *Oh, Jesus, it was vile, sour and warm, iron-tasting. There could be no doubt whatsoever that it was blood that oozed from the Punch and Judy stage!*

Staggering white-faced back to Liz, dragging her with him, desperate to be well away from here. Not looking back, not seeing the face that peered from between the parted curtains, the expression of sheer hatred; *only knowing that he was being watched.*

'I'm going mad!' Liz beat her fists together. 'I can't stand any more. D'you hear me, *I can't stand any more!*'

Roy looked at her helplessly, not knowing what to do. Should they keep on searching for Rowena or should they go back to the police station?

'We'll keep looking for another twenty minutes,' he tried to sound optimistic. 'Then if there's no sign of her we'll go back to the Beaumont. It could be that she's already back there asleep in bed.'

'And what if she's not?'

He did not answer. That was a problem he might have to meet very shortly.

'Can't you *feel* them?' Jane breathed as she and Rowena hung back in the shadows at the rear of the big amusement arcade.

Rowena looked with upturned face, trying to lip-read but it was impossible in this dark place.

'They are gathering all around us like storm clouds,' the Cheyenne girl went on. 'The fair should have closed an hour ago but there is no sign of it doing so. Schaefer is obsessed with greed and tonight he will let it remain open as long as people are prepared to stay and spend their money. This is what worries me. Darkness has already fallen and *they* will not wait much longer. *There are hundreds of innocent people in here.*'

The animals in the menagerie were roaring incessantly now, a fearsome medley that was louder even than the music.

'*The beasts know it,*' the fortune-teller muttered. '*They can sense it and they are wild with fear.* We can wait no longer. Come with me.'

Rowena followed in her companion's wake, heading in the direction of the menagerie. Milling crowds queued at roundabouts and dodgems, eager to spend the last of their holiday money. Out of the bright lights, shadows and reflections.

'The puppets,' Jane whispered, 'we must take them first. The others we cannot touch until the fairground is deserted. Be strong, Rowena, and help me to be strong, too.'

They saw the Punch and Judy theatre, all in darkness except for the lighted curtains, something moving behind them. Jane drew back, clutched at Rowena. '*All should be in darkness. Something is wrong*!'

The striped material billowed out, they saw a shadow, a figure with an oversize narrow head, pointed hat, in profile. A club raised. Coming down. *Thud*!

'The fiend is obsessed with killing. But we must try to take him.'

They rushed forward, Jane ripping the curtains wide, the rotten material tearing in places. She recoiled, stifling a scream.

'*The Wise One protect us. Punch has already begun*!'

The scene was like a miniature abbatoir, broken bodies which no longer seemed to be made of wood, expressions of agony and terror on upturned faces, blood running down the walls and forming pools on the stage floor, a crimson spottled Punch insane with lust and fury pounding the puppet corpses, splintering and smashing them.

'Oh, Manitou, this was never meant to be,' Jane's eyes closed briefly and then she was reaching out for the tiny murderer, her fingers red with blood as she grasped his slippery form. He did not resist, all movement seeming to have left him, a springy doll. Harmless . . . *except for his hate-filled bloodshot eyes which blazed into her own.*

Jane swung him aloft, held him suspended above her head, then dashed him to the ground with all her force, hearing him split like axed kindling wood. Stamping on him. Something wet splashed on Rowena's face; it could have been rainwater from the puddles except that it was warm.

Again and again, the Indian swung her foot, picked up a broken limb and snapped it in two in a frenzy of fear and desperation. A half-submerged face stared up at them from a deep muddy puddle, orbs that still glowed and fizzed in the water. Crunched to matchwood, Punch still lived!

Jane hunted around, found a jagged stone, slammed it down on the grotesque features, water and blood shooting high into the air, then grinding the remains of the splintered skull into the mud with her moccasin. They watched but it did not float up to the surface again.

'Oh, Rowena, indeed your powers have given me strength,' Jane's face was grim in the half-darkness. 'This fiend who took the form of a Punch is dead in the same way that he destroyed his stage victims. But there is no time to be lost. There are many more of them!'

Jane and Rowena broke into a run, then stopped. Behind them on the other side of the steel corrugated fence the captive creatures had begun roaring again, this time louder and fiercer than before, a note of triumph in their wild chorus. A tearing, cracking sound, heavy bodies crashing. A human scream that was suddenly cut short.

'Their evil has begun!' Jane paled, drew Rowena close to her. '*They have released the wild animals to aid them in their quest for human destruction!*'

Rowena was numbed with terror, holding on to her companion, aware that they were running again, back across the fair where the midnight revellers still rode the roundabouts and played the slot machines, oblivious that ferocious beasts of the jungle were loose in their midst.

Then suddenly came a chorus of piercing screams. Jane turned, knowing that the escaped animals were still on the promenade side. Nobody could have spotted them, yet . . . it seemed that everybody was screaming.

A roundabout, just four fancy painted horses that circled gently, appeared to have gone berserk. The speed had built

226

up gradually so that nobody was aware of it at first; now the machine was spinning crazily, a multitude of bright colours blurred into one; horses going faster and faster so that they gave an optical illusion of galloping abreast, shrieking children clinging to their carved manes. Wild horses, heads back, eyes rolling, the rotating axle screaming its protest at this unholy stampede.

A group of watching adults rushed forward but there was no way they could board the platform. Watching helplessly. A horse whinnied and they shrank back. So fast now that it was impossible to discern one animal from another. Horses bucked and reared, a rider was thrown, a child catapulted high into the air, bent and limp like a rag doll.

'The horses which I fashioned into evil beings with my own hands!' a cry of despair from Jane. 'Now I have unleashed them on innocent children. We are powerless to stop them!'

They watched horror-stricken. Horses and riders were airborne, flashing hooves crushing down on the helpless bodies of the thrown riders; the Four Horsemen of Apocalypse invisible on their mounts, red-eyed mustangs of malevolence.

Four broken tiny bodies, people rushing forward to stand and stare in horror. And even as they gathered, the devilish mounts came at them from above, death-dealing hooves unerringly finding defenceless skulls in a battleground of blood and death. And then the empty merry-go-round began to slow, a child's top that had run out of momentum, whining and creaking.

But nobody had stopped the music yet.

' . . . *the Comancheros are taking this land* . . . '

A tawny streaking form that was no roundabout horse, a bounding snarling ball of fury, leaping, slashing a path through the crowds like a scythe through grass, then pausing briefly to maul. Angry because its teeth were no longer sharp and resorting to its claws, spraying blood and entrails all around it.

Trapped crowds huddled in the remnants of the big-dipper wreckage, watching the feasting man-eater. Gasps of horror, not just because of Remus, and the horses which had killed so horribly, but because of the swinging giant form on the twisted girders above, a black gorilla that hung by one arm and beat its chest with the other, now snarling its hate and defiance. And further away, an elephant which trumpeted and slashed with its trunk, demolishing a tent. A loud explosion, louder than a gunshot; it had rested a foot on the inflated rubber Kiddies' Kastle.

'There will be a massacre!' Jane's arm crept around Rowena's face, but she could not stop the child from seeing. *'We are too late to prevent their rampage of blood and vengeance but there will be even more terrible happenings this night unless we destroy Okeepa and his brother who are one and the same!'*

Running again, a detour, glancing fearfully into every patch of shadow, aware of wooden eyes that saw and followed their progress, trying to stop them. The caravan, dilapidated but still intact, looking lifeless, deserted. A feeling of unease crept over Jane. I am a fool, I should have destroyed the totem-dolls first. I am to blame for all this, the blood of these people is on my soul.

She knew they would be gone even as she pushed open the door, squeezed Rowena's hand because she needed the child. Without her she might have been dead by now.

The music had stopped at last. Just the screams, hysterical cries of terror, heavy objects being smashed. The atmosphere was heavy with the stench of death and . . . *something else.*

Jane felt it catch in her throat, knew only too well what it was. *Smoke! Somewhere there was a fire!*

She hurried inside, saw the empty table. Despair but not shock, only a numbed realization of her worst fears.

'They have gone, Rowena,' her voice was weak, barely audible. 'I guessed as much. *Okeepa has gone to spread evil and death.*'

Rowena stiffened. A strange prickly sensation goose-pimpled her skin; the same vibration that she felt when she was close to Doll and he tried to impose his will upon her.

'Wait!' she pulled at Jane, led her back outside. 'Doll is

228

close, I know. I can *feel* him, a vibration like my hearing-aid makes when it is not fixed properly.'

And then Jane knew, too. The air was so cold, a lurking evil close to where they stood. She stared about her, saw the sudden leaping tongues of flame turning the cloudy sky a radiant hue. The amusement arcade was blazing, sending up a single pillar of thick black smoke and a shower of sparks. Another explosion, louder than the first. The coloured lights went out; the fire must have reached the main generator! Now there was just an eerie yellow glow from the blaze, the shadows deepening and closing in, hiding whatever they chose to hide.

But Rowena was turned in the opposite direction, seeing an oblong black shape that was just beyond the reach of the glow from the fire, tensing. Pointing with a shaking hand. Jacob Schaefer's caravan.

'There,' she shouted. '*Doll . . . in there!*'

And Jane, the Cheyenne, knew that what her young friend said was right. *Okeepa, the carved devil god of the Plains Indians, was only yards away from them*!

Roy Catlin pressed back into a heap of wreckage, Liz close to him, wondered if there was any chance of making it to the promenade exit. Behind them the arcade was a blazing inferno. They could feel the heat and the fire was spreading. It would come this way, devouring tents and shanty buildings as a freshening westerly wind fanned it. The petrol tanks of burning vehicles were exploding all around them.

The elephant was their greatest danger at the moment, though. No longer was it rampaging madly, its deep cunning now prevailed. Its trunk snaked amongst the debris, searching, feeling for trapped victims that still lived so that it could drag them out and trample them with its colossal feet. A crazed bull, but far more deadly now that its initial blind rage had simmered.

'If it wasn't for that damned elephant between us and the promenade we'd make it,' he muttered. 'As it is, we'd better sit tight. Surely the police will come soon and bring marksmen with them.'

'Where's Rowena, though?' Liz Catlin voiced her greatest fear, a question she knew that Roy would be unable to answer.

'Like I said earlier, she's probably safe asleep in bed back at the hotel,' he tried to sound convincing but made a poor job of it.

Liz closed her eyes, hoped that maybe it was all a nightmare. This sort of thing could not really be happening, those crazy roundabout horses behaving like untamed stallions, the Punch and Judy. . . .

Oh God, but it was real all right; you could feel the heat from the blaze, hear the tortured screams of trapped holidaymakers. Just like hell itself! The waltzers, a funeral pyre, slumped bodies in the burning chairs, their agonized terrified expressions frozen in death grotesquely reflected by the flames. Something exploded nearby, sent up a cloud of sparks; firework night with a host of Guy Fawkes effigies condemned to death by fire.

The elephant had overturned a generator van, was standing on it so that its sides buckled like a squashed tin can, bellowing his triumph, eyes glinting as he looked around for his next conquest. A small monkey was chattering from the top of a stark tent-pole, surveying the torn and crumpled canvas beneath it. Then with a screech it jumped, landed on all fours and gambolled off into the shadows. It didn't like this place one little bit.

Roy Catlin was watching the elephant closely. If the beast moved off elsewhere there was a chance they might make the promenade exit. But Attila did not seem in any hurry. It was almost as though he had been assigned to guard this last escape route.

And, if you listened closely, intermingled with the roaring of the escaped wild animals, the crashing of blazing debris, and the screams of those who huddled in the shadows, you could just hear the wailing of sirens. Fire, police, ambulance. But there was no way any rescue force was going to be able to get into Jacob Schaefer's fairground for some time yet.

*

230

The door of the fairground proprietor's caravan swung gently to and fro, creaking on rusty hinges. Jane stopped, a strangled cry in her throat, gripped Rowena's hand tightly. From inside she heard low babbling laughter; eerie, insane.

'*No!*' she hissed. '*It cannot be. It is impossible!*'

The child picked up something through her hearing-aid, could not be sure what it was but her flesh began to creep. It reminded her of Doll, the way he used to communicate with her, a kind of telepathic vibration.

The Indian girl hesitated, every instinct crying out to her to flee. *Some nameless terror lay beyond that door. Okeepa was determined to wreak his vengeance this night and he would call upon all the evil forces of darkness to help him!*

'I must go in there, whatever the consequences,' Jane muttered. 'Go, my child. Flee. Do not linger here, it was wrong of me to have brought you.'

But Rowena was not going to flee. She felt a sudden surge of hatred towards the malevolent power which made the carved figures do its bidding; she knew that in some way she was impervious to them. They had not been able to harm her, not in the forest, the Ghost Train, nor in that cave of indescribable evil. Even Doll, whom Jane called Okeepa, had been forced to concede to the will of one small girl. And she would confront him again, remind him of the manner in which he had betrayed her loyalty. No longer did she need him. *She wanted to destroy him!*

Jane pushed the door wide, stepped through the doorway. The glow from the blazing fairground illuminated the interior, flickering orange light that depicted the awfulness of the man who crouched snarling on the floor. And this time Jane could not hold back her shriek of terror.

It was Jacob Schaefer and yet it was not. The scrawny frame had thickened and filled almost beyond recognition; the filthy tattered clothing of fringed animal hide was similar to that which she herself wore. The grey hair and beard had grown black and bushy, a wild unkempt mane. Only the eyes remained unchanged, twin pools of glittering evil that burned with the intensity and fierceness of the raging blaze outside. A demon in human form, the slave of

231

Okeepa and his twin totem doll which watched with blank features.

This is the woman, Levine. Mistai who bore yet another Mistai, and she a further one, and so it continued. A child spawned to avenge — but now that the hour is nigh she is seeking to thwart us. You must destroy her, take her as you took her once before.

Schaefer was lurching to his feet, breathing heavily, lips twisted into a mis-shapen grimace, hands clawing the air. 'I let you live once. This time you shall die!'

Jane backed away, her vision swimming, blurring. This man, so familiar; she didn't know why she had not realized it before. *Schaefer was Levine, just as she was Mistai.* Another place, another time, all merging. A grove of trees, cottonwoods, the hot air tinged with the odour of death, stale sweat, and powder-smoke. He was advancing on her, lusting cruelly, a bull buffalo pawing and snorting at the rutting stand, eager to mate and then to kill.

'Squaw bitch, you'll make it good for me before I kill you!' He spat on the ground, a dottle of phlegm that raised a puff of dust, starting to unfasten the leather thong which secured his breeches.

Mistai cried out as she was flung to the ground, her body jarred, staring skywards, the distant cirrus cloud seeming to take on shapes. A face. So stark and hawk-like; inhuman yet living, moving. Laughter without mirth, whipping her like a sudden hailstorm with its venom.

Okeepa. The totem-god had arrived to give his blessing to the mating.

This time she wouldn't make it easy for him, would fight him every inch of the way, reject the sperm which carried within it the spawn of ancient evil vengeance. I deny you, Okeepa, even as I deny this creature sent to do your bidding!

You cannot, Mistai. My vengeance shall be complete within your womb as it was then, the bloodcurse of your own people.

The weight of his body crushed her own, his foul stinking lips pressed to hers, hands tearing at her clothing to bare her body. No longer could she see the sun and the sky, only an orange glow as though the sun set, Okeepa's laughter ringing in her ears.

And suddenly that laughter died away to curses, a noise like summer lightning splitting the sky, thunder rolling off the distant mountains. Thudding hooves that came and went, savage yells becoming fainter and fainter. Just sporadic gunfire that eventually petered away. Then nothing. Only silence.

Still she fought the man who lay astride her, pummelled with her fists, bit and clawed, spat something soft and spongy out of her mouth. But only his weight resisted her; no longer did he force her thighs wide and attempt to thrust between. A body that sagged, a head that lolled, sightless eyes staring at her when finally she managed to push him from her.

The cottonwoods and the blue sky were gone. Only the heat remained, a blistering burning heat that threatened to stifle her. As she tried to adjust her eyesight to the fiery glow she saw Jacob Schaefer and knew that he was dead. And Rowena Catlin standing there erect and trembling, a small kindling chopper in her hands. Both of them looking now, seeing the pile of splintered wood on the table, unrecognizable slivers and jagged chunks, sliced and sliced again like choped meat on a butcher's tray.

Okeepa and his brother were destroyed, their evil totem magic from the land of Manitou sent back whence it had come. The terror that had first been spawned over a century ago was no more.

'We have won,' the Cheyenne's voice was husky, the glow from the fire outside shimmering on dark eyes that were wide and wet. 'Just when it seemed we had lost, we have won. Now, my child, you must go. Follow the alleyway from here that leads behind the menagerie. The animals are away in the main fairground. Run, before the flames close in, and you will be safe. There is not much time left.'

'*No!*' Rowena stood her ground. 'I won't go without you, Jane.'

'You must. I cannot come. Whatever happens I must remain here. Go now, delay no longer. I will always remember you Rowena, a debt that can never be repaid.'

Rowena turned and left the caravan, not once glancing back, cowering at the sight of the wall of sweeping flames. Then running. Somewhere behind her a wild beast was roaring its wrath, a noise that might have been summer thunder rolling, pounding hooves that thudded and vibrated and died away. Gunfire, a volley of shots. Then came a few moments of silence when even the leaping devouring flames seemed unable to make themselves heard to one small fleeing deaf girl who clutched a tiny woodchopper to her as though it was a favourite doll.

The promenade, pushing her way through the large crowd which had gathered, vehicles with flashing blue beacons cutting a path through them. Rowena did not look back, she didn't want to see, tried to shut the vision out of her mind but it refused to go. The interior of a dingy untidy caravan. A dead man who was rawboned and frail again, with greying hair. A pile of splintered wood that no longer fused with latent evil. And a dark-haired Indian girl who sobbed her grief and stayed behind when she could have fled. Waiting for death because for her it was the only way.

The smell of thickening suffocating smoke, the hissing of foam and water sizzling on the flames, the beginning of a battle which would last for many hours but in the end would be won. And one final burst of rifle fire, a salute to man's supremacy over the beasts of the wild.

Rowena began to struggle and scream when strong fingers fastened over her arm, pulled her back. In her desperation she swung the axe with her free hand, but it was seized and wrenched from her grasp, clattering to the wet concrete.

'*Rowena!*' Liz Catlin's face, the surge of relief. 'Wherever have you been and what are you doing with that axe?'

Her father's features; grave, lined, trying to smile. And for the last time she heard Jane's voice as though it wafted on the smoky hot wind, *I will always remember you,*

Rowena, a debt that can never be repaid.

Then for the second time in as many days Rowena Catlin fainted.

16

SATURDAY MIDDAY

The sun had broken through the last of the low cloud around breakfast time, dispelling it completely, turning the grey sea to a sparkling blue, beginning to dry up the puddles on pavements and promenades so that by midday only patches of damp remained in the shade.

Roy Catlin finished roping the suitcases to the roofrack, not hurrying because the urge to be gone from this place had died. Had Mrs Hughes had any vacancies he would have been tempted to stay over until Sunday. Maybe Liz would even have been in agreement. But in the long run it was best that they left . . . and tried to forget.

Looking out across the bay you could almost tell yourself that it hadn't really happened. Until the wind brought with it the eddying black smoke from the smouldering skeleton of what had once been Jacob Schaefer's domain of evil. Then it all came back and you shivered in case those eyes were still watching you. But they couldn't be because everything that was wooden had been reduced to ashes. Everything was gone, total destruction. The only way.

Roy wondered wistfully about Jane, whether she had managed to get out. Maybe they would never know. The deathtoll was heavy and they hadn't finished counting yet. Tomorrow it would make the headlines of the Sunday papers but the real story wasn't even guessed at. Perhaps it was best that way, the dead left to bury the dead, the living left with their nightmares.

Liz was sitting on the bench seat in the Beaumont Hotel's tiny front garden, an arm around Rowena. She glanced at Roy but didn't even tell him to hurry, a half-smile on her freckled face. A lot of things had changed, some for better, some for worse. But life just went on.

The holiday traffic queues were already starting to build up, early arrivals clashing with late leavers, the police cordons across the promenade adding to the chaos, an auxiliary fire-engine driving with two wheels on the pavement until forced to stop behind a parked ambulance.

Rowena had been silent since breakfast. Suddenly she was on her feet, pointing excitedly in the direction of the harbour. Shouting shrill words which were almost lost in the general noise. But not quite. '*Birds . . . birds. . . .*'

Roy turned, looked where she was pointing. High above the harbour, wheeling, calling, diving, was a large flock of seagulls. Circling warily, going out to sea, coming back again. A reconnaissance, as though they had to be sure of *something*. Then, as if in answer to a prearranged signal, they swooped down, alighting on the railings, ruffling their feathers. Calling again, more birds arriving, specks in the sky that grew larger until they were recognizable as gulls. A joyous screeching homecoming that ended in the everlasting search for food as though they had never been away.

Roy grinned, walked across to Liz and Rowena. 'We're ready to roll,' he said, 'and even the gulls have come back. I guess everything's OK now.'

Liz nodded, squeezed his hand. 'And the sun's even shining. Did . . . did these things *really* happen, Roy?'

'I guess we'll never know the truth,' he pursed his lips. 'Perhaps only Rowena knows and there's always the chance that one day she might decide to tell us.'

One last look back as they climbed into the car. A single spiral of black smoke, mushrooming into the sky, the sea breeze pulling it to ragged shreds as though even Nature herself was determined to eradicate the last remnants of Okeepa, the Cheyenne totem-god, before a shape could form and be recognized, and those who knew might be reminded of what had been.

Richard Lewis

SPIDERS

Out of the earth crept mankind's oldest nightmare.

The Kentish countryside was bathed in golden sunshine. All around lay peace and tranquillity.

Maybe it was too peaceful, too ominously quiet, but who'd complain about that? Certainly not old Dan Mason, energetically tugging out weeds in the farmhouse garden.

What he'd uncovered there didn't alarm him. But it should have. For he'd just released a seething army of death . . .

Fiction

GENERAL

☐ The House of Women	Chaim Bermant	£1.95
☐ The Patriarch	Chaim Bermant	£2.25
☐ The Rat Race	Alfred Bester	£1.95
☐ Midwinter	John Buchan	£1.50
☐ A Prince of the Captivity	John Buchan	£1.50
☐ The Priestess of Henge	David Burnett	£2.50
☐ Tangled Dynasty	Jean Chapman	£1.75
☐ The Other Woman	Colette	£1.95
☐ Retreat From Love	Colette	£1.60
☐ An Infinity of Mirrors	Richard Condon	£1.95
☐ Arigato	Richard Condon	£1.95
☐ Prizzi's Honour	Richard Condon	£1.75
☐ A Trembling Upon Rome	Richard Condon	£1.95
☐ The Whisper of the Axe	Richard Condon	£1.75
☐ Love and Work	Gwyneth Cravens	£1.95
☐ King Hereafter	Dorothy Dunnett	£2.95
☐ Pope Joan	Lawrence Durrell	£1.35
☐ The Country of Her Dreams	Janice Elliott	£1.35
☐ Magic	Janice Elliot	£1.95
☐ Secret Places	Janice Elliott	£1.75
☐ Letter to a Child Never Born	Oriana Fallaci	£1.25
☐ A Man	Oriana Fallaci	£2.50
☐ Rich Little Poor Girl	Terence Feely	£1.75
☐ Marital Rites	Margaret Forster	£1.50
☐ The Seduction of Mrs Pendlebury	Margaret Forster	£1.95
☐ Abingdons	Michael French	£2.25
☐ Rhythms	Michael French	£2.25
☐ Who Was Sylvia?	Judy Gardiner	£1.50
☐ Grimalkin's Tales	Gardiner, Ronson, Whitelaw	£1.60
☐ Lost and Found	Julian Gloag	£1.95
☐ A Sea-Change	Lois Gould	£1.50
☐ La Presidenta	Lois Gould	£2.25
☐ A Kind of War	Pamela Haines	£1.95
☐ Tea at Gunters	Pamela Haines	£1.75
☐ Black Summer	Julian Hale	£1.75
☐ A Rustle in the Grass	Robin Hawdon	£1.95
☐ Riviera	Robert Sydney Hopkins	£1.95
☐ Duncton Wood	William Horwood	£2.75
☐ The Stonor Eagles	William Horwood	£2.50
☐ The Man Who Lived at the Ritz	A. E. Hotchner	£1.65
☐ A Bonfire	Pamela Hansford Johnson	£1.50
☐ The Good Listener	Pamela Hansford Johnson	£1.50
☐ The Honours Board	Pamela Hansford Johnson	£1.50
☐ The Unspeakable Skipton	Pamela Hansford Johnson	£1.50
☐ In the Heat of the Summer	John Katzenbach	£1.95
☐ Starrs	Warren Leslie	£2.50
☐ Kine	A. R. Lloyd	£1.50
☐ The Factory	Jack Lynn	£1.95
☐ Christmas Pudding	Nancy Mitford	£1.50
☐ Highland Fling	Nancy Mitford	£1.50
☐ Pigeon Pie	Nancy Mitford	£1.75
☐ The Sun Rises	Christopher Nicole	£2.50

Fiction

HORROR/OCCULT/NASTY

☐ Death Walkers	Gary Brandner	£1.75
☐ Hellborn	Gary Brandner	£1.75
☐ The Howling	Gary Brandner	£1.75
☐ Return of the Howling	Gary Brandner	£1.75
☐ Tribe of the Dead	Gary Brandner	£1.75
☐ The Sanctuary	Glenn Chandler	£1.50
☐ The Tribe	Glenn Chandler	£1.10
☐ The Black Castle	Leslie Daniels	£1.25
☐ The Big Goodnight	Judy Gardiner	£1.25
☐ Rattlers	Joseph L. Gilmore	£1.60
☐ The Nestling	Charles L. Grant	£1.95
☐ Night Songs	Charles L. Grant	£1.95
☐ Slime	John Halkin	£1.75
☐ Slither	John Halkin	£1.60
☐ The Unholy	John Halkin	£1.25
☐ The Skull	Shaun Hutson	£1.25
☐ Pestilence	Edward Jarvis	£1.60
☐ The Beast Within	Edward Levy	£1.25
☐ Night Killers	Richard Lewis	£1.25
☐ Spiders	Richard Lewis	£1.75
☐ The Web	Richard Lewis	£1.75
☐ Nightmare	Lewis Mallory	£1.75
☐ Bloodthirst	Mark Ronson	£1.60
☐ Ghoul	Mark Ronson	£1.75
☐ Ogre	Mark Ronson	£1.75
☐ Deathbell	Guy N. Smith	£1.75
☐ Doomflight	Guy N. Smith	£1.25
☐ Manitou Doll	Guy N. Smith	£1.25
☐ Satan's Snowdrop	Guy N. Smith	£1.00
☐ The Understudy	Margaret Tabor	£1.95
☐ The Beast of Kane	Cliff Twemlow	£1.50
☐ The Pike	Cliff Twemlow	£1.25

Fiction

SCIENCE FICTION

☐ More Things in Heaven	John Brunner	£1.50
☐ Chessboard Planet	Henry Kuttner	£1.75
☐ The Proud Robot	Henry Kuttner	£1.50
☐ Death's Master	Tanith Lee	£1.50
☐ The Dancers of Arun	Elizabeth A. Lynn	£1.50
☐ The Northern Girl	Elizabeth A. Lynn	£1.50
☐ Balance of Power	Brian M. Stableford	£1.75

ADVENTURE/SUSPENSE

☐ The Corner Men	John Gardner	£1.75
☐ Death of a Friend	Richard Harris	£1.95
☐ The Flowers of the Forest	Joseph Hone	£1.75
☐ Styx	Christopher Hyde	£1.50
☐ Temple Kent	D. G. Devon	£1.95
☐ Confess, Fletch	Gregory Mcdonald	£1.50
☐ Fletch	Gregory Mcdonald	£1.50
☐ Fletch and the Widow Bradley	Gregory Mcdonald	£1.50
☐ Flynn	Gregory Mcdonald	£1.75
☐ The Buck Passes Flynn	Gregory Mcdonald	£1.60
☐ The Specialist	Jasper Smith	£1.75

WESTERNS

Blade Series – Matt Chisholm

☐ No. 5 The Colorado Virgins	85p
☐ No. 6 The Mexican Proposition	85p
☐ No. 11 The Navaho Trail	95p

McAllister Series – Matt Chisholm

☐ No. 3 McAllister Never Surrenders	95p
☐ No. 4 McAllister and the Cheyenne Death	95p
☐ No. 8 McAllister – Fire Brand	£1.25

NAME...

ADDRESS...

....

Write to Hamlyn Paperbacks Cash Sales, PO Box 11, Falmouth, Cornwall TR10 9EN.

Please indicate order and enclose remittance to the value of cover price plus:

U.K. CUSTOMERS: Please allow 55p for the first book, 22p for the second book and 14p for each additional book ordered to a maximum charge of £1.75.

B.F.P.O. & EIRE: Please allow 55p for the first book, 22p for the second book plus 14p per copy for the next seven books, thereafter 8p per book.

OVERSEAS CUSTOMERS: Please allow £1.00 for the first book plus 25p per copy for each additional book.

Whilst every effort is made to keep prices low it is sometimes necessary to increase cover prices and also postage and packing rates at short notice. Hamlyn Paperbacks reserve the right to show new retail prices on covers which may differ from those previously advertised in the text or elsewhere.